FLIGHT FROM CHADOR

A novel by
Sigrid Brunel

New Victoria Publishers
Norwich, Vermont

Published by New Victoria Publishers Inc., PO Box 27 Norwich, Vt. 05055, a Feminist Literary and Cultural Organization founded in 1976.

Cover Art based on an original photo by Beth Dingman

Printed and bound in Canada.
1 2 3 4 1999 2000 2001 2002

Library of Congress Cataloging-in-Publication Data

Brunel, Sigrid, 1939–
    Flight from Chador : a novel / by Sigrid Brunel.
          p.   cm.
        ISBN 1-892281-06-6
        I. Title.
    PS3552.R7996F58   1999
    813' .54--dc21   99-25698
                                                              CIP

For my late parents

———————————

My thanks to New Victoria Publishers, especially ReBecca Béguin whose ideas were of great help.

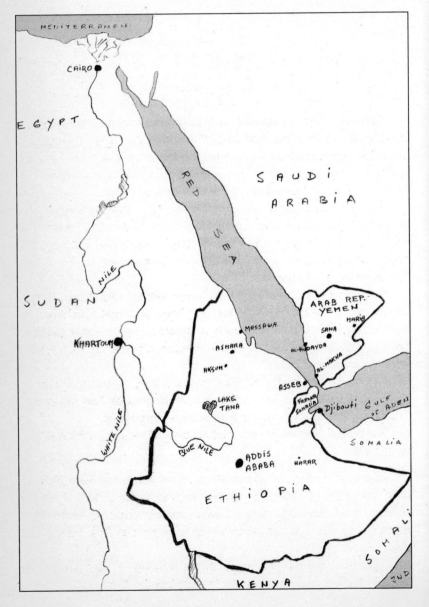

MEDITERRANEN

EGYPT

CAIRO

SUDAN

NILE

KHARTOUM

WHITE NILE

RED SEA

BLUE NILE

LAKE TANA

AKSUM

ASMARA

MASSAWA

ADDIS ABABA

HARAR

ETHIOPIA

SAUDI ARABIA

ARAB REP. YEMEN

SANA

MARIB

AL-HUDAYDA

AL-MAKHA

ASSEB

FRENCH SOMALIA

Djibouti

GULF of ADEN

SOMALIA

SOMALI

KENYA

JUD

4

Chapter One

Ethiopia 1970

Anouk pulled the control stick back, and with full throttle, got the Cessna up to a hundred and thirty miles per hour, then gently eased the stick forward and switched on the automatic pilot. Leaning back, she looked down at the mountainous wilderness where the Blue Nile wound like a dark ribbon through basalt rock.

Suppressing a yawn, she poured some coffee from a thermos. She was tired. Her cousin's letter had kept her awake most of the night. Stephanie usually only wrote at Christmas. This letter was a cry for help, but what Steph wanted was crazy. Dangerous. Forget it, her common sense told her.

Stephanie's mother and hers were sisters and from Egypt. Stephanie's father was from Yemen. They had met and lived in France, where Stephanie was born. Stephanie's father had a younger brother who had married a German woman in Hamburg with whom he had a daughter, Silke.

Apparently he had sold Silke, now a teenager, into marriage in Yemen without her or her mother's consent. Anouk had never met Silke who was much younger than she and Stephanie.

She reread Stephanie's somewhat jumbled message which ended with a plea:

Please, Anouk, think of something to get her out of there. Silke is only seventeen. She's been in Yemen for over a year now and is very sick and needs help. Her whereabouts have been kept secret from her mother who divorced her father years ago and who (what else!) has disappeared.

Silke was hospitalized several times. Finally the German doctor heading the hospital in a town by the name of Al-Hazm called Silke's mom in Hamburg. Irmgard flew to Yemen, saw her at the hospital, but couldn't get her out of the country. The German authorities can't do anything as Silke has become a Yemenite national through her marriage.

The doctor will contact you soon. So will Irmgard. She is willing to pay any price to get her daughter back. Silke's husband and in-laws don't know that we finally found her and that she saw her mother.

She's kept like a prisoner. Only you can help. You speak the language, you fly, you know the Arab customs. And you'll find a way. I just know it. Love and kisses, Steph.

Anouk drew a deep breath and folded the letter, remembering her childhood in Cairo, how her older sister Alifa and Yasmine, another cousin, had both been married away at sixteen.

Yasmine was dead and Anouk didn't know anything about her sister or her family because when her turn had come to be married away at sixteen, Anouk had chosen to escape.

When Alifa's and Yasmine's fates had been sealed by the cruel customs that robbed women of any say about their lives Anouk had been a child and helpless. But she wasn't a helpless child any longer. Here was another young woman of her family who had been forced into a marriage; she couldn't just let it go. Steph was right. She would find a way to get Silke out.

Chewing her lower lip, she fixed the controls without really seeing them. Suddenly she noticed the oil pressure gauge. It read zero. Swallowing a curse, she tapped it. But the needle remained frozen in its place. Think positive, she told herself. There is nothing wrong with the oil pressure. It's the gauge itself that's stuck. She checked all the controls, relaxed, kept looking at the scenery.

Flying was her life. She needed the feeling of freedom it gave her, the security on a column of air, the speed, and the sensation when earth vanished from under her with all its ties, ambitions, likes, dislikes. Only the craft's logic talked to her—and the logic of the cosmos—splendid, light, free. Up here was her real life. She almost wished she could stay up here forever.

As the miles continued to slip by, the sight of the stubborn needle began to get under her skin. She decided she had to do something about it and smashed the glass face of the gauge, then moved the needle to its proper setting—60 psi. Now everything not only was in order, but looked in order too.

Settling back again, she thought about Silke and how to get her out of Yemen, a country which still held on to restrictive Islamic laws. Silke would never be allowed to leave the house alone or show herself unveiled in public which would make it impossible to recognize or approach her. It was best to wait for the doctor to contact her, then take a trip to Yemen and scout the area where Silke lived.

Anouk would have to pose as a man to be able to move freely. But that had never been a problem with her tall frame, deep raspy voice, and androgynous looks, especially when she slicked back her short black hair. She had escaped from Egypt at sixteen posing as a boy in her brother's clothes, and she had posed as a man when traveling through Africa in a van with Hilde, a petite blue-eyed blonde and ex-lover, so they wouldn't be harassed by men.

Mount Amedamit stretching its ten thousand feet through a thin layer of clouds brought her back to the present. The southern tip of Lake Tana appeared and, soon after, Bahar Dar's tin roofed huts. She reduced speed and headed for the sandy strip.

Red dust whirled as the wheels touched down. Trailing a vortex of sand, she taxied toward a hangar from which people came running. She turned off the engine and climbed out of the plane. A tall Arab met her.

She greeted him in Arabic with, "Hallo, Ali," and handed him a mailbag. "So, where's the woman?"

Before he could answer, two men had put down a stretcher with a young white woman.

"She can't make the baby," one said in Amharic, Ethiopia's official language which Anouk spoke quite well.

Anouk looked at the woman who had her eyes closed and was as pale as the sheet covering her. "My God, is she alive? Who is she?"

Ali nodded. "Anya Munther. Her husband is one of the German engineers building the hydroelectric plant at the Nile Falls."

"Pregnant in that wilderness?" Anouk shook her head. "Where's her husband?"

"At the falls," Ali replied.

Leaves her to face the music, she thought. "What if she dies on me?"

"Won't be your fault," Ali said. "We've radioed the Menelik Hospital in Addis that she's coming and an ambulance will be waiting at the airport."

"Where am I going to put her? Nobody told us she'd be on a stretcher."

"We'll take out the seats."

Ali and the men climbed up into the plane and stowed the seats in the back. Then they hoisted the stretcher into the cabin with the woman's head next to Anouk's seat.

"Have a good flight," Ali said as Anouk climbed into the cockpit.

Minutes later she was airborne. When she reached altitude and speed, she put on the automatic pilot and looked at the woman. "Anya? Can you hear me?" No answer. Stroking the woman's hair, she asked, "Anya, do you speak English?" Then she repeated the question in German.

Anya answered with a moan.

"We'll be in Addis in three hours, Anya. You'll be all right."

Anouk leaned back, remembering the oil pressure gauge. She had forgotten to mention it to Ali. The needle was still at 60, where she had moved it. She shrugged, certain from her knowledge of the plane and its maintenance that the gauge itself was faulty.

She looked at Anya lying with her eyes closed, not moving. Anouk wondered if she was sedated. She remembered reading that unconscious people were still able to hear, so she kept relating what she saw from the air to soothe the suffering woman.

The sky over Addis Ababa was clear and sunny. She put her earphones on, got into contact with the airport tower, then touched down gently as if the runway were made of glass. Pulling up to her spot near a hangar, she saw Sergio, her boss, next to an ambulance. Sergio was a tall, dark Italian in his forties, and one of the few men she'd run into who didn't suffer from an inferiority complex. Ever since he had given her a job five years ago, she had enjoyed his live-and let-live attitude and become his close friend.

"We've arrived, Anya" she said, turning off the fuel and switches. The woman made no sound.

Sergio and one of the Italian mechanics helped unload the stretcher. The waiting doctor and nurse had a short look at Anya and covered her face with an oxygen mask.

"Didn't know it was that bad," Sergio said, looking after the howling ambulance.

They walked toward a small office with the sign *Ras Dashan Airlines*. Anouk mentioned the oil pressure gauge.

Sergio gave her an amused look, hearing what she had done to it. "The Egyptian way to fix things?" he teased, alluding to her nationality.

"Sergio."

"Yeah? Something bothering you?"

"It's…well…remember you once told me how you smuggled a cousin of yours out of Yugoslavia by tying him under the car?"

Holding the door to his office open for her, he said, "That was quite a few years back. Why?"

"Do you think it's possible to airlift someone out of a country?"

Sergio sat down at his desk. "Okay, what are you trying to tell me?"

Anouk told him about Stephanie's letter.

His temper flared. "That woman's out of her mind to propose anything that crazy. And Yemen of all places! Airlifting a woman or, better, kidnapping an Arab's wife…that's against international law."

"So? What about you smuggling your cousin out of—"

"His life was at stake for writing against the regime."

"Apparently Steph's cousin is quite sick and needs help. And she's kept like a prisoner. You know women there have the rights of a goat."

"She must have known what these Arabs are like. Why did she marry one in the first place?"

"She was tricked by her father, a Yemenite. Her mother's German and divorced from him. Silke grew up in Hamburg. She was still in high school when he sent her to Yemen during summer vacation to see his homeland. Just think what it must be like for her in Yemen." Anouk sat down on a chair in front of his desk, combed back her hair with her fingers and sighed. "I wish I knew what to do."

Bending forward, Sergio looked her in the eyes. "Anouk, attempting something like that is courting the undertaker. Forget it. And don't ask me for a plane because the answer is no. I'm not going to let you fly into disaster. Besides, I don't want to lose my best pilot."

Anouk gave him a mirthless smile. "I wasn't going to ask you for a plane." Twirling a pencil, she murmured, "There must be a way…"

"Why do you want to stick your neck out for someone you don't even know?"

Anouk dropped the pencil. "I'm distantly related to her and there was a time when Steph helped me."

"Airlifting you out of a marriage?"

"Well, not quite. But close."

Sergio studied her for a moment shaking his head, then glanced out the window at the airfield.

Back to business, Anouk looked at the flight schedule on the wall.

"I see I fly to Djibouti the day after tomorrow."

"Yeah, hope you don't mind the change. I had to send Murath to Asmara, and Fabbio's in the Omo Valley with a bunch of tourists. Anyway, there's an American to pick up—a Miss Jensen."

"An American? Why is she coming via Djibouti?"

"All I know is that she took a French ship from Marseille. The American consul made the reservation personally."

"Oh la la, an important lady," Anouk said in a mocking tone.

Sergio shrugged. "Doing anything tonight? The Milnos are giving a party."

Anouk groaned. "Oh God! The same faces, same conversations…"

Sergio lit a cigarette. "What else is there to do here? Besides, a stiff drink might get you off that crazy idea of abducting a woman from the Arabs."

The villa was at the outskirts of Addis. Anouk squeezed her steel grey Land Rover between a Mercedes and a Fiat, then walked up some steps to a terrace. In the dimly lit parlor beyond, soft music filtered through chatter and laughter. A few couples were dancing.

Mr. Milno, a dark bulky Hungarian with troubled eyes and neatly trimmed black and silver hair, moved toward her with extravagant gestures. "My dear, dear Anouk," he purred and kissed her hand. "So nice to see you."

Another sweep of his hand summoned a servant with a tray of drinks. Anouk took a scotch on ice. Mrs. Milno, her hair dyed a vivid red, floated close in a green cocktail dress revealing her ample bosom. She held out her hands melodramatically. "Anouk, how are you?" she twittered, glancing up and down Anouk's black silk shirt and slacks which emphasized her height.

Anouk smiled, exchanged a few words with her, then ambled on, greeting people on her way to the piano where Sergio stood toying with ice cubes in a tall glass.

"Hello, handsome," she greeted him. "Having fun?"

"In a way, yes. It's like watching a comedy." He gave her an appreciative glance. "You're looking sharp. Too bad you don't like men or I'd propose this minute."

"Get lost," she said, chuckling, then asked, "Where's your new flame?"

"We had another fight."

"That's the problem with hetero relationships," she joked.

He gave her a shrewd smile, then turned serious. "It's the lack of selection here."

She knew what he meant. He was divorced from a wife who had hated Ethiopia and returned to Italy, and it was difficult to find a compatible woman in a country where single, educated women were scarce.

Loud laughter shifted their gaze to a bleached blonde with bright red lips, looking like a cheap copy of Marilyn Monroe. She was on a young man's lap, her tight black dress half way up her thighs exposing not so perfect legs.

"Mrs. Thompson's at it again," Anouk remarked.

"Yeah, a few drinks and she's slopping over every young man she can grab."

"Has she ever grabbed you?"

"I make sure I'm not close enough. Always wondered that her husband doesn't mind."

"Maybe American husbands are more liberal," Anouk said, glancing at a tall man with grey hair who looked like a scientist and was the representative of an American pharmaceutical firm. "Who's the couple he's talking with?"

"The American consul and his wife."

Anouk took in the robust stature and ruddy complexion of the man who appeared to be in his late thirties, and the well-rounded woman.

Sergio took her arm. "Come, I'll introduce you. They might as well know who's picking up their friend from Djibouti."

"A woman pilot?" John Peters exclaimed.

"Do you have a problem with that?" Anouk asked, her ebony gaze sinking into his pale eyes.

He smiled. "Hardly. It's just amazing how more and more women invade men's territories these days."

Anouk's eyes flashed. "These territories as you call them, have been artificially created by some men to seize the best of life for themselves."

"So true," Nora, the consul's wife threw in.

Mr. Thompson let out a little laugh. "I'd like to see a woman build an airplane, let alone invent one."

"Why? Could you?" Anouk retorted. When he didn't reply, she added, "A lot of genius has been lost by having kept women uneducated and subjugated."

"I won't argue with you there," John Peters conceded. "Anyway, our friend, Karen Jensen, is also a very independent spirit. So you two should get along well."

"Yes," Nora added. "She's my best friend. We grew up together and went to college in Philadelphia. She was working as a fashion model to put herself through college. So gorgeous! Now she has moved to the other side of the camera just as effectively."

Anouk smiled at the woman's pride about her friend. "I'm looking forward to meeting Miss Jensen and shall take good care of her."

Someone put a new record on and a tango drifted through the room.

"How about a dance with your boss?" Sergio asked Anouk, taking her arm and leading her to the floor.

"Any idea what this Karen Jensen's going to do in Addis?" Anouk asked.

Sergio shrugged. "No. Maybe she missed her chance in the States and came here to catch a husband. There're certainly enough bachelors."

Anouk gave him a mocking smile. "You wish."

He smiled back. "Let's see how beautiful she really is." And swept her up into the dance.

The record ended and they ambled to the buffet where Anouk took some shrimp salad and a cracker.

"Hello, Anouk," someone said next to her.

"Oh, Baron!"

Baron von Wieninger, a rotund, short man with a red face and curly brown mane kissed her hand. "The elusive Anouk back in Addis. May I invite you to my party the day after tomorrow?"

"Uh, no can do," Anouk replied. "I have to fly to Djibouti to pick up Miss Jensen."

"Ah yes, I heard she's arriving."

The word's out, thought Anouk, amused. Here was another possible candidate for marriage.

As if reading her thoughts, Sergio smiled at her, then turned to the baron and for awhile the two men discussed the baron's flying lessons.

Tired and bored, Anouk finished her drink, excused herself, and left. She drove back to town and parked in front of a small white stone house in a side street. An attractive woman of Italian-Ethiopian birth opened the green door before Anouk reached it.

"I thought I heard someone drive up," she said, smiling.

"Hallo, Thula," Anouk greeted her, coming up the stone steps to the porch.

"Nice to see you, Anouk. Come in. Something to drink?"

"No, thanks. I'm coming from a party and had enough. What I need is a good massage."

Thula smiled slyly and put a fresh sheet on a flat couch while Anouk undressed in the restless light of a candle, then lay down on her belly. As soon as Thula's hands touched her, she fell into a trance and a soothing warmth rose from her feet to her face. As Thula rubbed oil into her skin, gently palming her back, Anouk's thoughts dissolved. Everything moved far away.

"Would you like some smoke?" Thula asked.

"No need," Anouk murmured.

Thula massaged her shoulders, the muscles along her spine, her buttocks, her strong thighs. She kneaded, rubbed, tapped Anouk's feet and pressed her knuckles into the soles, then brushed them with rotating movements, making the blood pulse, stimulating the nerves centering in the sole of the foot. Anouk was overcome by a prickling sensation which ran all the way to the crown of her head.

"Wonderful," she groaned.

Thula's hands returned to her buttocks, brushing her sex as if by accident, and a tremor run through Anouk.

"Turn around," Thula whispered.

She feathered Anouk's small breasts, flat abdomen, moved to her dark pubis, fingers teasingly skimming the silky lips, spreading wetness.

Anouk groaned again, opening her legs. She began to tremble, feeling Thula's tongue and fingers penetrating her and before long, spasms shook her entire body. Slowly returning to reality, Anouk sat up.

"That was just what I needed, Thula. You're as good as ever."

"You sure you don't want something to drink now?"

"I only want my bed." Anouk got into her clothes, put a few bills on the table, kissed Thula on the cheek. "Until next time."

Chapter 2

Anouk lived in a house she rented at the edge of town. Tucked among eucalyptus trees, it was built in the colonial style with a corrugated tin roof and encircling verandah. Masses of purple bougainvillaea robed it on one side. Papaya and banana trees grew in the small garden along the fence.

Wrapped in a white terry cloth robe, Anouk sat on the verandah, sipping coffee. On a table next to her were the empty shells of a papaya and soft-boiled egg, a piece of toast. She waved at the flies buzzing around the plates, and called her servant. Leaning back, she gazed at the garden, drinking in the morning quiet, her aimless thoughts eddying in the honeysuckle air. The sun was not yet above the trees and it was cool. She enjoyed these mornings on her days off when she didn't have to rush and could linger over breakfast. Tadessa, a stout Ethiopian woman in her forties, appeared with a tray and began to clear the table.

"By the way, has the *zabanya* repaired the fence?" Anouk asked. *Zabanyas* were watchmen and a necessity. Otherwise *zabanyas* from other houses would break into hers.

Tadessa nodded. "He did this morning." Brushing crumbs off the tablecloth, she asked, "Anything special you want me to cook for lunch?"

Anouk shook her head. "I have errands to run and will grab a bite in town. Tomorrow morning I have a flight to Djibouti. I'll be back in the evening. Please see to it that I have two clean uniforms."

Shortly after, she left the house in white slacks, a light blue shirt, and loafers, and drove down Queen Elizabeth Street where she stopped to buy a bouquet of flowers before driving on to Menelik Hospital. She asked for Anya Munther's room at the reception desk.

"The German woman?" the nurse said.

"Yes."

"Are you a relative?"

"I'm the pilot who flew her to Addis yesterday. Why?"

"I'm sorry, but she passed away this morning."

"Oh God," Anouk whispered. "What about the baby?"

"The doctors were able to save it by a Caesarean. A girl."

Anouk looked at the flowers, murmuring, "How sad." And handed them to the woman. "Give them to someone."

She drove to the center of town where tall new buildings rose at random from a huddle of mud shacks. Cadillacs and Mercedes mingled with donkeys and cows, as did well-dressed business men and beggars in rags. Browsing in a bookstore, she bought a tourist guide of Yemen, then entered an Italian cafe to study it.

"Anouk!" a tall, slender brunette called from a table.

"Carla! What a surprise," Anouk exclaimed, slipping the book into her pocket.

Carla, a vivacious Italian from Asmara whom Anouk had met at a cocktail party, stood up to embrace her.

"You're looking good," Anouk said. "That a new hairdo? It's very becoming."

Carla's hand went to her short, stylish hair. "Thanks. I was going to call you. How are things with you? You looked a bit glum coming in."

Anouk told her about Anya.

"Yeah, it's always us women getting the shitty end of everything. It isn't fair." She pulled out a chair for Anouk as she hailed the waiter. "Another tea and a cognac, please. What would you like, Anouk?"

"Same," Anouk replied. "So…what're you doing in Addis?"

"My husband's here on business and I came along. I needed a change."

"Is anything wrong?"

Carla shrugged. "Just a little bored…with the house, the kids; sometimes I wish I had your independent life." She sighed. "But unlike you, I didn't run when my parents pushed me into a marriage I didn't really want."

Anouk waited till the waiter had put their order on the table and left, before saying, "Being single isn't always milk and honey. I can get quite lonely."

"Lonely? You?" Carla laughed and stirred sugar into her tea.

Anouk also laughed and poured some cognac into hers. "All right, so I have a few flings here and there; but that's only sex, not companionship."

"Isn't there anyone in this town for you?"

"Foreign companies don't give contracts to women. And if they did, the chance that she'd be gay would be slim. So, yeah, it can get lonely, believe it or not."

"I have a cousin in Italy who's gay. He's smart and lots of fun. Of course the whole family pretends ignorance." Carla had a sip of tea. "Have you always known you were gay?"

"I always knew I didn't like men. When I lived in Paris, a woman ten years older realized what I was and took me to a private club. It was a revelation seeing all those women who were like I am. I felt as if I had come home."

"How old were you?"

"Seventeen." Anouk smiled, recalling all the women who had helped her come to grips with her sexuality, especially Yvonne, a true femme who had shown her how to please a woman. Yvonne had given her names of clubs in London where she had moved a year later to learn English. London was where she had met Hilde.

"Good memories?" Carla asked, smiling shrewdly.

Anouk picked up the cognac snifter and looked into the oily amber heart of the drink, thinking of her success with all the fair-complexioned women who had loved her dark exotic looks in those days. "Yeah, very good," she said, and drank.

Carla emptied her glass, then looked at her watch. "I have to go. We're meeting friends for lunch. Are you ever going to fly to Asmara again? I miss our talks."

"I will. Tomorrow I fly to Djibouti."

"Ah, the duty-free French boutiques and white beaches," Carla sighed, and tried to pick up the tab.

Anouk stopped her hand. "My treat."

"Thanks," Carla said, kissed her, and left. "Come see me soon."

Djibouti, the capital of French Somalia on the Red Sea, could claim white beaches and a few chic boutiques but was otherwise as inhospitable as the desert surrounding it. With few decent hotels, anti-tourism was at its purest. The air was so hot it was like breathing fire after the cool Ethiopian highlands.

Anouk took a taxi to town from the airport. She walked in the shade of white-washed arcades past street merchants who offered a multitude of objects, mostly of very bad taste, and entered a small hotel. The lobby was full of French soldiers and their women sipping cold drinks at tables under whirring fans. Tall Somali waiters in long white shirts and red fezzes whisked around with trays as she made her way to the reception desk and asked an older French woman for Miss Jensen.

"She rented a Land Rover and left his morning for Lake Assal," the woman told her.

Anouk took off her sunglasses and gazed at the woman in surprise. "Miss Jensen did?" The woman's grey curls bounced as she nodded, and Anouk exclaimed, "Alone? Why didn't you stop her?"

The woman shrank back. "But how could I?"

"Didn't you warn her? About the salt desert, the temperatures? This isn't the USA. What if she has car trouble?"

"I can't tell people what to do or what not to do," the woman said indignantly.

Anouk ground her teeth. "I can't believe this. The nerve of her. Didn't she know she was to be picked up to fly to Addis today?"

"I wouldn't know, Madame."

"May I make a call to Addis, please? Charge it to Miss Jensen." Moments later, Anouk was talking with Sergio.

"Lake Assal?" he exclaimed. "But that's crazy."

"It's inconsiderate. What shall I do now? Twiddle my thumbs until Her Highness decides to return?"

"Calm down, Anouk. The best thing would be to rent some four-wheel drive and go after her."

"You can't be serious."

"We can't just let her get into trouble, now can we?"

"We're not her babysitters."

"Please drive after her. And don't worry about expenses. I'll bill the American consulate."

Resigned, Anouk rented a Land Rover, bought three ten-gallon cans of extra fuel, three of drinking water, as well as a supply of dry and canned food. It was noon when she started out, the sky a blazing white, the sun a fluid-yellow fury. Thirty miles west of Djibouti, she got off the paved road and took a track, abandoned and deteriorating further with every mile.

After difficult crossings over dry riverbeds and two gruelling hours of inching around boulders and holes, the track to hell climbed a small pass and opened to a vast landscape.

Lake Assal spread its magnificent deep blue water between

17

impressive arid mountains of black lava. Anouk stopped to take in the view, emptying a bottle of water before her thirst was quenched. She then refilled her fuel tank.

Out of nowhere, three Somali men appeared on top of a plateau with heavily loaded camels. They hardly took notice of her, and responded to her wave with an indifferent nod before vanishing behind rocks.

Her progress became increasingly difficult. Foot after foot, the wheels spun over sharp lava rocks or sank into patches of salt. Perspiration drenched her shirt, stung her eyes. Karen Jensen, I could strangle you, she moaned. She wondered about the woman who was probably trying to make an impressive entry like some newcomers did. Thinking they could conquer their fears of Africa's wilderness they threw themselves heedlessly into it, sometimes with disastrous endings. Well, she will have a surprise when she sees the costs she has incurred, Anouk thought smugly.

Finally she reached the famous depression of Lake Assal.

Awed, she gazed at the expanse of a disconcerting universe. Among chaotic mountains lay an immense plain, half blue, half white, reflecting sunlight. A dark spot stained the immaculate white surface of salt and Anouk reached for her binoculars.

"Miss Jensen," she murmured, relieved at seeing a Land Rover.

The track continued towards the lake over crevices, and she advanced slowly with an eye on the distant vehicle seemingly frozen in white space. The water's deep blue picked up a thousand hues from the salt bank adorning its shore. Behind, volcanoes of black lava accentuated the contrast which the azure of the sky could not temper.

Karen Jensen's hands holding the camera sank. Frowning, she watched the approaching car, wondering who was at the wheel. She had tried to make out the driver through her zoom lens but the vehicle was too far away and constantly disappearing behind some boulders. She was sure the other driver had spotted her Land Rover and was heading for it. Slightly apprehensive about this intruder, she kept out of sight behind a pillar of gypsum and waited. Tires crunching, the car labored around a bend in the track and came into view, then stopped. She pressed further into the column and watched someone in a sweat-stained khaki uniform getting out. Tall, strongly built, dark-skinned, the face hidden by a visor hat and sunglasses. Darn, she thought. Who is this? And what does he want? As the hat and sunglasses were flung onto the back seat, Karen saw that it was a woman. And she's not in the best of moods. What's she so mad about? Karen watched the woman wipe perspiration off her handsome face and look out at the striking scenery, eyes dark and electric. Karen decided it was time she showed herself. She came from behind the pillar. "Quite spectacular, isn't it?"

Anouk stared at the willowy woman with a camera who slowly walked toward her. Her gauzy white blouse revealed the shadowy contours of small breasts, the red of the setting sun warmed the golden tones of her hair cupping her head like a helmet. "Miss Jensen?" she asked in disbelief.

Karen took off her sunglasses and offered her hand. "That's me. And your name is?"

Anouk took her hand, gaze lost in eyes like deep blue pools and a sunny smile that defused her grudge. "I'm Anouk Turabi," she said, speaking less sharply than she had intended. "Your pilot. Miss Jensen, we should be in Addis by now."

"Call me Karen, please," Karen said, thinking, so that's why she's mad. "I thought I was to be picked up in two days. I wrote to the Peters I wanted some time here to take pictures."

"They told us…oh, never mind."

"Come, let's drive to my car and have a drink. You must be thirsty. Did you come here especially for me?"

"What else? We were worried about you."

"Who's we?"

"My boss and I. This isn't America, you know."

"I appreciate your concern and am sorry to cause you trouble."

They got into the car and Anouk drove up to the other Land Rover. "You were going to spend the night here?"

"I brought a tent. There's room for two. And I have enough food and water."

"In that case we can have a banquet. I brought some too."

"Look," Karen said, gesturing to the west.

"Yes, it's beautiful."

The sun was setting, sending a shimmering path of light across the lake towards them before dropping behind volcanoes, leaving a mesmerizing tranquillity.

"This your first time here?" Karen asked.

"Yes, thanks to you." Anouk laughed, then said, "Sure wish I could take a swim."

Karen poured water into cups, handed Anouk one. "You'd be pickled. The water's saturated with salt. Three hundred and thirty grams per liter or so my guidebook says. Mind helping me set up the tent?"

It was getting dark and they worked fast. Karen lit a hurricane lamp, hung it from a pole she had attached to the Land Rover.

Anouk observed her. "Weren't you afraid to camp out here alone?"

"Afraid of whom? Who'd be crazy enough to come here?"

"You."

Karen threw her head back, laughing. Anouk chimed in. Karen took in her wide smile, the brilliant teeth, the deep, raspy voice, and wondered what her accent was.

"I need to wash." Anouk walked to the car, stripped, and poured water over herself from a canister.

Karen noticed the perfect golden cast of her skin, the firm small breasts with dark points. Beautiful, she thought, asking herself if Anouk could be from Italy or France. But her accent didn't match. The Middle East? No, too emancipated to be from there. Maybe Israel. She got out of her clothes, picked up another canister, and began to wash too.

Anouk had left her personal things and spare uniform at her airline's office at the airport, not knowing she would have to make this little side trip. "Do you happen to have an extra shirt?" she asked, turning to Karen. "Mine's stiff from perspiration." Wow, she thought, caught off guard by the slim figure and fair skin, a real blonde that one. Hands off the straight ones, she warned herself.

Karen handed her a T-shirt along with a towel. "How about slacks?"

"Hmmm, I doubt I can get into yours."

"These are pajama pants and quite loose on me. They should fit."

Anouk slipped into them. "A bit tight and short, but who's looking?"

Karen also got into a fresh cotton shirt and stone-washed designer jeans which showed off her flawless body.

Refreshed, they prepared a meal, opening cans of cheese and meat, opening bottles of beer, unwrapping bread, and slicing tomatoes. Karen lifted her cup. "Here's to us."

Not likely, thought Anouk, and drank. "I don't know how to say this, but I pictured you quite differently. Not at all the way you are."

20

"Is that good or bad," Karen wondered.

"You're different from Americans I've met."

"Yet a while back you were mad at me."

"Frankly, yes."

"Was it the consul who made you drive after me?"

"I don't think he and his wife are aware of your little side trip. What made you come out here if I may ask?"

"Sure. As I said, I wanted to take photos. I intend to create a picture book of Ethiopia because when I decided to come to Addis, I looked for one to learn about the country and couldn't find one."

"Good idea. Ethiopia's many facets definitely deserve to be put into a book. Have you published anything?"

"I've sold photos to magazines. Ethiopia will be my first book." Karen had a sip of beer and resumed, "I used to be a model, but after a while I got tired of being the object and wanted to work behind the camera. So I went to school to study photography."

"What made you think of Ethiopia of all places?"

"My friends, the Peters. I always wanted to see Africa and since Nora and John invited me, I decided to begin with Ethiopia."

This was only part of the reason, Karen thought. The other part was that she had confided in her sister that she was attracted to women. Her sister then told one of her brothers.

All hell had broken loose when her father, a renowned conservative lawyer in Philadelphia, had found out. "My daughter's a pervert," he had hollered, and ordered her to get psychiatric care. She had chosen to leave when faced with electric shock treatment.

She looked at Anouk who was studying her, wondering what her reaction would be if she told her she was attracted to women. But no, she wouldn't make that mistake again. She only felt safe with people in the art and fashion world where many were gay. Most people only pretended to be liberal, like her sister. From her looks and manner Anouk could also be a lesbian. But how to be sure without asking? She had asked once, sure the woman was gay and would never forget the reaction. Being in another country with people of different cultures, she would have to be more careful to keep her tongue as well as her tendency to rebel in check

"Why so silent all of a sudden?" Anouk asked.

Karen shrugged. "Just thinking, and wondering where you're from."

"Egypt. I was born in Cairo."

"Really? Do you still have family in Cairo?"

"I guess."

Karen frowned. "Don't you know?"

"I haven't been there for sixteen years and know nothing about my family because I choose not to know about them."

"How did you end up in Ethiopia?"

"Via Europe and South Africa. It's a long story."

"Do you like living in Ethiopia?"

"It's been home for the last five years." Anouk watched Karen finish her sandwich, thinking of all the bachelors who would be standing in line to get to her. And sooner or later she will end up with one. Too bad. Such an attractive and pleasant woman. One should save her from those clods. She finished her beer. Well, it was none of her concern.

"It must be late," Karen remarked, yawning behind her hand.

"Past ten," Anouk said after a glance at her watch.

They put the food into the coolers, wrapped the garbage in plastic bags and stowed it in one of the cars, then turned off the hurricane lamp. The lake was dark and there was utter silence. In the sky, constellations spread out like the lights of a city—Orion, Cassiopeia, Auriga, Ursa Major. No glow from earth obscured their brilliance. Anouk and Karen shivered as the night grew cold and crawled into the tent, sharing the air mattress and a blanket.

"Good night," Anouk said, turning away to lie on her side.

"Good night," Karen repeated. "And thanks."

"What for?"

"Coming out here—it was very kind."

"You're quite welcome," Anouk murmured.

Chapter 3

In the late afternoon, after returning to Djibouti and taking a siesta, Anouk and Karen took a taxi to the airport. As the long shadows lifted the heavy heat and brooding silence from the town, the streets became alive with people. They watched tall and slender Somali and Ethiopian women stroll under arcades, their gaze far away, their brown flesh a sensuous promise under a flow of filmy cloth.

Anouk sighed inwardly, regretting she hadn't had time to visit a special friend on this trip.

The driver slowed for a crowd that was gathering around something burning in the square.

"Oh no," Anouk groaned, "not another one."

"What?" Karen cried, alarmed. "What are they burning?"

"Don't look," Anouk murmured, clenching her fists to control her emotions.

"What do you mean don't look?" Karen protested, then her eyes widened in shock. "Oh my God! It's a woman! They're burning a woman! Driver, stop!"

The driver, a middle-aged man, drove to the curb and left the engine idling. He glanced at the burning woman and sat waiting, his face an unreadable mask which Ethiopians put on when working for foreigners, pretending not to listen or care about their business.

Eyes averted from the gruesome scene, Anouk explained in a low, tremulous voice, "It's a suicide," then asked the driver to go on.

"No! We have to stop her," Karen screamed, trying to open the door.

Grabbing her firmly, Anouk held her back, ordering the driver to go on. Karen tried to wriggle out of her grasp. "We can't just let her do this…why—?"

"She's burning herself to protest," Anouk said, holding on to her.

"Protest? Against what?" Karen cried, looking at the kneeling figure wrapped in flames.

Anouk sighed. "Violence, or the tyranny of parents, infibulation,

23

an arranged marriage, an unpunished rape, a child forced into prostitution. It could be any or all of these. And she's not the first, or the last. Now let's get away from here."

But Karen didn't listen and reached for her camera. "I'm going to take pictures. The world should know about this."

"The world doesn't give a damn," Anouk said through clenched teeth and tightened her grip on Karen's arm. "And you'll end up beaten and your camera smashed. Driver, will you finally move on?"

"No! Don't!" Karen cried. I can't let this happen—"

"Karen! In God's name, you can't take pictures! They'll kill you!"

"They can't kill me!"

The man looked at them struggling in the back seat, then shrugged and stared ahead again, face impassive.

Anouk gripped Karen more fiercely, her voice low and warning, "They can do anything they want. And nothing will be gained because they *will* kill you if you aim your camera at this woman. Now will you pull yourself together and stop making such a scene?"

Tears spilling, Karen cried, "You're insensitive!

"Insensitive because I am trying to keep you out of trouble? Besides, is it sensitive to take pictures of a dying woman and sell them to the Western papers so they can feed their readers' appetite for sensationalism?"

"Oh…" Karen growled. "How can you believe that this is the reason I want to—"

Voice rising, Anouk interrupted, "Karen, whatever your reasons, it is not possible. Now put your camera away and calm down."

"You're cold—"

At the limit of her patience, Anouk shook her. "Listen," she snapped vehemently. "I've lost family and my country because of these crimes against women. I know better than you what it's like. So be quiet now and do me the favor of keeping your thoughts about me to yourself, because you know nothing about me or my feelings. Driver, now go on. Please."

The car began to move again. Karen sank back, furiously wiping at tears and sniffling, then sitting quietly for awhile before saying in a choked voice, "I didn't mean to insult you…I'm just so shocked about all this."

Anouk frowned at her. "You better grow a thicker skin if you want to live in this country because you can't change things or meddle in people's affairs." She handed her a handkerchief.

Karen blew her nose and after a deep breath asked, "What's infibulation?"

"A procedure where the inner surface of the labia are slit open, then pulled together and stitched up to assure virginity."

Karen's expression changed to shock. "Are you serious?"

"Most girls have to submit to this procedure when they reach puberty. It is performed at home with a simple needle and thread, and out in the bush with a cactus thorn. Needless to say, many die of infections."

A new wave of outrage swept over Karen. "B...but what about the bodily functions? Or when they marry?"

"Two small openings are left so the girl can urinate and menstruate. On the wedding night the groom simply rips her vagina open with a knife. Most of the time he's drunk, too."

Remembering weddings to which she had been invited, Anouk related how they were a celebration for the groom and not the bride. After the ceremony the bride did not join the wedding party but remained in a tent usually with an older woman. "Once I visited a bride in such a tent and saw her shake with fear anticipating the moment when the groom would appear to claim his rights."

"Isn't there a law against this?"

"My dear, this is the law."

Karen gasped for breath and tried to say something but her voice failed her.

"The worst is," Anouk went on tonelessly, so she wouldn't choke with emotions herself as she couldn't afford that anymore, "that in the twelve days following the wedding, the groom is required to keep the gaping wound of his wife's sex open or his virility will be questioned and he'll be the laughingstock of the whole clan."

Karen shuddered. "What about the woman?"

"You mean does anyone consider what she's going through?" Anouk's laugh was harsh. "Nobody gives a damn about the woman."

Karen pressed a hand against her mouth, trying to smother another onrush of emotions.

"Feeling better?" Anouk asked, speaking loudly over the roar of the Cessna's engine.

Karen nodded.

"We'll be in Addis just in time for dinner," Anouk shouted.

"Are we flying over Ethiopia already?" Karen asked, looking at mountains below.

"We left French Somalia a while ago. It should get greener down there."

"It does. I can hardly wait to see and photograph this country."

"Do you have a publisher?"

"Two showed an interest. I'll send them sample pictures as soon as I can. I see a river. Could it be the Awash?"

"Yes. You know a lot about the country already."

"I studied everything I could about Ethiopia and was surprised to learn that it has as much history as Egypt. What's Addis Ababa like?"

"It's a big small town. There're still many Italians living there, leftovers from the Italian colonial times which lasted only five years. Italian is still spoken by the natives, especially the old ones. There's also a big French colony because of the railroads, and plenty of Greeks and Armenians most of them born in Ethiopia. Then there are the whites on business contracts, quite a pretentious and arrogant bunch. Their contracts provide furnished homes, cars, two-months vacations in their countries every two years. And they can afford servants, something they can't back home. It all goes to their heads. You'll find out."

"Oh well," Karen sighed. "I'll be busy traveling around to take pictures for my book. I see a railroad."

"That's the *chemin de fer Franco-Ethiopien*."

"You speak French well."

"We spoke French at home and we girls went to French school in Cairo. I also lived in France for a while."

"French seems to be like a second language in Egypt."

"I hear it's English now. But in my day it was fashionable for the upper classes to speak French at home. And girls were usually sent to French schools, boys to English schools. My brother was."

"How many children in your family?"

"Just two girls, one boy. My brother is the youngest."

"I'm the youngest," Karen said. "We're two boys, two girls. All of them married except me."

"How old are you?"

"Twenty-nine, and you?"

"Thirty-two."

"Where did you live in France?"

"In Dijon with my aunt, a sister to my mother, and Stephanie, my cousin. I also lived in Paris for a year, two years in London, then Duesseldorf."

"You've been around. How did you ever get to Duesseldorf?"

"With Hilde who was from there and sponsored me so I could get a student and working visa. I went to the Goethe Institut to learn

German, and worked at all kinds of jobs." Anouk smiled to herself, thinking of her time with Hilde, a quirky woman who was always ready for a good time.

"I also went to the Goethe Institut in Frankfurt," Karen said. "I lived there for six months with my grandmother, my mother's mother."

"Oh, so you speak German?"

"Enough for a little conversation. My mother tried to speak it to me but I didn't want to be different from the other children and refused to speak German and she gave up. Later in college I regretted it when I took German."

"What's your father's background?"

"Danish and English. I'm a typical American mix. What about you?"

"Pure Arab, as far as I know." Anouk glanced down. "We're reaching Awash Park. Let's do a little sightseeing." She carried out a few maneuvers and the plane lost speed and altitude. They circled over the eastern edge of the rift valley overlooking the Danakil depression. Then they flew over the southern boundary, partially formed by the Awash river with its waterfalls and gorges.

"Zebras!" Karen cried in delight. "And over there giraffes. What are those small houses?"

"They belong to the Kareyu lodge. A nice little hotel in the wilderness. You should go there one day. And there is Mount Fantalle, a semi-dormant volcano."

"You're a good pilot," Karen said as Anouk swung around once more, flying still lower and stirring up a herd of kudus and a few people too.

Anouk laughed. "In South Africa I'd get fired for doing this." She flew back to a civilized altitude.

"How did you get to South Africa?" Karen asked.

"In Hilde's VW van which we outfitted like a camper." Anouk was careful to skirt her true relationship with Hilde or that she had travelled as Hilde's boyfriend most of the way. "We went through Spain, Morocco, West Africa. It took us almost a year to reach Cape Town where the van died, and Hilde got sick with hepatitis and flew home."

"And what did you do?"

"I took a bus trip east along the coast. In Port Elizabeth I ran out of money and got a job as a waitress and bartender at a ritzy club. That's where I met a woman who had a flying school. I took lessons from her." Anouk fell silent, thinking of how she had met Diana, a dynamic woman in her early forties, and the four beautiful years they had lived together in the small community of lesbians outside Port Elizabeth. Some women had worked for Diana, others had their own shops, or were doctors, lawyers, and one an entertainer in a nightclub.

She remembered the conversations, the barbecues, the picnics, the sailing, and above all the lovemaking with Diana. How she missed all that. How dull her life seemed now in comparison. She didn't like to think about it. But Karen's curious questions stirred it all up. She usually kept her old life well buried and fobbed off passengers with a joke or some other distraction when they tried to know too much about her. Why was she revealing herself to this straight woman?

Karen asked, "And you got your pilot's license?"

Anouk nodded. "Yes, I became a commercial pilot."

"When did you leave South Africa?"

"Five years ago," Anouk replied, recalling the day Diana had crashed because the elevator unit of her plane had broken. Diana's death had been the end of the world for her.

Diana had willed her the house, but it carried too many beautiful memories. She couldn't go on living in it and sold it. Life had never been the same since. The terrible grief had been replaced by a dull pain, but nothing had filled the emptiness Diana's death had left. "I traveled to Tanzania," Anouk continued, hurrying the topic to an end, "and Kenya, then on to Ethiopia and got this job." She pointed to mountains ahead. "It won't be long now. We've reached the Entoto mountains. Addis lies beyond them."

"I enjoyed this flight," Karen said. "Could you also fly me to other places?"

"Of course. I fly people around the country all the time, especially to places where the big planes of Ethiopian Airlines can't land. And we have good package deals. Just make a reservation a few days ahead of time." Anouk fished for a business card from a pouch next to her seat and handed it to Karen. "We're three pilots. If you want to fly with me, just tell Sergio, that's my boss."

The sun dramatically highlighted the edges of plateaus and tormented outlines of mountains. When the first houses appeared, Anouk said, "Here's the New Flower, that's what Addis Ababa means." She throttled back. "It's about the size of Paris with a population of eight hundred-thousand and its elevation is close to a mile above sea level, making it pleasantly cool."

"Yes, Nora wrote about that and that the air is scented with eucalyptus." Filled with excitement, Karen looked at the sprawling town.

In touch with the tower now, Anouk made a big circle on her approach to the airport. Karen continued to look at the jumble of roofs amid patches of eucalyptus trees. Not long after, they roared down the runway. Taxiing into the parking area, they saw Nora Peters waving next to Sergio.

The next day was a Sunday; Anouk was off and decided to go to the horse races, one of the few diversions available. The racetrack was out of town, bedded between hills, and appeared fresh and vast, its rich green lawn in contrast to the deep blue sky.

To her surprise, she met Karen with the Peters at the gate. Camera slung over her shoulder, Karen smiled broadly at her. Nora Peters shook her hand. "Thanks for driving into that horrible desert and getting this crazy friend of mine."

"Actually she was doing fine and didn't need rescuing," Anouk countered with a smile.

Laughing and joking, they strolled towards the track. In the center of a green field was a cluster of people with brightly colored hats, scarves, parasols and binoculars. Not far away rose the grandstand where more people had already taken seats.

At their approach, a movement rippled through the crowd. Faces turned to examine them, especially Karen in her dress of mint-colored linen. The Baron in a straw hat and white linen suit adorned by a pink carnation left a roly-poly blonde to greet them. He kissed Karen's hand and gave her a carnation with a "Welcome, beautiful lady."

"Do I hear a German accent?" Karen asked.

"Yes, I'm from Vienna," he replied, bowing gallantly. A black horse and jockey riding by diverted the Baron's attention. "I put my stakes on Black Diamond," he exclaimed. "A gorgeous beast, isn't he?"

"My dear, dear friends!" Mr. Milno in a beige suit and Panama hat came towards them with outstretched arms. He stopped short in front of Karen and with lips pursed took her hands, saying dramatically, "So happy to meet you." Then planted a kiss on each.

His wife, in a white and green voile dress, sailed close behind, one hand holding an apple-green prima donna hat that an increasing breeze tried to lift off her fiery hair. "Welcome to Addis," she said, slightly out of breath.

More people approached to have a good look at Karen, including a few bachelors of different nationalities. Karen seemed to enjoy the attention.

"I think I just fell in love," Philippe, a Frenchman with the face of a voluptuary, sighed. "Isn't she lovely?" he asked, addressing no one in particular.

Dumb ass, Anouk huffed to herself.

The loudspeaker made several announcements and a light hush fell over the crowd. Some people headed for the stands, others clustered along the track. Karen joined Anouk and they strolled along the turf.

"Enjoying yourself?" Anouk asked casually.

Karen picked some lint from her sleeve, then opened her camera to set it. "It's all right." Anouk's mildly mocking gaze made her uneasy. "What's so funny?"

"I can see some of the men eating out of your hand already."

Karen shrugged. "And you think I care?" She smiled, then added in a low voice, "Little do you know."

Anouk's brows raised quizzically, and she studied Karen as if trying to read beyond the words.

Karen looked away. Careful, she warned herself, don't run off at the mouth. "By the way," she said, "the Peters plan to give a party next Saturday. You're invited of course."

Here we go, Anouk thought. The obligatory party to properly introduce Karen to the boys. Instead of a book, she'll end up pushing a pram.

"I'll come if I'm in Addis," she said evasively.

Mrs. Milno, who had given up her fight with the wind for her huge hat, and Mrs. Donner, a bleached blonde who pretended to be descended from Prussian aristocrats though everyone knew she had been her husband's servant in Beirut at one time, joined them. The start signal was given and everybody's interest veered to the track, the murmur of voices died.

In the sudden quiet the beautiful afternoon seemed milder to Anouk. The dust free air, not vibrating with sunrays any longer, let everything appear in tender clarity into which crept a light melancholy. The hills with their bluish tinge looked transparent on the gilded horizon gleaming like a glassy river.

Coats shining like satin, the horses raced past, their jockeys' shirts inflated with air, and people began to cheer for their favorites.

Karen was taking pictures. Anouk caught sight of Sergio and waved, glad to have an excuse to get away from these people and their pretentious ways.

God, what a zoo. And what a display of hypocrisy. Everybody acting so friendly when they all hated each other. How different things had been with Diana who had wit, charm and strength. She longed for a woman like her and people like herself. She knew the rumors about her sexuality were rife in Addis and that she had these people guessing. Being Egyptian added to her mystery, as did her flying and that she kept to herself.

All that whetted their curiosity. She had never tried to pass for someone she was not, but neither did she flaunt her sexuality or beliefs which were no one's business. After all, she didn't care what they did in bed and with whom. She had often thought of returning to Europe where she could be among her own kind. However, she wouldn't easily find a job as a pilot, being a woman. Besides, she preferred the freedom her job provided and the empty wilderness of this country rather than overpopulated Europe.

Anouk, she sighed to herself, you can't have everything.

"What's eating you?" Sergio asked when she reached him.

"It's these people," Anouk sighed. "I can only take them in small doses."

Sergio laughed and put an arm around her.

"Where's your girlfriend?" she asked.

"I broke it off," he said with a sigh, and looked at her affectionately. "It's just too bad they can't create a heterosexual version of you."

Anouk laughed merrily. "Don't tell me you have crush on me."

"What else?" he sighed melodramatically, then suddenly became serious and took a piece of paper from his pocket. "I almost forgot. This is a message that was left at my office for you from a Dr. Korda from Yemen. He's staying at the Ras Hotel."

Anouk stared at the paper, murmuring, "Yemen, that must be the doctor who took care of Silke. I'd better leave. See you in the morning."

Frowning, he watched her run to the parking lot. Near the grandstands, Karen, who was pretending to listen to Philippe's attempt to impress her with some intellectual prattle, also watched her leave and swallowed her disappointment.

She had hoped Anouk would accept an invitation to have dinner with her.

Chapter 4

Anouk gazed around the crowded lounge of the Ras Hotel, saw a blond man sitting by himself at a window table, and walked toward him. "Dr. Korda?"

He jumped up eagerly. "Yes. Miss Turabi?" He shook her hand and pointed to a chair. "Please sit down. What would you like to drink, Miss Turabi?"

"Call me Anouk, please," Anouk began in German.

"I will if you call me Klaus."

"All right, Klaus, a scotch on the rocks would be nice."

He ordered two, then said, "You speak good German."

She thanked him, taking in his deep tan and candid face. "So, you're the doctor who took care of Silke."

"Yes, I was heading a hospital in a town called Al-Hazm-al-Jawf. I had a three-year contract with the Yemen government which ended this month." A waiter brought their drinks and they drank to each other's health.

"It sounds as if you left Yemen for good."

He nodded. "I have, I'm sorry to say, so I can't help you much. Anyway, I met Silke at that hospital, and came to Addis strictly to see you at Silke's mother's request. Although now that I'm here, I'll tour the country before returning to Germany. I hear it's quite a fascinating place."

Anouk handed him her business card. "Consider our airline. We fly to all the historic and scenic places and upon request, also act as tour guides. We have good package deals."

"Thanks, I certainly shall do that." He slipped the card into his breast pocket. "About six months ago, an old Arab came into my office followed by a veiled woman whom he introduced as his daughter-in-law. He complained that she was constantly sick and thinner than any of his goats, and that after a year of marriage hadn't given them a son.

He left after exchanging a few words with the woman. You can't imagine my surprise when she lifted her veil and I saw a European looking teenage girl with blue eyes who spoke German with a Hamburg accent. Silke was pale and emaciated and I had her put into a private room where she broke down and cried as I've never seen anyone cry. I guess you know that Silke's mother is from Hamburg, her father from Yemen?"

"I do," Anouk said.

"Silke's mother is divorced from her father. Growing up, Silke continued to see her father on weekends and had a good relationship with him. When she was sixteen, her father offered her a trip to Yemen during the summer school vacation and Silke was overjoyed, wanting to see her father's country after having listened to his colorful tales for so many years."

"Didn't the mother suspect anything?" Anouk interrupted.

"Apparently they were on good terms and she had no reason to, I guess. Anyway, her father didn't travel with Silke, but entrusted her to good friends, a couple who had worked in Germany for years and were returning to Yemen to retire.

"An uncle picked up Silke at the Sana airport and brought her to Marib, a dusty town two hundred kilometers from Sana and surrounded by desert. She was left with a family who lived in primitive huts. Silke's father had promised she'd be staying at a house on the beach and Silke sensed that something was wrong.

"In the evening Silke was introduced to a short, thin man of twenty and was told that this was her husband. When Silke protested, she was shown a marriage certificate which her father had signed and which stated that he had received the sum of three-thousand D-marks for his daughter. She cried and fought and tried to run away. But they locked her up and threatened to tie her to the bed if she refused to sleep with her husband."

"Incredible," Anouk breathed, and took a sip.

He also took a sip and resumed. "Needless to say, Silke's German passport has been taken from her and she is never allowed to leave the house alone or to write to her mother because they fear the mother will try to get her daughter back."

"She told me she stole some money from her husband's wallet once, and tried walking to a neighboring town in order to call the German consulate in Sana to ask for help. But her brothers-in-law caught her and she received a severe beating from her husband. So she decided to die and stopped eating. When she began to have fainting spells, she was brought to me.

"She perked up after talking with her mother on the telephone and ate again. I kept Silke as long as I could in the hospital, telling her husband that she was sicker than she was, so she could see her mother who arrived within a few days. Of course we kept the mother's visit secret. Her mother, Irmgard, hadn't known of her daughter's whereabouts for over a year and all her letters to the Yemenite government had been fruitless. They couldn't apprehend her ex-husband as he had vanished."

"And the German consulate couldn't help?" Anouk asked, gulping her drink.

"Irmgard went to the German consulate in Sana but was told they couldn't do anything because Silke had become a national of Yemen through her marriage and any interference would cause a scene. The fact that Silke had been married without her consent didn't matter. According to Yemen's laws, the marriage was valid. And as you probably know, a woman can't divorce a husband there."

Anouk emptied her drink in one swallow. These events were ripping open the past buried deep within her. Gritting her teeth in fury, she waved to the waiter for another drink. "Was there no way to secret her out as a member of a German family or diplomatic employee? Surely—"

Klaus laid a hand on her forearm in sympathy. "It was a very painful situation. Irmgard was frantic—to be so close to her daughter and not be able to take her home. Believe me, we thought of all kinds of schemes to smuggle her out. But as obvious foreigners, nothing was realistic, and we had no clout with the embassy to do it illegally. To make it short, the mother had no choice but to return to Germany where she went to the highest authorities to get her daughter back, but was told again that Silke was out of Germany's jurisdiction and that they couldn't do anything.

"In the meantime Silke had to return to her husband. We had kept her as long as we could. A month later she was brought to me again, this time badly hemorrhaging. She had ruptured her uterus with a wire coat hanger to cause an abortion."

"My God," Anouk exclaimed. "Did her husband know she had done that?"

"Absolutely not, or he would have killed her, I think. I know how strictly the Koran as well as the law forbid even a necessary termination of a pregnancy. No, she had done it secretly at night in the out-house and everyone believed it was a natural occurrence.

"Anyway, she begged me to sterilize her. She was afraid that if she had a child she would never get out but that they would eventually get rid of her if she were sterile.

"Finally, after repairing the damage she had caused to herself, I tied off her fallopian tubes, an operation which can be reversible, afraid that she would repeat this and kill herself.

"In the meantime, in Hamburg, her mother and grand parents haven't gotten anywhere using official channels and, indeed, have now decided to get Silke out illegally." He smiled. "And that's when your cousin in France, is it Stephanie—?"

Anouk nodded.

"When Stephanie thought of you. She told Silke's mother that you were a pilot and the only person she knew who had the guts to get Silke out."

"If I listened to my guts, I'd refuse right away," Anouk retorted, feeling that they were all tied up in knots of anger and anxiety. What was she getting herself into here? Just because she had lucked out and saved herself so long ago didn't mean she felt brave or cunning now. Yet she knew she had no choice—she couldn't leave Silke to her fate in Yemen. Her motivation was deeply personal.

"Silke's mother and grandparents are willing to pay well. They have a dry-cleaning chain in Hamburg and are well off. They're aware of what you'll risk and will pay your price. The big question is, how can it be done?"

Anouk leaned on her elbows, thinking. "First, how can Silke even get away from her husband and his family?"

"That's something we don't know. I know where she lives. Silke made me a drawing of the village and the house." He took a piece of paper from his pocket and handed it to her. Anouk glanced at it. "And this is a snapshot I took of Silke at the hospital. Although it won't be of much help since Silke is veiled and cloaked when she's allowed to leave the house with her mother and sisters-in-law."

Anouk studied the picture of a young woman who looked more like a disturbed child, with big frightened eyes in a thin face framed by long brown hair.

Handing her a business card, he said, "And this is from a friend of mine in Sana, a crazy Swede by the name of Ulf Joergensen who'd do anything for a little diversion. You've no idea how monotonous life for a single guy is there. Anyway, he's met Irmgard, Silke's mother, and is willing to help."

Anouk was pensive. "First we have to find and contact Silke. I wish you hadn't left Yemen."

"It was that or renew my contract for another three years. I just couldn't face that. Anyway, how could I have helped?"

"Silke could've faked another illness in order to be hospitalized and we could've smuggled her out of the hospital and hid her in your friend's place."

He considered it slowly shaking his head. "I don't think it would have been that easy because there were always some of her in-laws visiting and watching. And I would've been held responsible. But aside from all that, how would you go on once you have Silke away from her in-laws?"

Anouk sighed. "You're asking me too much too soon."

"We thought that perhaps with a small plane—"

"That's out of the question. How and where would I be able to land without being picked up by radar?"

"Good question. What about a boat?"

"I've thought of that. But again, the minute we enter Yemen's territorial waters we'll be discovered and accosted by their coast guard. And via land is out too. We'd have to cross the entire Arabian peninsula which is mostly desert and we would be caught for sure."

"Are you trying to tell me you don't think it can be done? You're Irmgard's last hope."

"No, it's just that I haven't found a way yet." They lapsed into silence, sipping their drinks.

"This is difficult," he muttered.

"It is," Anouk agreed. "But not impossible."

"No more ideas?"

Anouk shook her head, glanced at the business card he had given her. "I'll fly to Yemen within the next few days and look up your friend, Ulf. I'll also drive to the village where Silke lives and check it out. Who knows? Maybe I'll be able to make contact with Silke somehow."

"I must warn you that the law in Yemen requires that women must be veiled and cloaked in public which will make it difficult for you to travel. Ulf will have to drive you around."

"I don't intend to travel as a woman," Anouk said, and drained her glass.

He looked at her surprised, then smiled. "I see. Well, Stephanie

36

was right. You do have courage." He glanced at his watch. "It's dinner time. Would you like to join me? Please do," he said, when she hesitated. "It's been three years since I had the pleasure of dining in the company of a woman. You could tell me what to see in this country."

Anouk smiled. "All right."

The next day, Anouk walked into a store selling electric appliances.

"Is George here?" she asked the Ethiopian clerk.

"Just a moment," the woman said, and went into a room in the back. Moments later, a slender man appeared who looked like a playboy of the twenties with pomaded black hair and a Clark Gable mustache. He was Armenian with a special talent known only to a few initiates.

"Hallo, Anouk," he greeted her, holding out his hand which was hairy and bore a heavy signet ring. "What can I do for you?"

"Can I talk to you for a moment? In private," she asked.

"This way." He led her into his office and closed the door. "So…?" he asked when she was seated at his desk.

Anouk pulled out an Ethiopian passport she had acquired two years before and handed it to him. "I need my name and sex changed."

He leaned back in his chair, perusing the document. "Am I assuming correctly that you intend to cross a border?"

Anouk nodded.

"Then you need a new passport. Because no forgery, no matter how good, will pass an x-ray undetected. And most international airport x-ray passports these days."

Anouk considered this for a moment. "All right. How much would a new passport cost me?"

"For you a thousand."

"Isn't that a little steep?"

He smiled, exposing a gold tooth. "I don't get those passports for free. And my work is the best."

Anouk drew breath. "I might also need an Egyptian passport in the near future. Is that possible?"

Again he smiled. "Everything's possible if the money is right."

"Let's do the Ethiopian first."

"When do you need it?"

"As soon as possible."

"Is two days good enough?"

Anouk nodded.

He picked up a piece of paper. "Which name do you want?"

"Amir Turabi, sex male, the rest can remain as on the original."

He looked at her with dark brows raised but asked nothing. Anouk got her wallet from the inside pocket of her jacket and pulled out a couple of hundred Ethiopian dollars. "That's all I have on me."

"I trust you." He took the money. "See you the day after tomorrow."

Chapter 5

A week later, Anouk got off the airplane at Sana airport and stepped into the cool mountain air of Yemen's central highlands. The rainy season had started and humidity was high, yet a gust of wind brought dust.

She followed the other passengers into the terminal, looking like an Arab man in a suit and tie. A headcloth held by a goat hair band covered her slicked-back hair and fell loosely down one shoulder. Her breasts were bound flat under a long-sleeved shirt.

Going through passport control, she had a tense moment as the official studied her passport, then her. "You're originally from Egypt," the officer said, speaking Arabic.

"Yes, sir," Anouk replied, keeping her voice at its deepest level.

"And you've taken the Ethiopian nationality?"

"I've been a permanent resident of Ethiopia for many years and travel a lot. Having an Ethiopian passport saves me from having to get exit and entry visas each time I leave the country."

"For how long are you planning to stay in Yemen?"

"Five days, sir."

"Where are you going to stay?"

"At the Sana Palace Hotel."

"What is the purpose of your visit?"

"I'm a history teacher and would like to visit a few archeological sites in Yemen."

He seemed to be satisfied, stamped her passport, and handed it back to her. Relieved, she stuck it into her pocket and picked up her suitcase. The terminal was crowded with a motley variety of people: Bedouins in long white shirts and headcloths with black goat-hair bands, Omani men also in long shirts and embroidered caps, Yemenite men in shirts and jackets and colorful futas—skirts ending at the knees—some men wearing turbans. There were Indian businessmen, and a few Europeans. Women were totally absent. She gazed around and saw a tall, blond man in his thirties scanning the arriving passengers.

His searching glance briefly brushed her.

"Ulf Joergensen?" she asked when she reached him.

"Yes?" he said, frowning, then his face lit up. "Anouk Turabi?" he asked, surprised, speaking English with a Swedish accent. "You could've fooled me."

"I just fooled the immigration official," she said, smiling and taking in his blue eyes and rugged good looks.

"You're the first Arab woman in this country whose face I've seen," he said, taking her hand. "Can you believe that?"

"Don't say it too loud," she warned. "Someone might hear you."

He picked up her suitcase and she followed him outside to his car.

"Do you have a hotel reservation?" he asked, driving out of the airport.

"Can you recommend something that's not too expensive?"

"My guest room," he said, grinning.

Anouk thought about it for a moment, then said. "All right."

"You won't regret it because I live in the center and have a splendid view of the old town." He turned south and drove through a hilly area along fields of vegetables and orchards of almonds, walnuts, peaches, apricots and lemons. "Is this your first trip to Yemen?"

"Yes," Anouk replied, gazing at a village and large vineyard. "I avoid Arab countries if I can. Is wine being made here?"

He laughed. "No way. Alcohol is strictly forbidden. Why is it you don't like Arab countries?"

"Too many bad memories."

He remained quiet for a while, then said, "Sana's quite an enchanting place. According to Yemenite folklore, it was founded by Noah's son Shem and is one of the first sites of human settlement."

"I know the legend," Anouk said. "Apparently Shem came from the north seeking somewhere to settle and chose the place shown to him by a bird. I also know that Sana was the capital of the Himyarite kingdom in the first century AD, and in 525 AD the Aksumites from Ethiopia conquered it. The city was either the capital or else destroyed by new sultans seizing power from old rulers. It was also ruled by the Mamelukes of Egypt, then taken by the Turks in 1548."

He gave her an appreciative look.

Anouk grinned. "History's my passion. Anyway, how has life been here since the Yemen Arab Republic was proclaimed three years ago?"

"It's finally peaceful. Of course the military's still quite active and there are roadblocks to control papers to assure no royalist rebels are trying anything. But for us Europeans working here it's all right. Our contracts give us some kind of immunity."

"What do you do?"

"I'm an electrical engineer and have a contract with the government."

"Do you like it?"

He shrugged. "The pay's good, but the social life stinks. No women, no bars or night clubs, no alcohol." He shook his head. "I'll never understand the Arabs." He grinned again. "But I have a good friend who's a pilot and smuggles in beer and wine. So we'll have a cool beer when we get home."

"Aren't there any European women?"

"A few wives of men on contract like me. But most of them don't last long. They can't stand all the restrictions, especially the strict dress code they have to follow. Women can't show themselves in public and have to wear the abba or chador, a heavy black all-enveloping cloak which is quite unbearable when it's hot. I understand you're from Egypt so you must know."

"The dress code is less strict in Egypt and only the more traditional, mostly lower class women veil themselves."

They reached the outskirts of the city where the streets were bustling with people and cars.

"So how's Ethiopia?" he asked, driving around a farmer and his two donkeys.

"To begin with, less dusty," Anouk said, coughing, and loosening her tie. "Have you ever been there?"

"Not yet. I heard from Klaus Korda that it's a fascinating country. I understand he toured it with your airline." He honked at some boys, then slowed to let a car pass. It wrapped them in another cloud of dust, and Anouk rolled up her window.

"Haven't they thought of paving their streets?" she asked.

"Unfortunately not. And the cement factories just outside the city don't help either."

Anouk looked around. "I have to admit, the houses are beautiful."

"Yes, the architecture here is distinctly different from anywhere else in the world."

Anouk gazed at walls ornamented with elaborate friezes, and windows with a complex fretwork of superimposed round and angular alabaster panes.

"Lit up at night, all those colorful panes make the town look quite fabulous," Ulf said.

Two women cloaked in black walked along the street with their heads turned away. As they passed, Anouk noticed that their faces were also covered by a black veil. Looking ahead again, she noticed Ulf repeatedly glancing at her. He's starved and checking out the merchandise, she told herself, planning to make her sexuality clear as soon as the moment was right. He drove to the side of the street and parked next to a four-story building.

"We've arrived," he announced.

His apartment was on the upper floor with a magnificent view of the old town and its many graceful minarets.

He showed her the guest room and the bath. "As the Arabic saying goes, my home's your home, so feel free to do as you like."

At last in the bathroom Anouk could take off the headcloth, get out of her suit, untie her breasts, wash her face and hands and loosen her hair.

He was sitting on the couch when she joined him in the living room, having changed into a galabiya—a floor-length, long-sleeved white shirt men wore in Arab countries.

"You look more like a woman now," he remarked with a swift glance at her breasts showing through the thin cotton.

She sat down in a chair. "I'd like to warn you that although I am a woman, I don't care for men sexually."

"I was afraid of that," he said, then shrugged. "I still enjoy your company. How about a cold beer?"

"Gladly," Anouk said.

He got two bottles from the refrigerator and glasses from the kitchen.

"Delicious." Anouk sighed after drinking, then leaned back. "So, let's come to the point of my visit—Silke."

He nodded. "Ya, that's quite a problem."

"I assume you've never met her?"

"No. Klaus and I usually saw each other in Sana. He told me about Silke when she was brought to his hospital in Al-Hazm-al-

42

Jawf. He was quite shocked when he learned what happened to her and called Silke's mother in Hamburg. A few days later I met the mother at the airport and drove her to the hospital. I also drove her to the German Embassy here, but, as you know, they were of no help."

"I understand the mother's visit was kept from Silke's husband and in-laws?"

"Definitely. The mother-in-law and one of her daughters camped at the hospital like watchdogs. Klaus had to literally throw them out of Silke's room a few times to examine her. Or he had her taken to his office to have some privacy. That's also where Silke and her mother visited. They had to be so careful."

"What's her mother like?"

"Irmgard's an attractive and gracious woman," he said with a wistful smile. "She stayed with me for a few days. It was quite dramatic when she had to leave without her daughter after trying to find her for over a year. She cried all the way to the airport." He finished his beer. "We're corresponding, but unfortunately I can't write her anything about her daughter. I wrote her that you'd be coming to Sana, though."

"I also wrote her," Anouk said.

"So how do you plan to find Silke?"

"First, I need a map and a car. I thought that you could rent one in your name for me so I didn't bother to get a forged driver's license stating that I'm male. I understand women aren't allowed to drive?"

"Right, and car rental in the Western sense is out, too, because you'd have to rent one with a driver, which I'm sure you wouldn't want. I'll organize a company car for you." He went to a desk, got a map, and unfolded it. "Here's Al-Hazm in the Al-Jawf province. That's where Klaus lived and worked. It's about a two hour drive from Sana. And here's Marib, the village where Silke lives. It's in the easternmost province of Yemen and bordered by the ar-Ruba al-Khali desert. It's also the land of the Bedouin."

Anouk studied the map, shaking her head. "She couldn't be in a more isolated place. I know that there's a new Marib and an old Marib which is Yemen's most famous archaeological site."

"Silke lives in new Marib."

"Klaus gave me a drawing Silke made of the village and the street where she lives."

"How about another beer?"

"Thanks," Anouk said, and emptied her glass.

He went to the kitchen. "Okay, so we know the address. How are we going to recognize Silke all veiled and wrapped up?"

"That I don't know," Anouk replied. "And don't think of going with me. You'd only draw attention and make everyone suspicious."

"I could wrap myself in chador," he suggested half-jokingly, opening two more bottles.

"You'd be the tallest woman Yemen has ever seen," Anouk said, laughing. "How tall are you? Six foot five?"

"Six foot six," he said almost ruefully.

"With the short people here even I'd stick out at nearly six feet. Besides, women seldom leave their house alone and never linger in the streets. That's considered immodest. So even if you were short and covered up you couldn't just walk up and down Silke's street without causing suspicion." She had a sip of beer. "I have to drive there and see."

"What will you do once you've found Silke?"

"I'll try to contact her somehow."

"How?"

"I don't know. I only know that I must be very careful, because if her husband and his family suspect anything, they'll make Silke disappear and make sure we never find her again."

They became silent. The room had dimmed and the double glass door of the balcony was filled with a resplendent sky. From the tower of a nearby mosque a muezzin called believers for prayer.

"By the way, who are your neighbors?" Anouk asked.

"Next to me are two Dutch men, they're involved in a development aid program. And downstairs are two German engineers whose wives returned to Europe not long ago. A building of lonely bachelors," he sighed. "We meet a couple of times a week for a card game, and from time to time go out to have dinner at the hotels here."

"Do you have a servant?"

"Yes, a houseboy who comes Mondays, Wednesdays and Fridays from six till eleven. Why?"

"That means he was here this morning." Anouk concluded. "I have a few things that could give me away as a woman. Besides, I don't want to be seen by him so he doesn't come to any conclusions later when the big search for Silke is on."

He showed her a cabinet with a lock where she could stow special items, then asked, "What shall we do about dinner?"

"I've been wondering that myself," Anouk said. "I'm hungry."

"I have things for a cold plate: eggs, chicken, vegetables, olives, goat cheese, bread, and fruit. And beer. Or would you like to have a glass of white wine?"

"I'll stick with the beer," Anouk replied.

Getting the things from the refrigerator, he said, "Tomorrow night we could eat at the Taj Sheba Hotel down the street. They have excellent food."

"Tomorrow night I'll be in Marib," Anouk said.

The next morning he procured a white Peugeot for her, and by noon she drove north through an agricultural region which had elaborately built irrigation terraces of ancient origin. Mountain slopes were covered by terraces bearing all kinds of crops.

The road wound through the Eastern mountains, crossed parts of a wadi, a dry seasonal river, and went over several passes, then descended to the desert, very steeply at first and offering spectacular views. It became hot and the dry lands were alternately strewn with sand dunes or black lava rocks, crossed by small wadis. Vegetation consisted of small shrubs and grasses, acacia and tamarisk trees among which grazed herds of goats watched by boys. She reached the Bedouin country which was forbidden to tourists and had been a stronghold of royalists during the civil war. She was stopped once by a Bedouin patrol, but after she showed her passport and told them she was a teacher, they let her pass.

Two hours later she reached Al-Hazm, modern capital of the province and of no particular interest. She found the hospital and parked. Before getting out of the car, she checked her face in the rearview mirror. Ulf had brushed some soot from the kitchen stove onto her chin and upper lip, then wiped it off again, leaving only her pores black to suggest the shade of a beard.

"You look like a handsome Arab man," he had said before she left his apartment. "Some father in the village might offer you his daughter."

A young man sat at the reception desk of the hospital and she asked for Dr. Klaus Korda.

"Dr. Korda doesn't work here any longer. He returned to Germany," the clerk told her.

She feigned surprise. "Who's his replacement?"

"Dr. Hamid Shahatta."

"That sounds Egyptian."

He smiled. "Yes, like you. Would you like to see him?"

Anouk shook her head, thanked him, and left.

An Egyptian, she thought, disappointed, returning to her car. She had hoped Dr. Korda's position would have been filled by another European. Certainly she couldn't expect any help from an Egyptian doctor. So she discarded her idea of smuggling Silke out of the hospital and turning south headed for Marib.

The land became more arid; the sparse vegetation equalled the population. She encountered a few trucks with Bedouins but they didn't stop her and only returned her wave. After passing a few villages, she reached Marib an hour later. The village still bore the traces of the civil war, but well-irrigated fields growing vegetables and grains promised a hopeful future. The streets were dusty, the houses of mud brick. Some houses in the center were of white stone.

There was a small mosque, a hotel, a gas station with a hand-cranked pump, a market, a cafe with peeling blue and white paint.

A few men sat at wooden tables in front of the cafe; the roads belonged to half-grown boys and skinny dogs.

She counted six cars—all models from the fifties—parked along the main street. Women were invisible. Finding the street where Silke lived, she drove along high fences hiding dwellings and assuring complete privacy. After rechecking Silke's map, she slowed in front of a fence of mud bricks behind which she made out the reed roofs of several huts. She heard the cackling of chickens, the bleating of a goat. Otherwise there was no noise.

It was early afternoon, the heat heavy, and everyone probably still taking a siesta. She drove on, fearing she would attract attention if she remained too long. She returned to the center of the village, parked in front of the cafe, and sat down at a table outside.

An older man in a shirt and red and white striped futa appeared. "Your visit honors me, sir," he said in Arabic

"The honor is on my side," Anouk answered, noticing that conversations at the other tables had stopped and everyone was listening.

"Ah, you are Egyptian," the man who appeared to be the owner, continued.

"Yes, I am," Anouk said.

"Welcome, and may Allah bless you and your great country."

"May Allah preserve you and your house," Anouk answered,

46

and ordered Turkish coffee.

He left and she gazed around, aware of being watched by the other patrons. From the looks of it, this village didn't get many visitors, which made everything still more difficult. She wouldn't be able to make a move without everyone knowing.

"What brings you to our humble village, sir?" a man from a neighboring table asked.

"I'm a history teacher," Anouk said, "and want to visit the sites in old Marib."

"Allah is good and has sent us many teachers and doctors from Egypt," he said, and his two companions nodded in agreement.

I wish he'd send me an idea how to find Silke and get her out of here, she thought. So far it looks pretty hopeless. "It isn't often that you get visitors?" she asked.

He shook his head. "Our town is too small, sir."

"It is small but pleasant," she said, to justify her stay and future ones. "Its peace is like balm for the heart after the noisy cities I have visited. May Allah keep it that way."

The owner returned with the coffee, a strong brew in a short glass, and she asked, "Do you serve evening meals?"

"It will be my pleasure to have a meal prepared for you, sir."

"May Allah increase your possessions," Anouk answered. "I shall look at the surroundings and will be back at sundown."

She finished her coffee in three sips, put money on the table, and returned to her car, knowing that by evening everyone would have heard about this conversation. Driving a good distance out of the village, she parked under a tree, pondering.

For all she knew, she might have talked to Silke's husband or in-laws at the cafe. But even if she could get invited to their home, she wouldn't see Silke. When men entertained other men in their homes, the women remained out of sight. She hated to be so helpless. And she hated to fail.

After driving and walking about, taking in the land, the day was finally ebbing with a splendid sunset. She drove back to the road where Silke lived and saw four men enter the compound. Three were younger, one older. The father and his sons, one of whom was Silke's husband. She knew it was useless to wait any longer. At this time of day no woman would leave her house. She checked into the only hotel which was cheap and as filthy as Ulf had predicted.

Following his suggestion, she had borrowed a set of sheets from

47

him and spread them over the dirty ones on the bed, then returned to the cafe and was greeted with great reverence by the owner.

"Have you enjoyed your drive around, sir?"

"I have. It is a beautiful area."

He put plates and a glass on the table. "Are you teaching in Sana?"

Amused by his curiosity but on guard, she said, "I am."

"Do you have a bride?"

"I recently married," Anouk replied, afraid he might offer her his daughter.

"Ah, may Allah grant you many sons."

He hurried into the back to get the food. It was surprisingly good. A fiery stew with lamb and lentils, beans, chickpeas on a bed of rice, thin Arab bread brushed with clarified butter and a paste made form fenugreek and coriander; figs and peaches from the region and coffee. There was no silverware and Anouk ate with her right hand, leaving the left 'unclean' hand in her lap.

"You are an artist in your trade," she said, wiping her mouth and dipping her hand into a bowl of water. "May light shine on you at all times."

He bowed. "Your praise is generous and exceeds my worth."

She was up before dawn, not having slept much, as she had to sit most of the night on a chair with her feet on the table after discovering that the mattress was crawling with bedbugs. She went down the hall to the squat toilet which was stopped up and had fat flies buzzing all around. Retching, she hurried from it. The bathroom next to it hadn't been cleaned in decades from the looks of it. She only washed her face and brushed her teeth, careful not to touch anything. She doubted that complaining would change much and decided against it.

The sun rose while she got dressed and with it, as if on cue, the muezzin's voice from the nearby mosque. 'There is no God but God and Muhammed is the Prophet of God,' he sang in long cadences to call believers to prayer. It reminded her of Egypt where they had lived near a mosque in Cairo. As with all religions, many Muslims were practicing while others were not, like her father who was a believer but didn't pray five times a day as the Koran demanded. It was perfectly permissible to pray at home or elsewhere; only on Fridays was one supposed to pray in the mosque. That's when her father usually went, and when her brother was old enough he had been taken along. Women were not allowed in the mosque and had to pray at home.

Pores freshly clogged with soot, she went to the cafe, ordered coffee and asked for a newspaper.

The owner shook his head. "Sorry, sir, no one reads here."

Anouk remembered reading about the high illiteracy rate in Yemen. Women were not educated at all. She shuddered, imagining what it must be like for a modern young woman from Europe to live in these primitive conditions.

She finished the coffee and drove to the market, already bustling with men and cloaked women buying food for the day while children, dogs, and goats ran everywhere. Filled with hope, she drove to Silke's street and parked some distance from the fence, acting as if she were studying a map.

Her pulse accelerated when she saw the gate open and three women come out, one carrying a basket. They were heavily cloaked with a veil of black gauze covering their faces—shapeless, faceless shadows with no status, identity, or freedom. Indistinguishable aside from their sizes, they approached the car with heads lowered and turned away as a sign of modesty. With an eye on them through the rearview mirror, she drove to the end of the street, made a U-turn and slowly drove after them. Close to the market, she passed them. The women kept on walking with their heads lowered and faces averted.

Anouk parked and, pretending to look at baskets, watched them arrive, wondering if one of them was Silke. As they walked past her into the milling crowd, she turned away so she wouldn't appear to be staring which would have been an offense. They walked from merchant to merchant, looking at vegetables and fruit. Anouk stayed close enough to hear the shortest and heaviest of the women bargaining with a merchant. Her voice sounded old and she spoke the Arabic of the region without an accent. Anouk concluded that it must be Silke's mother-in-law.

The merchant wrapped beans, green peppers, and a bunch of herbs into newspaper, then took money from the woman whose hand looked dark and as old as her voice sounded. While the merchant made change, one of the other women took the package and put it into the basket. Her hand was also dark but young.

Anouk followed them as they continued from stand to stand, watching the woman whose hands she hadn't seen yet. If it was Silke her hands would be paler. At times the women were hidden by other women and it was difficult not to lose them in this crowd of identical looking black cloaks.

The women lingered before a stand selling scarves and the woman Anouk had thought might be Silke picked one up. Her hands were small and also dark. Finally the women were done shopping and left the market.

Disappointed, Anouk returned to her car. It would have been a miracle if she had found Silke on the first try, she reasoned. Maybe tomorrow.

But the next morning only men and a half-grown boy appeared from Silke's dwellings. She drove along other streets as if doing a little sightseeing, then returned to the cafe.

"You are up early, sir," the owner greeted her.

"I have been to the market," Anouk replied. "It is quite impressive with good produce and crafts."

"It is the biggest in the region," he said with pride. "People come to shop here from all the nearby towns."

She ordered coffee, thinking of all the questions she couldn't ask without causing suspicion. Full of hope that the next and last day of her stay would bring results, she drove around and read at the cafe, then spent yet another miserable night at the hotel. But in the morning only two women showed, the short, heavy one who was the mother-in-law and one whose hand holding the basket was dark. She didn't bother following them. Driving back to Sana, she regretted that she couldn't stay longer in Yemen and wondered if Silke was ever allowed to go to the market.

Chapter 6

The day was fading and it was getting cold. Anouk had just returned from her trip and looked forward to a quiet evening. She felt worn out and her mind was still buzzing with images of Yemen. She took a long, hot shower and was getting into a comfortable white sweater and black corduroys when she heard a car driving up to her house and the *zabanya* talking to someone.

Still brushing her hair dry, she went out on the verandah.

"Surprise, surprise," she said to Karen who was coming up the stairs.

Karen also wore a sweater—hers dark blue wool—and white slacks. Anouk noticed that she looked pale. Might be the sweater's color.

"Hope you don't mind my dropping in like this," Karen said. "But I called earlier and got no answer. Then I ran a few errands in town and thought—"

"Stop making excuses and come in," Anouk interrupted, more curious than annoyed by this unexpected visit.

"This is nice," Karen said, looking around.

The living and dining rooms were separated by an arch. A Persian carpet partly covered the wooden floor. Lit by two floor lamps, wicker furniture with sand colored upholstery and colorful cushions was like an island in the center of the living room. A few paintings depicting Ethiopian figures graced the walls. The dining room had a table with six chairs.

"Simple and chic," Karen said, sitting down on the couch.

"It's home." Anouk studied her. "Is everything all right with you?"

"Yes, I'm a bit tired, that's all. Must be the altitude."

"It takes a while to get used to it. Can I offer you something? I have fresh orange juice, wine, beer, scotch."

"I'll have a glass of wine if you join me."

"I will." Anouk went into the kitchen. She returned with the drinks on a tray and a bowl with assorted nuts. "So what's been happening with you?" she asked, setting the tray on the low table before the couch.

"I took pictures of Addis and the surroundings. I also went to the Rift Valley Lakes for a week. They were fabulous. Otherwise..." Karen let the sentence trail off and shrugged.

Anouk handed her a glass, took the other and sat down in a chair. "How was your party?" she asked, after they toasted.

"You should've come. It turned out quite nice."

"I was away."

"You must be away a lot. I never see you."

"Well, it's due to my job, and I tend to stick pretty much to myself."

"Don't you ever get lonely?"

"Of course."

Karen studied her for a moment. "What do you do when you're lonely?"

Anouk smiled, thinking of a few places around town which helped her out of the dumps, but she couldn't tell Karen about them. "I read, listen to music, or see a film."

Karen picked a couple of almonds from the bowl. "I can only read so much. And the films they show here leave much to be desired."

"I thought you'd be swamped with invitations."

"That gets old, too."

"What about your book?"

"My friends are against my driving to Omo Valley. They say it's too dangerous. Is that true?"

"Yes, it's the country's most vast and remote wilderness with tribes still living as they did in the Stone Age. You shouldn't go alone or drive there. The roads are mere tracks. Why don't you take one of our tours?"

"All right, I'd like to fly with you."

"Omo Valley's really Murath's specialty. He knows the area like no one else. He's a good pilot."

They lapsed into silence, hearing eery cackles coming from the hills behind the house.

"Hyenas," Anouk said, seeing Karen's surprise.

"They sure come close."

"They're hungry."

"Don't you ever fly to Omo Valley?" Karen persisted, wanting to be with Anouk again.

"I do. But my specialty is history and I mostly do the north of the country which is its most historic part. In fact I'm flying a group of Swiss to Massawa and Asmara the day after tomorrow. There's still room for one passenger."

"Reserve it for me, please," Karen said eagerly, and rose. "Well, I've taken up enough of your time. Thanks for the wine. I'll see you at the airport the day after tomorrow."

Anouk went outside with her, watching her drive away. Something struck her as odd about Karen. Aside from appearing lonely, she sensed that there was something else. She didn't quite seem to fit in with the other whites or be too interested in associating with them.

And this visit was more than just a social call. But of all people, why would she seek me out? she asked herself. Could it be that she heard the rumors and is herself…no, impossible. Surely I would see it somehow, in her eyes, her demeanor.

The Peters house was at the other end of town and Karen drove slowly, in no hurry to get back. Nora and John were probably reading or watching TV. Although she liked her friends, she looked forward to having her own place. These past two weeks she had been looking for an apartment. There were few available and finally something had come up in a modern building near Mexico Square; she'd be able to move in on the first.

Driving along the dark and empty streets, she thought about Anouk, wondering what kind of woman she was. She had hoped that they'd become good friends, do things together, after they had started out so well in Djibouti.

Anouk had seemed warmer, friendlier then. Or had that been part of the customer service? She was a bit cool and distant tonight, as if she were preoccupied with something. Maybe she shouldn't have just dropped in on her. She seemed to be a recluse with no need of friends. Too bad, because she was more interesting than all the people she had met so far. Maybe she'd warm up to her on this trip.

She thought about the dinner parties she and her friends had been invited to and how every host had tried to outdo the previous one. How empty the conversations were, how affected the behavior of some people.

The tea parties of the women to which Nora had dragged her were the worst. She knew she was only invited because of her friendship with the Peters, although the fact that she had been a model impressed the old bats. And the conversations during those afternoons were even deadlier. Most of the time they gossiped about other people, making her wonder what they were saying behind her back. She was also tired of hearing laments about the lack of amenities in Ethiopia. One would think they had all been millionaires in Europe and lived in palaces.

And those bachelors Nora always tried to match her up with! The worst was the Baron. No, Philippe actually. God, what a wishy-washy excuse of a man.

Nora was reading on the couch when she arrived at the house. John was in his study, their six-year old son in bed.

"Where have you been?" Nora asked, putting a book down and glancing at the clock on the wall. "I was beginning to get worried."

"Come on, Nora. It's not even nine and I'm an adult," she said, annoyed. "I'm quite able to take care of myself."

"Still, this is Africa and you're a white woman."

"And black men have rape on their minds the minute they see one of us," Karen jeered. "Really, Nora. This town is probably safer than most in the States. Besides, judging from how well the bordellos here are visited by white men, it's rather black women who have to watch out for white men—wouldn't you say?"

Nora looked vexed. "No reason to get angry. I only meant well."

"I know you do, and I love you for it. But I wish you'd limit your mothering to your son." Karen slumped into an arm chair. "Anyway, I visited Anouk and will fly north with her the day after tomorrow. I have to go on with my book."

"Anouk, huh?"

"Yeah, why?"

"You know the rumors about Anouk?"

Karen frowned. "What rumors?"

"Apparently she isn't normal."

"She seems quite normal to me."

"You know what I mean. She's supposed to be *different*—you know."

Karen swallowed and sat momentarily transfixed. Nora looked

at her inquisitively and Karen felt color rise to her face. Then bold resentment filled her. "You mean she's a lesbian? Who told you that?"

"We've heard it from several sources—one man actually saw her come out of a bordello."

Taken aback, Karen remained silent.

"A little shocking, isn't it?"

"Why should it be more so than if a man goes. Obviously whoever told you that also went. And who knows if it's true. He might've mistaken someone else for Anouk. After all, they all sneak to those places in the dark."

"Whatever the case may be, we've heard about Anouk from several sources. They can't all be wrong."

Karen's tone turned belligerent. "Well, there's nothing wrong with gays. I've worked with plenty of them in the fashion business."

"Gays, huh?"

"Or dykes, queers, fags if you prefer."

Nora gave her an odd smile. "Why so defensive suddenly?"

"Why that smile?" Karen asked back.

Nora threw a glance towards the study and said in a low voice, "You are, too, aren't you?"

Karen stiffened. "Nora, if this is a problem, I'll move to a hotel right now."

"Don't be ridiculous! I always had an inkling."

"You had an inkling? And still tried to fix me up with those jerks here?"

"I thought that maybe if you met the right man…"

"Among those debauched alcoholics? I thought you were my friend."

Nora threw her hands up in defeat. "All right, all right, I plead guilty."

"How come you never told me you knew?"

"Come on, Karen, one doesn't talk about these things easily, and what if you weren't? You never brought it up, and I thought it was up to you. Besides…" Norma smiled embarrassed.

"Besides what?"

Nora giggled. "You always had a definite boyish air about you with your short blonde hair, and you were always so daring, so powerful and unpredictable which made you somehow mysterious. And you never talked about boys, only your adventures, always putting me in the role of the girl you had to save."

"Do you still think I'm boyish?"

Nora nodded. "Must be that short hair although your long lashes and those blue eyes confound the impression as does your full mouth. And when you smile, you're downright beautiful and feminine. That's why they liked you as a model."

"Because all the photographers were gay! But thanks. I'll try to smile more often." Karen grimaced the way she did when she had to smile for a photo session in her modeling days.

Chapter 7

"Massawa means the 'calling place' in the Tigré language," Anouk explained to Karen and a group of Swiss, some dressed in hiking boots as if ready to climb their Matterhorn. Karen was in white shorts, a light blue shirt, and sneakers. Anouk wore her khaki uniform consisting of slacks, and a tailored shirt with epaulettes, gold buttons and an insignia of gold wings pinned to her breast pocket.

"It is one of the most important ports of the Red Sea," Anouk went on, "and one of the hottest places on earth."

It was dawn, the sun barely up, yet it was hot already. Anouk led her flock to the suq or market, noisy with bleating goats, cackling chicken, bargaining women and men, and boys in long white shirts offering glass and plastic jewelry and small toys to the tourists. They continued on to the old section of town, following narrow, dusty streets lined with white-washed stone houses where maimed beggars and skinny dogs slunk around in hopeless apathy. After visiting the colorful harbor of the ninth century with its dhows and fishing boats, the Swiss wilted and asked to be returned to their hotel.

Karen looked at her watch. "It's only ten. What shall we do with the rest of the day?"

"How about a swim in one of the islands beyond the reef?" Anouk asked. "Let's get our bathing suits, then rent a boat."

Glad to be alone with Anouk, Karen agreed.

Anouk rented a Chris Craft and they motored to Dahlak-Kebir, the biggest of the low-lying coral islands. Karen sat next to her, enjoying the speed with which the boat flew over the glassy water. She glanced at Anouk who looked straight ahead, hair brushed back by the wind. She was more and more intrigued by this impenetrable woman. Although Anouk was more congenial, Karen hoped it wasn't only based on customer service again.

Reaching the island, Anouk beached the craft and they strolled on a white beach, watching tropical birds through Karen's zoom lens, then got into bikinis, Anouk's black, Karen's emerald green, and swam in warm, turquoise water. When they had their fill of exercise, they stretched out on towels in the shade of some palms. Karen's skin had taken on a pink hue and she rubbed sunblock onto her face, arms and legs. Handing Anouk the bottle, she asked, "Would you put some on my back, please?"

"Of course," Anouk said.

Karen closed her eyes, savoring the touch of Anouk's large yet graceful hand.

"Would you mind doing this for the next two hours?" she sighed. "It feels divine."

Anouk just laughed, gave her a gentle slap, and put the cap on the bottle.

"Let me rub some on you."

"I don't burn easily. I get very dark in no time."

"You already have. Wish my skin would do that."

Anouk lay on her back, eyes closed. Karen remained sitting with her legs pulled up, arms around them and looked at Anouk's well-shaped arms and her wide brown shoulders. She couldn't stop looking at that bronze body, and felt a powerful longing to touch it. She also longed to know whether the rumors were true and Anouk really was a lesbian, but was afraid to ask. What if it wasn't true and Anouk would be insulted?

Or didn't want it to be known? She remembered her fear of discovery at college after a fellow classmate had been expelled. What a complicated world we live in, she thought. Why couldn't one simply ask others about their sexuality without anyone feeling threatened or indicted?

"Have you ever been married?" she tried.

"No," Anouk answered. Her eyes were closed, her thoughts rotating around Silke and possible ways to get her out of Yemen. It seemed that was all she could think of lately.

"Do you plan to?" Karen continued to ask.

Anouk briefly opened her eyes. "Plan what?"

"To get married."

Anouk chuckled. "No."

"Neither will I."

What's she trying to get at? Anouk wondered. Then her thoughts returned to the letter she had received from Irmgard who was prepared to come to Ethiopia. But as long as she didn't have a concrete plan, it would be a wasted trip. She planned to return to Yemen again soon to try to make contact with Silke somehow. From George she had ordered an Egyptian passport, this time with a different name. She feared she had to make several trips to Yemen and that the Yemenite officials would get suspicious if they saw too many entry stamps in her Ethiopian passport.

"I have the feeling we have a lot in common," she heard Karen say.

"Oh, I'm sure we have," Anouk replied, wondering what would come next.

To hell with this, Karen thought and decided to go all out. "I think that we're two of a kind, what I mean is—"

Voices and the sound of a luffing sail cut her short and made Anouk sit up. A dhow was heading for their island, its lateen sail patched and bloated from a hot breeze.

Anouk frowned. "Looks like they're heading for us."

"A fishing boat?"

"I don't know."

The boat was coming closer rapidly, and they could see that it was crowded with Arab men in long white shirts and turbans.

"We'd better leave," Anouk said. "I don't like the looks of them."

The minute the men saw them moving around in their bikinis, they began to holler more and wave.

"What're they saying?" Karen asked nervously.

"Nothing nice. Let's get away from here."

They gathered their things and hurried into their boat. As they zoomed away, Karen saw the men shaking their fists after them. She sighed at the interruption because it was obvious by Anouk's preoccupation with the boat that the discussion was closed.

With no further chance to be alone with Anouk, Karen resigned herself to the tour group. The next morning their trip went on to the Eritrean highlands by air. Karen sat in the co-pilot's seat; the Swiss, visibly relieved to get out of this 'hell-hole', as they called Massawa, filled the seats behind them.

Karen remained quiet most of the trip, pretending to look at the scenery. From time to time she threw a furtive glance at Anouk who looked sharp in a fresh khaki shirt and slacks that showed off her strong thighs.

She felt heat between her own thighs and had to force herself not to touch Anouk's. Damn it, this woman is driving me insane. And damn those Arabs in their dhow yesterday who fouled it all up. Who knew when another opportunity for such a conversation would occur? Especially since Anouk seemed preoccupied and businesslike.

"Asmara," Anouk announced flatly. "Fasten your seat belts, please." She put on her earphones and flew a wide circle over the town, heading for the airport's windsock. After sizing up her wind direction, she maneuvered the aircraft a good distance from the air strip and headed straight in.

Waiting on the ground were three taxis which took them to the Albergo Italia where reservations had been made for the Swiss.

"We need one more room for Miss Jensen," Anouk told the young man at the reception desk.

"Was the reservation made under this name?" he asked, scanning the ledger.

"No reservation."

He looked apologetic. "I'm afraid I can't help you. We're booked solid."

Karen looked at Anouk. "I wouldn't mind sharing your room, if you don't mind."

" I'm staying at a friend's house," Anouk said. "Let me call her."

Karen watched her saunter to the wall phone with a light, bouncy stride, put a coin into the slot, and dial. Leaning nonchalantly against the wall, Anouk talked into the phone, her face split into a wide mischievous smile that changed the rhythm of Karen's heart and made her wonder who that friend was who could produce such a smile from Anouk.

"It's settled," Anouk said, returning. "You'll come with me to Carla's."

Another taxi took them to a house which was at the outskirts of town, amid an abundance of trees and flowers. Carla came running and hugged Anouk.

"Finally! I thought you'd never come to Asmara again," she cried, speaking English with a charming Italian accent.

Anouk introduced Karen while a servant picked up their luggage and carried it into the house.

Shaking hands with Carla, Karen noticed her smart haircut, the casual chic of her dress. "Thanks for letting me spend the night at your house."

"Of course, Anouk's friends are my friends," Carla said, leading them to comfortable chairs on the verandah. On the table were three glasses and a pitcher. "I prepared Campari and orange juice," Carla said, pouring. "I know Anouk likes it. I hope you do, too, Karen. We'll have wine with lunch." She sat down, lifted her glass. "Cheers." Then sighed happily. "We have the house to ourselves. My husband's away on business and the kids are at their grandmother's. How divine."

Anouk chuckled. "Seems women are always happier when their old man's gone."

Carla's eyes rolled skyward. "You'd understand if you had one. Gino's not a bad guy, yet I always feel under pressure when he's around. And lately I'm tired of this house, of being married, even of the kids. Don't know what it is." Turning to Karen, she asked, "Are you married?"

"No, and I don't intend to ever get married," Karen said. "I came to Ethiopia for the adventure and to photograph the country to create a picture book."

"Another independent spirit," Carla exclaimed, looking from Karen to Anouk.

"Yes, I think Anouk and I are quite alike," Karen declared, looking at Anouk whose vague smile and dark gaze lingered on her. "And in more than one way," she added in a low voice, holding Anouk's gaze and smiling back."

"Well, good for you," Carla remarked, then laughed. "Except in Anouk's case that means something quite different, uh, maybe I shouldn't have..."

"That's all right, Carla," Anouk said. "I have a feeling the rumor mill has been working just fine in Addis and that Karen knows about my sexual persuasion, or perversion." Her head back, Anouk laughed. Reassured, Carla joined her.

Karen flushed and stammered, "Well, that's true. I was told, but the point is I am a lesbian myself."

Anouk grinned. "Yes, and you wanted to tell me on the island, I know! 'I have a feeling we have a lot in common,'" Anouk said, mimicking Karen's American accent. Seeing Karen's growing embarrassment, she added quickly, "Forgive me, Karen, I'm just making light of something that is made awkward too often."

"You two are luckier than you seem to know," Carla threw in wistfully. "I also meant to have a career and stay single till my late twenties. I wanted to travel, taste life a bit before getting married. But my mother kept pushing me to marry Gino as if she couldn't wait to get rid of me. She sure was different with my brother. He was her god and no woman on earth was good enough for him."

"Don't I know!" Anouk exclaimed. "In Arab homes, the boy is the jewel of the house, the ornament of his sisters, the treasure that has to be protected. My brother could do or say anything he wanted. He kicked us girls, pulled our hair, broke our toys. My mother never intervened. 'That'll make a man out of him,' she'd say, and punish us if we retaliated in defense. Don't think it took me long to figure out I was going to be independent."

"What about your father?" Karen asked.

"He only had eyes for his son. My mother should have looked out for us. The only thing she did was to forbid that we be circumcised."

"What do you mean?" Karen asked, puzzled.

"Circumcision on women is actually a clitorectomy. Anyway, my mother's interdiction didn't do my older sister much good. One day Alifa went to visit our grandmother, my father's mother, in upper Egypt. She came back sick and weeping. We couldn't understand— visits to grandmother were always such fun. Finally she told us that one morning my grandmother came into her room with a bunch of women who grabbed her and opened her legs. One woman, a mid-wife, cut off her clitoris and some of the labia with a razor blade. The pain was hellish. My mother was furious. The wound was infected and Alifa needed medical care for weeks. When my mother confronted her mother-in-law, she replied, 'I only wanted the best for the girl.'"

Karen shook her head in disbelief. "How utterly cruel to mutilate a healthy woman and rob her of her right to sexual pleasure."

"Ah, but her biological function is to produce sons, not to feel pleasure," Anouk mocked.

Karen's hackles rose. "How come the women don't rebel?"

"How much room is there for the few rebels like me?" Anouk asked, her tone still sharp. "Who can risk that? Is it any easier in America?"

"Well, not around my family, that's for sure," Karen had to concede. "They'd just as soon force me into a quick marriage. Can you imagine?"

"Much too easily," Anouk said darkly.

"Women have never had any say about their bodies," Carla said. "It's as if we belonged to everyone else but ourselves."

"Right," Karen agreed. "We've been told how we must look or behave by the churches down to the fashion designers."

"And most comply," Anouk said, "mainly because they have no choice. In Arab countries for example, women are still being stoned or beheaded in public for adultery, abortion or if a father suspects his daughter isn't a virgin any longer. All of which is a great deterrent for the rest of the female population."

Karen nodded. "There's a political term for that—sexual fascism. I've been reading new political theory by women in the States, about men ruling women's bodies and sexual lives. Birth control and abortion are hot political issues now—the laws are just becoming more liberal—it's much easier to get an abortion."

"Which Islam strictly forbids as well as birth control," Anouk said. "Any woman caught practicing it gets the death penalty."

"That's not any different from what the Catholic Church says," Carla threw in. "Birth control is considered a mortal sin."

"So, how did you escape, Anouk?" Karen struggled for words. "You know, from being circumcised? You did escape, didn't you?"

Carla burst out laughing.

Also laughing, Anouk exclaimed, "Karen! You're quite surprising, I refused to visit my grandmother after that. Carla, stop laughing, will you?"

Karen looked at them, embarrassed.

"I'm sorry, Karen," Carla hooted, "I'm not laughing at you."

"It's me she's laughing at," Anouk said, waving a fist at Carla. "Me the abominable pervert who dares to be sexually active."

Carla smiled shrewdly; Karen wondered where and with whom Anouk was sexually active, then remembered Nora telling her that some man had seen her come out of a bordello. She still couldn't quite believe that, yet felt an unreasonable stab of jealousy.

They were interrupted by a servant who appeared at the door and said something in Amharic. "Well, we'll have to carry on this conversation over lunch," Carla announced, and they moved into the dining room.

Chapter 8

"Carla, this was a delicious lunch." Karen wiped her mouth on the starched napkin. "Thank you."

"Beats the best restaurant in town," Anouk agreed.

They left the table to sit in the spacious, richly furnished living room to have Turkish coffee and petit-fours. In the drowsiness of noon, their conversation simmered down. They sipped silently, enjoying the quiet, only occasionally broken by bird chirping from the garden.

"Well, I'm ready for my siesta," Carla said, putting her cup down. "Do you take siestas, Karen?"

"Yes, I got into the habit since living in Ethiopia."

Carla rose. "Let me show you to your room. You too, Anouk?"

Anouk finished her coffee. "I'm going to leave for a while. Have to run a few errands. May I borrow your car?"

"Oh, do run those errands of yours. The keys are in the car."

Karen didn't miss Carla's mocking tone or the collusive smiles between the two. She followed Carla upstairs to a spacious room with twin beds. Their bags sat on the carpet between them.

Carla pointed at the bed to the left. "Anouk usually sleeps in that one."

"Then I'll take the other one," Karen said, heart leaping in anticipation of spending a night close to Anouk again.

Carla wished her a good siesta and left. Still feeling the heat of the conversation, Karen got a few things from her bag and went into the bathroom. Looking into the mirror, she wondered about the errands Anouk had so suddenly to run.

Humming with smug anticipation, Anouk drove across town to a small stone house and gave a short blast with the horn. The bright blue door opened a crack and part of a face appeared. At Anouk's smile and wink, the door flew wide open.

"Anouk! Anouk!" A young, very pretty black woman cried, and came running to hug Anouk. She was Eritrean, from the north of Ethiopia where women have more freedom.

Several children gathered around them and Anouk gave an older boy a few cents to watch the car.

Inside the house, which had one room and a small kitchen, Anouk lifted the lithe woman and whirled her around. "Adama, *habebee*—darling, how have you been?"

"How have I been?" Adama pouted. "Miserable. Why did you stay away so long?"

"My job, Adama," Anouk muttered, well aware that Adama really missed the generous amount of money she gave her every time she saw her. But she played along, kissing her throat, cheeks, eyes, whispering, "I missed you, too," then carried her to bed.

She opened Adama's dress exposing her full breasts. "So beautiful," Anouk murmured, and took one in her mouth.

Adama began to writhe. "Oh, Anouk, I've been longing for you."

"And I for you," Anouk said and helped her out of her dress, then began unbuttoning her own shirt.

"Let me," said Adama.

Anouk's pulse accelerated. "You're beautiful," she said in a hoarse voice, holding out her arms. Adama lay on top of her, wriggling and rubbing her cunt against Anouk's thigh. Anouk's cunt began to throb wildly and she sucked Adama's lips, drawing her tongue into her mouth. Moaning endearments, she pushed Adama on her back and let her hands travel along smooth curves, feeling her warmth, as if molding Adama's body like clay. Hips rising and sinking, Adama moaned and whispered delicious obscenities which fired Anouk's lust to ever greater heights.

She spread Adama's legs and slipped inside her. "Oh, Adama, your little cunt makes me die," she sighed. Then, leaving a trail of kisses, she glided down to the curly mound. She parted the dark lips and dove her tongue into the pink, moist flesh. A sound came from deep within Adama, and her voice cried with need and awe. Anouk felt her tremble, then buck, and pressed her pounding groin into Adama's. After a furious ride, brought them both to a shattering orgasm.

"Habebee, you're the best," Anouk murmured, chest heaving.

"You are, for me," Adama said.

"I bet you say that to everyone," Anouk teased. "Did you really come or did you fake it?"

"I don't fake it with you like with men. You know that I don't enjoy men."

"Still, I'm just a customer," Anouk continued to tease.

"A special customer. With you I don't feel I'm working."

Anouk was inclined to believed her. Adama was a lesbian but had to prostitute herself to men to survive. To be with Anouk was a respite from her work. And unlike many Ethiopian and Arab women, Eritrean women weren't circumcised and could enjoy sex. She also knew that Adama had a steady lover, another prostitute with whom Adama had set up Anouk on occasions when Adama wasn't well.

Adama kissed her face. "Would you like some wine? Someone left a good bottle from France."

"No, I had enough at lunch." Anouk sat up.

"Are you leaving already?" Adama asked, alarmed.

Anouk drew her close, laughing a low contented laugh. "No chance. I'm still hungry and I'll be here all afternoon. Or do you expect someone?"

"Yes, at three-thirty. I'll pretend to be sick and send him away."

"Good girl." Anouk reached for her wallet on the table next to the bed and pulled out a few bills. "That enough?"

Adama greedily counted the money and nodded. "Sleepy?" she asked, seeing Anouk stretched out with her eyes closed.

"Just resting a bit. Come lie close to me. But don't let me fall asleep like last time when I had to cancel a flight because it was too late to fly out."

Anouk remembered the outraged tourists who had to be driven back to the hotel, the phone calls that had to be made to keep hotel reservations at their next destination, the excuses she had to invent for being late.

"So you're flying out again later?" Adama asked.

"No, I have a dinner obligation," Anouk said, although she didn't feel it was an obligation. She always liked to visit with Carla and was looking forward to tonight's dinner and another good conversation with Carla and Karen.

Karen and Carla were on the verandah when Anouk returned. Carla threw her a taunting smile and asked what she wanted to drink.

Anouk smiled back. "A scotch on ice would be nice. But first I'd like to take a quick shower."

Karen watched her running upstairs, taking two steps at once. She looks all mussed up, she thought. If she hasn't come from a lover, I'll eat every broom in Carla's broom closet. Jealousy bored its ugly sting deep inside her.

When Anouk reappeared, she wore a yellow shirt over white slacks, and leather slippers. Her hair was wetly plastered to her head, emphasizing her androgynous looks.

"So where's that scotch?" Anouk asked, sitting down and stretching her long legs.

"Are you that impatient with everything?" Carla asked, laughing.

"That depends on what I'm doing," Anouk retorted, and took the drink. They toasted, then Anouk leaned back, smiling her wide smile, her dark eyes flashing with pure delight.

Karen observed her, fascinated by her exotic appeal, her boldness. She couldn't remember ever having known anyone like her.

"What're your plans for tomorrow?" Carla asked.

Anouk looked at Karen. "I guess we're flying on to Gondar and Lake Tana, aren't we?"

"Yes, and I'd like to do all the historic sites and the Semyen Mountains, too. Is that possible?"

Anouk looked surprised. "Possible yes, but it wasn't scheduled. What made you decide to change your plans?"

"I thought I might as well do it all while I'm up here," Karen said. The truth was that she couldn't bear the thought of being back in Addis in a few days and not seeing Anouk, who probably couldn't have cared less.

"All right, in that case I'll call Sergio." Anouk sauntered to the phone, wondering why Karen was extending her trip. Well, why not see what this American lesbian is about, she thought.

Carla also rose. "I'm going to check things in the kitchen."

Karen finished her drink in one draught. It was her third and she was beginning to feel high. Damn it, I'm falling in love with her, she mused. And the more I'm with her, the deeper it gets, and the more difficult it will be when this trip is over. Oh well, the trip wasn't over yet.

They stayed two days in Gondar, the ancient capital, embedded in green hills and eucalyptus trees, visiting the many ancient castles in a rented Land Rover, then drove on to Lake Tana. It had rained during the night and the wet landscape glistened in the morning sun. Anouk drove, Karen sat next to her, writing in her notebook, her camera close and ready. They passed small settlements and wide fields where thin cattle grazed watched by thinner shepherd boys.

From time to time, Karen cried, "Stop," and Anouk did so she could capture a particular scene on film.

Karen put a new roll of film into her camera and changed lenses, then asked Anouk to stop once more so she could take pictures of the charming tukuls—the round huts with their conical roofs of reed grass.

No sooner had they stepped out of the car then they were surrounded by yelling children. Anouk said something to them and gave them a few coins to pose for pictures.

Karen zoomed in on their faces, some with snotty noses and flies gathering at the corners of their eyes and mouths.

Adjusting her camera, she said, "Stand next to the children, Anouk."

"You want me in the picture?"

"Why not?" Karen focused her camera and took several photos, then zoomed in on Anouk's face with its wide smile that was so full of mischief and caused so much trouble to her heart.

They drove on, descending, and the closer they got to the lake, the hotter and more humid it became.

"Can we swim in this lake?" Karen asked, seeing the first distant shimmer of water.

"I wouldn't advise it. You'd risk an infection of bilharzia parasites."

By noon they reached a small town at the shores of the lake and stopped at a restaurant, a mere shack stitched together by a muddle of materials. Its floor was pounded mud, covered by some mats. Gasoline cans contained sorry looking palms. As it was stifling inside and thick with flies, they chose to sit on the verandah. Its floor boards creaked with every step they took to a table near the railing.

A waiter with a stained apron around his substantial waist came to take their order. He spoke little English and Anouk ordered lemonade and cheese sandwiches after consulting with Karen.

When their order was delivered, Karen took a sip and made a face. "Don't they have mineral water? And ice? This tastes like pee."

"No to both questions. Their refrigerator conked out. This is

Africa, Karen."

"Sorry, I didn't mean to complain. I'm enjoying it tremendously out here. Much more than Addis."

"Glad to hear it."

"You seem different, too. I find you more relaxed and outgoing. You seemed more distant in Addis."

Anouk's brows rose. "Oh? My apologies, I didn't mean to be. I have a busy schedule and don't enjoy socializing in Addis much."

"I want you to know that I like you, Anouk."

Anouk's gaze rested on Karen for a moment. *Could it be that she has a crush on me?*

Karen was beautiful and fun, but Anouk never mixed business and pleasure, above all not in this case—not with a visiting friend of the local American diplomat and the tight circle of people Karen associated with. Not only would it cause a scandal, it would be stupid to get involved or allow Karen to get close. Especially now when other matters were hanging in the balance.

"I like you, too, Karen," she said evenly.

"Enough to become good friends?" Karen asked.

"But aren't we already?" Anouk picked up the tab before this became something she couldn't get out of without hurting Karen's feelings. "We better go on. There's still some road ahead of us."

Karen followed, disappointed, wondering what kind of women Anouk liked.

The sun was setting, and an immense peace enfolded the placid expanse of the lake. Anouk drove slowly alongside fields which sloped gently down to the lake's marshy shores and dense, tall reeds. Ahead, a few lights gave away the small town of Zeghie.

They stopped at the lodge where two rooms had been reserved for them. It had been the same in Gondar. Karen had hoped they would share a room and wondered who was paying for Anouk's.

Karen took a quick shower to wash off the dust of the day and joined Anouk, also freshly showered, in the dining room. They ate a simple but good meal, then lingered in the lounge for a while, sipping a sweet dessert wine, discussing the itinerary of the following days.

"Well, I'm going to call it day," Anouk said after a glance at her watch.

"I'm tired, too," Karen admitted.

Karen was stretched out on the bed when she thought she heard the door of Anouk's room open and jumped up. She carefully opened her door a crack and saw Anouk walking down the corridor.

Where is she going again? she asked herself, closing the door and leaning against it. God, she's like a prowling tomcat. Envious of whoever received Anouk's caresses that night, she curled up under the covers.

"Slept well?" Karen asked at breakfast.

Buttering a slice of toast, Anouk nodded, thinking of her steamy night. "Yeah, very well. How about you?"

"Same," Karen answered, although she hadn't slept much and heard Anouk returning to her room shortly after five. She bit into her lower lip to suppress a laugh. It was actually funny, but also aggravating because she wanted so much to give what Anouk sought somewhere else. And it had been months now since she had lain in the arms of a woman. But no matter what interest she showed, Anouk seemed oblivious. She probably wasn't her type.

Back in her room, Karen brushed her teeth and was drying her face when Anouk breezed in and said enthusiastically, "I've got the manager's seaplane."

Delighted, Karen dropped the towel on the bed. "Really?"

"We'll fly over the whole lake and its islands. There's lots to photograph, so bring all your equipment."

The grey sky was streaked with pink and the air still cool and filled with voices of birds when they left the hotel with a young male employee who led them to a high-wing monoplane moored at a dock.

Anouk jumped on a pontoon, crawled into the cabin, and took Karen's bag with the camera and lenses.

"I've never flown in such a thing," Karen remarked, getting in next to Anouk. "The water's perfect. Like a mirror."

"I hate to tell you, but glassy water is the greatest hazard for a seaplane," Anouk muttered, turning switches. She gave the Ethiopian a sign to untie the mooring lines. "It's also been a while since I've flown a seaplane. Afraid?" she asked, catching Karen's concerned look.

The plane glided along the water, and Anouk continued, "The bitch with calm water is that you have a hell of a job breaking the suction of the pontoons when trying to take off. But there is a way…"

With the plane far enough from shore, Anouk circled around on the water to kick up a wash, then headed for the waves she had made in the hope that this would break the suction sufficiently for her to get the pontoons on the 'step' to go.

"So far so good," she said, hydroplaning for some while with the pontoons partially out of water to gain speed.

"Made it," she sang when they were airborne.

The lake seemed an endless blue plain. Karen pointed to a dark dot below.

"Kabran Island," Anouk said. "It has a round church dating back to the 1300's."

"Have you been on it?"

"Yes, and on the other islands. All are rich in history and have churches and cloisters with an inestimable wealth of scrolls. In times of war, especially, people and priests took refuge on these islands, hiding religious scripts from the enemy."

Karen made a few entries in her notebook. "I'd like to go to such an island."

"Let's fly around a bit. I want to get the feel of this bird. You mind?"

"Of course not," Karen said, and kept looking around.

Anouk gazed straight ahead; Karen noticed that faraway look and wondered where Anouk was in her thoughts.

"A seaplane!" Anouk suddenly cried out. "My God, that's it! It'll be possible with a seaplane."

"What?" Karen looked puzzled.

"Just thinking aloud," Anouk said quickly.

"What's possible with a seaplane?" Karen insisted.

"Karen, I'm sorry, but I can't talk about it."

Karen turned away.

Anouk took her hand. "Don't be angry, please. It's something I have to do and I can't—"

"You don't have to explain," Karen interrupted.

Anouk withdrew her hand, regretting her outburst. But the sudden answer to her problem of how to get Silke out of Yemen had struck her like a lightning bolt. However, she couldn't risk telling Karen or anyone else about this, fearing that eventually it would leak out to the authorities and foil everything. Only Sergio knew and she fully trusted him.

Elated that she had found the answer to one part of Silke's escape, Anouk flew a wide circle and pointed to an island below.

"Here's Kabran again. And there's a slight breeze giving a nice chop to the water. We better take advantage of it and land."

"Why is a chop better for landing than smooth water?" Karen asked, her voice flat.

"Because it's very hard to focus your eyes on a sheet of calm water so there is such a good chance of smacking right into the water at an angle that will take you to the bottom of the lake. A nice chop, on the other hand, makes the surface very easy to pinpoint so you can cut the keel of your pontoons into the water."

Anouk circled her destination and located her landing site alongside the shoreline. She inspected it for underwater hazards, then came in on a fairly level approach to the water with the tail of the seaplane slightly lowered. She skimmed over the water, gradually cushioning down so that the 'step' on the bottom of each pontoon cut gently into the water. Then she slowly eased the stick back.

"I guess I haven't lost my touch." She laughed that deep, raspy laugh that made Karen's skin tingle and taxied toward a small beach. "Hope you don't mind getting your feet wet."

"I'm not made of sugar," Karen retorted, and rolled up her slacks.

They waded to shore where Anouk tied the plane to a tree, while Karen took pictures of fishermen in reed boats that had sailed close.

Chapter 9

In the following week, Anouk and Karen traveled to several historical sites and to the source of the Blue Nile in a swamp near Lake Tana.

Karen shot yards of film; her notebook was full. The constant moving around was taking its toll though and she was beginning to feel tired. She had lost weight and felt a strange pulling sensation in her abdomen.

Anouk asked her on several occasions if she wanted to take a break, but Karen stubbornly insisted they go on. Anouk flew them to Axum.

Anouk explained, while driving a rented car, "Axum was once the capital of an empire whose power stretched from Arabia to the Nile, ranking in status with Babylon, Rome, and Egypt."

Karen gazed around the sleepy town nestling, forgotten between rolling hills. A certain sad almost hidden splendor still shrouded its tombs and ruins.

Anouk parked the car and they walked among the historic rubble. "Christianity reached here in the fourth century," she went on. "And ever since it has been considered the holy city of Ethiopia. It was also the residence of the fabled Queen of Sheba whose legendary union with King Solomon led to the birth of Menelik I, from whom Haile Selassie claims direct descent."

Karen, who had been taking pictures, smiled. "You're a great resource for my book. Don't know what I'd do without you." She tucked her camera away and sat down on a broken column. Anouk sat down next to her.

"Glad to be of help. History's my hobby." Noticing Karen's pallor, she asked, "You feeling all right?"

"So so," Karen admitted, pulling her jacket tighter.

"Are you cold?"

Karen nodded. "I think I'd like to return to the hotel."

The hotel was swarming with tourists and they had to share a room. Anouk got out of her jacket and threw it on one of the twin beds. "Shall I order some herb tea?" she asked.

Karen shook her head, picked up some toiletries. "I think a hot shower will do me more good."

Anouk gave her a worried look. When Karen came out of the bathroom wrapped in a robe, Anouk was sprawled in a chair in careless ease, legs apart. Her features had assumed a somewhat sullen, withdrawn expression and her black eyes were staring. She seemed to be engrossed in thought.

Her eyes suddenly focused. "Feeling better?"

"A little," Karen said, and lay down.

Anouk sat on the edge of the bed and tucked the blanket tightly around her, then patted her cheek. As they looked at each other, some kind of communication sprang up, a mutual response at some deep and complicated level, a glowing spark of contact, delicate and precious. Anouk's dark eyes shone with a penetrating light in which Karen saw tenderness and longing. Anouk parted her lips as if to say something and Karen held her breath, aware of the great silence in the room as if the world around them had ceased to exist.

Then the moment passed. Anouk sucked in her breath and the light in her eyes died with a startling abruptness. She shifted and looked away, saying softly, "Try sleeping a little."

"What are you going to do?"

"Don't worry about me. I'll find something to do. Now go to sleep. I'll wake you for dinner."

Anouk hurried from the room, ran to the car, and sat inside. God, what was that back there? She panicked, her fingers raking her hair. That's all I need. Getting all mushy over Karen.

Not that she hadn't been wanting another meaningful relationship instead of hopping from woman to woman and paying for a few hours of sex. But with the upcoming rescue of Silke it was better if she had a clear head. Besides, with the risk involved, it wasn't the right time to start a relationship. There was also the fact that Karen was in Ethiopia only for a limited time, so why should she invest feelings? Damn it, there was only one cure for these emotions.

She started the car, slammed it into gear, and tore out of the parking lot. A while later she walked through a curtain of glass beads into a bar. Except for two young women and a heavyset older woman behind the bar, it was empty.

The two young women jumped from their chairs against the wall

74

and ran to her. Anouk hugged them. They were pretty with cropped hair, dark golden skin and barely reached her shoulders. The older woman smiled, her brilliant teeth gleaming against the dark color of her lips and face as she came around the counter.

Anouk also embraced her. "Hirut, how are things going?"

"We're surviving. What can I get you?"

"Open a bottle of champagne. But make sure it's a good one. And bring glasses for all of us."

"What are you celebrating?"

"Being alive, I guess."

They moved into the back room which had a big bed in one corner, a couch and two armchairs around a low table. Anouk saw that the sheet on the bed was clean. A young woman on each arm, she sat on the couch, feet on the table, joking and laughing.

"My two favorite girls in all of Ethiopia," she said, kissing them. Nuzzling the women's necks, she asked, "So which of you two wants me?"

Squealing, they went for the buttons of her shirt.

"I guess I'll have both of you," Anouk said, laughing. She took some money from her billfold and gave it to Hirut. "Bring us more champagne, then leave us alone."

It was dark when she arrived back at the hotel. She went to the bathroom in the lobby, splashed her face with water, rinsed her mouth and brushed back her hair with her fingers, then went to their room.

Karen was dressed and sitting in a chair. Anouk took in her pallor, but also her fine face and bearing. So lovely, she thought, feeling the old mysterious tugging deep inside her chest. She had liked Karen from the moment she met her and the feeling was turning into something deeper. Under different circumstances she would give in. It was the first time since Diana that she felt herself falling in love.

But this was the very time when she needed to keep her feelings at bay and remain free from any of the emotional involvement which she knew Karen would want. And how can I possibly give her what she needs with the habits I have now, she wondered. She is so different from the women I'm fooling around with. No, there were too many obstacles to a successful relationship.

Keeping her voice even, she asked, "How do you feel?"

"Better, thanks."

"Ready to eat something?"

Karen nodded, wondering how Anouk had spent the afternoon. She searched Anouk's eyes, but saw only neutral concern. So what she thought had passed between them earlier had been an illusion.

She resignedly slung her purse over her shoulder and followed Anouk out of the room. They didn't talk on the way to the dining room, and not much during the meal.

Karen had some soup, steamed vegetables and herb tea—a light meal she had to force herself to eat. She couldn't figure out what was wrong with her. Never had she felt so tired, so cold, so miserable.

Anouk ate a large meal.

"Where do you get your appetite?" Karen asked, smiling.

Anouk smiled back, spreading her arms. "Look at this big carcass of mine. It needs to be fed."

Karen couldn't help laughing.

"You also should eat more," Anouk scolded. "You've lost weight. Living at this altitude takes it out of you."

"Do you think I'm too thin?"

"You certainly were a little more padded when you first arrived," Anouk said, and Karen vowed to gain back every ounce she had lost. "You'll need energy for the trip into the Semyen Mountains tomorrow," Anouk went on. "Are you sure you're up to it?"

"Quite. You'll see. A good night's rest and I'll be like new."

But in the early morning hours, Karen suddenly jerked up from a deep sleep and ran into the bathroom. Moaning, she doubled over with the first attack of dysentery knifing through her.

Alarmed, Anouk also got up and waited by the bathroom door.

Shaking and covered with cold sweat, Karen staggered into the room. Anouk caught and helped her into bed.

Shivering, Karen groaned, "I'm so cold."

Anouk tore the blankets off of her own bed and piled them on top of her, then slipped into a robe. "I'll see if I can get a hot water bottle."

When she returned, Karen was on the toilet with hands clenched into fists, moaning and squirming in pain. Anouk put a hand on her shoulder, not knowing what else to do.

"Go away," Karen cried, embarrassed.

"Don't be silly. No one smells like roses."

Karen gritted her teeth as another attack tore through her. When her intestines had calmed down, Anouk washed cold perspiration from her face. "No hot water bottle," she said, piling more blankets

76

on top of Karen. "I got some herb tea, though. You need to keep drinking."

As soon as the tea reached Karen's stomach, she cried out and ran to the toilet. Back under the covers, Karen was shaking uncontrollably.

"Don't you have charcoal or Kaopectate or Lomotil in your kit?" Anouk asked, her concern growing.

Karen shook her head. "I didn't think I'd need it—I should've been more careful—it must've been that lemonade." Her words turned into a moan.

Anouk held her. "My God, Karen! What am I going to do with you at this hour?"

"This is the worst thing I've ever had," Karen groaned.

"I don't think there's even a doctor in this town. I wish we were in Asmara. But at this stage, I can't fly you there. We need to get you medicine."

"Sorry to be such a mess."

Anouk took Karen's face in both hands. "Don't say that," she murmured, and kissed her on the forehead.

Dawn was pushing its grey light into the room and Anouk went to the room phone. "I'll order breakfast and clear broth for you."

"I don't want anything," Karen said.

By the time the food was delivered, Karen was in the bathroom again. Anouk coaxed her into taking some of the broth. But it had the effect of the tea, and Karen refused to eat or drink anything more.

"I'm going to see if I can get some medicine," Anouk said, and hurried from the room. She was back thirty minutes later. Karen lay on her side holding herself, her pallor frightening. "I got something from a pharmacy which would have delighted a voodoo priest," Anouk said, and poured some dark powder into a glass of mineral water. "It must have charcoal in it. Want to try it?"

"Why not? At this point I don't care what I die from," Karen sighed, and swallowed it. It was bitter and she shuddered sinking back into the pillows.

In spite of the remedy, the attacks persisted throughout the morning and in the end Karen's intestines produced only bloody slime and excruciating pain.

Anouk paced the room, furious at her helplessness. "You must drink more or you'll dehydrate. I know it's hard, but you must!" Anouk held the glass of mineral water for Karen to sip.

After Karen had managed the glassful, Anouk sat next to her, holding her hand. Karen squeezed it, whispering, "Thanks for taking care of me."

Anouk bent over her. "You're welcome." And kissed her on the cheek. "Do you think that powder helped a little?"

Your kiss just did, Karen thought. "I'm still so cold," she breathed.

"I'll keep you warm." Anouk got under the covers with her and put her arms around Karen. "You do feel icy, poor lamb."

Karen pressed her face into the hollow of Anouk's throat and pushed her hands up under Anouk's arm. Anouk's warmth enfolded her; the tension from the cold changed to soothing relaxation as her body absorbed the warmth of Anouk's. Slowly she stopped shivering and was able to doze off.

Anouk lay thinking. This was the first time in a long time that she was holding a woman without having sex. Karen was very desirable but her sickness and pain pushed all desire to the background. Anouk felt compassion, concern and pity, but there was also that dark vibration of feeling from deep within and the harder she tried to suppress it, the more it pushed to the surface. How easy it would be to let herself fall in love. With a sigh she pressed Karen closer, caressing her head, filled with a tenderness she had thought she could no longer feel.

Later, Karen's intestines revolted again finally only producing a few drops of blood.

"To hell with it," Anouk growled. "You're not making any progress. I'm flying you to Asmara before you get worse." She went to the desk and put in a call to Carla.

Carla picked them up at the airport and drove them to her family doctor.

"You have a severe case of bacterial dysentery," he said, looking at Karen over the rim of his glasses. "You must've drunk unfiltered water." He wrote out a prescription. "Two pills every two hours today, then two every four hours."

They picked up the medicine on the way back to Carla's home. Anouk helped Karen upstairs to the guest room and into bed.

Shivering, despite down quilts and a hot water bottle, Karen lay in silent agony. Carla helped her sit up, and handed her the pills with a glass of water. "This is filtered," she said, smiling.

"Have you ever had dysentery?" Karen asked.

"No, we're immune, I guess. But most newcomers get it. It's not only in the water, it's also on certain vegetables. These pills are good. They'll calm your intestines."

"I feel as if I don't have any left."

When Karen woke some time later, Anouk was sitting next to the bed. She bent forward, caressed her face. "Better?"

Karen nodded, took Anouk's hand and pressed it to her lips. "Thanks for everything."

Carla came in with a tray and stopped short at the door, looking at them.

Jaws tensing, Anouk walked to the window.

"I brought you some soup," Carla said. "You have to keep eating, Karen, so you won't lose more weight and energy."

Karen sat up to make room for the tray on her lap.

"Good girl," Carla said, when Karen had spooned the bowl empty. "Now try to sleep again."

Drowsy from the hot soup, Karen snuggled under the covers. For a moment she tried to hold on to what she had read in Anouk's eyes just before Carla brought the soup, then she fell asleep.

Anouk called Sergio who told her that there were passengers to be picked up from the hotel the next day, and some cargo at the airport. "You sound down," he finished.

"I'm all right," she replied, and rang off.

Carla had made drinks and sat waiting when Anouk joined her on the verandah. "Cheers," Carla said, lifting her glass.

"Yeah, cheers." Anouk's voice was low.

Anouk remained silent, watching some moths flying around a lamp. Carla's daughter and son were watching TV and her husband was reading in his study. From the kitchen came the voices of servants and the wafting smell of cooking food.

"You're unusually quiet," Carla remarked.

Anouk sighed, "I've a lot on my mind."

"It's Karen, isn't it?"

Anouk nodded, chewing her lower lip. "In part."

"She's like you, so what's wrong?"

"The fact that no one in Addis would believe she is a lesbian and that I didn't corrupt her. Imagine me, the pervert, snapping up the most beautiful woman from their midst. They'll crucify me."

"They have never done anything against you."

"No, as long as I don't cruise in their circles; which I've never been interested in doing anyway."

"Well, how deeply are you and Karen involved?"

"We're not. And it's got to end before it starts. I don't need to be involved in a scandal, especially now with this job coming up."

"What job?"

Anouk finished her drink. "I promised to do something which is a little risky and I don't want Karen to invest feelings in a relationship when I'm taking a chance. It wouldn't be fair."

"My God, Anouk! What are you involved in?"

"I can't talk about it."

"You scare me."

"Sometimes I scare myself. But it has never stopped me before. May I borrow your car?"

"Anouk, do you think that's a solution?"

"Please, Carla, let me handle it my way."

"No reason to get mad. The keys are in the car as always."

"Thanks." Anouk touched Carla's shoulder. "And sorry. I didn't mean to snap at you."

The pills worked, and Karen was able to sleep through most of the night. Looking at the other bed, she saw that it hadn't been touched, and wondered where Anouk was and where she had slept. She longed to see her.

The door opened and she looked up expectantly.

"Good morning," Carla said, bringing a tray with herb tea, a soft boiled egg, and two slices of buttered toast. "How do you feel?"

"Much better, thanks," Karen said, propping herself on an elbow. "Where's Anouk?"

"Taking a shower downstairs." Carla put the tray on the night stand. "She also slept there. She didn't want to disturb you."

"She wouldn't have," Karen said.

Carla didn't answer and helped her sit up, then put the tray on Karen's lap. "I'll be back in a while."

Karen had finished eating when Anouk came into the room, looking immaculate in a fresh uniform, and smelling of shampoo and lotion.

"You look much better," she said, smiling that wide smile that made Karen's heart miss a few beats. Anouk sat down on the bed. "I have to return to Addis, Karen. I'll be back in four days to pick you up. In the meantime you stay here and get well."

"I'll miss you," Karen said.

Anouk's gaze darkened as she bent forward and kissed her on the cheek. "So long."

The room seemed to resonate with Anouk's presence even after she was gone, to hum with it like the last vibrations of a tuning fork.

Karen was up and about a day later and called the Peters to let them know what had happened and that she was all right. During her convalescence she became good friends with Carla's family. While Carla's husband was at work and the children were at school, Carla showed her around Asmara with its strong Italian flavor.

But whenever she was by herself, Karen daydreamed about Anouk, yearning for the day when Anouk would pick her up. At last on the fourth morning the phone rang and Carla waved at her. "For you."

"Hi, Anouk?" Karen said, breathlessly into the receiver.

"Miss Jensen?" a male voice said. "I'm Murath, a pilot with Ras Dashan Airlines. I understand you've been sick. How do you feel?"

"Much better, thank you," Karen replied, puzzled.

"Is it all right then if I pick you up this noon to fly you back to Addis?"

Karen swallowed hard, trying to make sense of this.

"Hallo? Miss Jensen?"

"Yes, I'm here. I thought Anouk was going to pick me up."

"She has left the country."

"Left the country? Why?"

"Frankly, I wouldn't know. Anyway, is today at noon all right?"

"Yes, of course. I'll be at the airport," Karen said in a toneless voice and hung up. As the shock slowly wore off, an angry ache of resentment filled her.

Carla looked at her in silence.

"Did you know Anouk wasn't going to pick me up?"

"I didn't or I would have told you."

"She didn't tell you she was leaving the country?"

"I didn't know that either."

"What is she doing?"

"I have no clue. I don't always know about Anouk's business," Carla said, although she believed it had to do with the risky venture Anouk had hinted at. But she wasn't going to tell Karen that.

Chapter 10

This time Anouk dressed like an Egyptian businessman in a black suit and white shirt with a beige and blue tie. She handed the immigration official at the Sana airport the Egyptian passport stating that her name was Hamid Ali Said.

"The purpose of your visit?" the official asked after a brief glance at her.

"I'm an electrical engineer and am here to meet with colleagues of the Electric Works of Yemen."

He gave her an appreciative look. "How long are you going to stay in Yemen?"

"A week, sir,"

He stamped the passport and handed it back. "Have a nice stay."

Ulf was standing by the glass doors of the reception hall. As she passed him, they nodded briefly at each other. Then Anouk went outside to a taxi, seeing Ulf go to his car.

A half hour later, they were settled in his living room. Anouk had changed into the galabiya and they were drinking a cold beer.

"Anything new on your side?" she asked.

"No. Irmgard wrote that you still had no solution."

"I do now. I wrote to her just before leaving Ethiopia," Anouk said, and had another sip.

"So, what's the solution?"

"A seaplane. If Silke were in a small boat about a mile offshore I could pick her up with a seaplane."

He leaned back and crossed his legs. "My God, what an idea!"

Eyes vibrant, she bent forward. "Once we have Silke, we'll hide her in your place. When I'm ready with the plane, you'll drive her to the coast and get her into a boat north of Al-Hudayda where there's a long, lonely stretch of beach. It'll take me an hour to fly from Asseb, where the plane would have to be berthed, to that beach. So if I left at five in the morning I'd be at that beach at six. You put Silke into a boat half an hour before and I'll swoop down and pick her up, then zoom away before any radar or coast guard boat can detect me."

He smiled. "Sounds almost too easy. A small boat's hard to see from the air."

"Not if we provide Silke with half dozen flares."

"What if the sea is rough?"

"It's summer and the Red Sea is dead calm in the early morning."

"It's still risky."

Anouk shrugged. "Of course. The whole venture is. But there's no other way. Can you organize a small motorboat and the flares?"

"Yes, that's no problem."

"And teach Silke how to use them?"

He nodded. "So we've solved one part of this venture. Do you know how you'll get Silke away from Marib?"

Anouk sighed. "Not yet. That's the most difficult part. Could you borrow a car for me again so I can drive to Marib tomorrow?"

"Sure. How about that Peugeot?"

"That'll do."

Dressed more casually again in a white shirt over khaki slacks and a headcloth, Anouk arrived in Marib and checked into the hotel.

The innkeeper greeted her, bowing. "I see Allah has brought you back in good health," and ordered a young boy to carry her luggage upstairs to the room.

Anouk gave the lad a few coins, opened the louvered shutters to let fresh air into the smelly room and retrieved a tall can of insecticide from her bag, then sprayed the mattress thoroughly.

Coughing, she went to the window to take several deep breaths. In the street, four half-grown boys admired her car. When they noticed her looking at them, they whispered something to each other and respectfully retreated.

As the fumes of the insecticide slowly dissipated, she got a towel from her bag, flung it over her shoulder, and went down the hall to the toilet. Knowing from her previous visit what awaited her, she took several deep breaths before going in. Holding her breath, eyes closed, she relieved herself, then rushed into the adjoining bathroom where she bent over the small sink till her stomach had stopped heaving.

The loose faucet yielded only a thin stream of water no matter how wide she opened it. She splashed her face as best she could, then tried the faucet of the grimy tub in the hope it would give more water. But it only sputtered air and rust. She hung her clothes on a nail, moistened a corner of the towel and wiped herself down.

In her room, the mattress smelled strongly of the insecticide and she noticed bugs on the floor. Most were dead. She stepped on the ones that still moved, sprayed the mattress one more time, then grabbed a history book of Yemen and left.

She ambled to the cafe which was well-visited with only a few tables vacant outside. The owner saw her and came running.

"Welcome back," he exclaimed, and held a chair for her. "What is the reason for your visit this time?"

Anouk greeted him and sat down, putting the book on the table. "I'm now writing a thesis on archeology of this region and need to revisit the sites for more detailed study."

She was sure he didn't know what a thesis was. But he was impressed, as were the other patrons who had been listening.

"So how long will you stay this time?" he asked, wiping crumbs from the table with his hand.

"Unfortunately my profession doesn't allow me to stay more than a few days at a time and I'll have to come back several more times to accomplish this work. Right now I'm thirsty and would like to have a bottle of mineral water and coffee. I'd also like to dine by sundown, is that possible?"

"Everything shall be according to your wish, sir," he said, and hurried inside.

Anouk leaned back and picked up the book, hoping to avoid further conversation.

"Excuse me, sir," a young man from another table said. "Do you need a guide to the archeological sites?"

Anouk considered for a moment. "Not at this time," she said, thinking it would be risky to get too close to anyone in this town. "I'm quite familiar with most of the sites, but I'm sure that I could use your help in the future."

"It would be my pleasure to assist you," he said.

The owner returned with the water and coffee, and she thanked him, reopening the book so they would leave her alone. Before she knew it, she was engrossed in a chapter and actually reading. The afternoon drew to an end and there was some relief from the heat.

As the sun was slowly sinking, the muezzin's song resounded from the mosque's minaret. She bent forward to see an old man with a long white beard and a turban. Arms stretched out, he kept calling to believers in a monotonous, almost wailing tone. Around her the tables slowly emptied. The men were either going to the mosque or home. Maybe she, too, should go to the mosque. It would be a good way to blend in. She knew all the prayers by heart, but as a girl had never been allowed to go to the mosque. She decided to go and put a few coins on the table for her drinks. Ambling to the mosque, she wondered how these men spent their evenings. Did they talk with their wives? Play with their children? Or did they entertain each other apart from the women? And what did the women do? She thought about Silke, imagining her constantly confined behind that mud wall day after day with no intellectual stimulus, and shuddered.

The mosque was a simple stone building, the hall cool. A few men knelt on small prayer rugs and were bending towards Mecca, mumbling verses of the Koran. She didn't have a rug and knelt on her headcloth and pretended to go through the ritual, feeling quite awkward and like a Pharisee as she couldn't believe in a doctrine or a god which had such contempt for women and wanted them veiled, crushed, and silent.

Feeling in no way purified, she returned to the cafe. A delicious aroma of cooking food drifted from the inside of the cafe and she knew her dinner was being prepared. A young boy brought plates and bowls and, after greeting her, set them on the table. A while later, the owner brought the food.

"May this meal agree with you," he said, and left.

She was hungry and ate heartily, enjoying every bite. Inside the restaurant a radio was on and a wailing voice sang about lost love. Then, to her surprise, an Egyptian song came on which she, her sister, and Yasmine had sung as teenagers. She stopped eating, and leaned back. The song brought back happy memories and suddenly she had to fight tears.

She was up early the next day. The insecticide had worked, nothing had bitten her and she had slept fairly well. She hurried through the ordeal in the toilet and bathroom, and drove to Silke's street at the time when she had seen the women going to market before. Driving slowly, she observed men, boys, and cloaked women appear from behind their high fences and walk toward the market.

The men and boys looked at her, while the women all turned away as she drove past. She stopped at the other end of the street and looked at Silke's dwellings through the rearview mirror.

But only four men, a donkey, and two boys carrying a basket each came out of the gate. She assumed the men went to work in the fields, the boys to the market.

So it won't be today, she mused. She waited a while longer, then drove along other streets and on to the market where she bought a kilo of fruit. Eating some, she strolled from stand to stand looking at the different wares and talking with merchants.

At one stand she fell in love with an exquisite ceramic vase and bought it. She brought the vase back to the hotel, then decided to visit old Marib.

Although the place was oozing with history and impressive, the day was long and hot. She returned to the hotel in the evening, tired and sweaty, aching for a long, hot shower. But all she could do was wipe herself down with a washcloth.

Praying that the next day would bring some kind of result, she put on a fresh shirt, slacks, and a headcloth and went to the cafe to have dinner.

Filled with hope the next morning, she drove to Silke's street. Again the men on the streets in Silke's neighborhood looked at her curiously. She knew she had them wondering and that she couldn't do this too often without making them suspicious.

She parked down the street across from Silke's wall, her car pointed in the direction of the market, and again pretended to look at a map. Men and boys walked past her car, then some women with faces averted. Throwing furtive glances at the gate, she waited. Without warning it opened and three women emerged, one with a basket.

Seeing her and the car, the women looked away as they passed and headed for the market, except one who quickly turned to give her a brief second look.

Anouk held her breath. Was it Silke who had seen something unusual in the car and wondered? She doubted any other woman would have shown enough interest in a strange car to dare turn and look, something that was against all etiquette. She tried to put herself in Silke's place. After her mother's visit she must be hoping day and night for some help to appear. That hope would keep her alert to any kind of change in the village.

Anouk waited till they had reached the end of the street and drove after them. Close to the market, she passed them and parked the car with an eye on them in the rearview mirror. She lingered in front of a stand selling rugs to watch them arrive.

They walked to a vegetable stand and she followed closely, afraid to lose them. Again it was the heavyset woman with the old voice who carried the purse and bargained with the merchant. She bought garlic, onions, peppers and carrots, which the merchant wrapped in paper. The old woman handed him the money, saying something to one of the other women who reached for the package, her hand dark. At the next stand the woman bargained for millet, walnuts and raisins. Again it was the young woman with the dark hands who put the package into the basket.

Anouk looked at the tallest of them, who stood silently with her hands under her cloak. As more women crowded around them, Anouk had a hard time keeping track of them, and stayed as close as propriety permitted. They stopped at a stand with fruit, and while the old woman negotiated with the merchant, Anouk asked his younger assistant for a kilo of peaches.

She surprised him by quickly paying the price he asked, and continued to observe the women. The old one and the merchant had come to an agreement, and while the merchant made change, the silent woman reached out and took the wrapped fruit. And Anouk saw that her hand was young and light skinned.

Silke! Anouk almost cried out.

The older woman was in the lead as they went on, and Silke was now carrying the basket, her pale hand in great contrast to the black cloak.

Going after them, Anouk asked herself how she could get Silke's attention, and bumped into children chasing a goat. When she looked up again, other women had moved between her and Silke, and she feared she had lost her. Then she saw the pale hand carrying the basket and breathed again.

The women stopped at another stand to buy rice and dried beans. Cradling the package in one arm and eating a peach, Anouk trailed them, sometimes closer, sometimes at a distance, pretending to be interested in the general hustle and bustle while keeping her gaze on them and racking her brains over what to do.

The women lingered in front of baskets of bread, so she walked closer. Voices rose and there was some shoving and pushing as two boys chased a dog which had stolen a loaf of bread from a merchant further down. She stepped into the dog's way as if to catch it and when the dog escaped between her legs, feigned a stumble, bumping into the women and letting her peaches spill to the ground.

The dog disappeared with the yelling boys in hot pursuit. Anouk straightened, apologizing profusely to the women who remained stock-still.

"May Allah forgive me for my clumsiness," Anouk said, avoiding looking at them directly to show respect. Gathering peaches from the ground around their feet, she kept murmuring excuses in an Egyptian slang she knew they wouldn't easily understand, inserting in German, "Your mother sent me." And in between more curses against the dog and boys, "We'll get you out of here soon."

She picked up the last peach from the ground, and got out of their way. The women also walked on. Biting into a peach, Anouk watched them stop at another stand and while two of them fingered some cloth, one turned to look directly at her. Anouk moved the peach away from her face, nodded and smiled almost imperceptibly.

She imagined Silke's shock at hearing German from an Arab man. But the first contact was made and Silke would recognize her. But so would the other two women.

Anouk and Ulf sat down to have dinner in Ulf's dining room, Anouk freshly showered, and triumphant.

"That's incredible!" Ulf exclaimed, turning the radio off. "I would've never thought you'd make contact that fast." He put on a record, asking, "Do you recognize this?"

"Mozart," Anouk said, listening.

He nodded, smiling, and joined her at the table.

Anouk had a sip of beer. "It's an overture."

He kept smiling and she cried, "The overture of the Abduction from the Seraglio." And laughed.

Ulf also laughed. "Yeah, I thought it'd fit the occasion."

"Well, in our case it's more an escape from a hovel. Poor Silke." She bit into a piece of spicy lamb.

He filled his plate with rice. "So, what's next?"

"Somehow I have to get Silke away from Marib," Anouk said, draining her glass.

"First you have to talk to Silke so she can cooperate. How are you going to do that?"

"Good question." Anouk sighed. "Another one is how can I get her to Sana without being chased by the whole village?"

"And lynched when they catch you," Ulf added laconically.

"Decapitated," Anouk corrected. "That's the punishment in Arab countries for abductions."

"Whichever you prefer," he said, laughing.

"Any ideas?" she asked.

He shrugged. "Sorry. By the way, when's your plane leaving tomorrow morning?"

"Eight. I have to be at the airport at seven."

"No problem. Any idea when you'll be back?"

"Not yet. But I'll keep you posted."

Chapter 11

Karen drove up the steep Churchill Road to the Piazza, parked behind a five-story building, and walked up to the second floor to the photo lab of Stavros Minakis from whom she rented a darkroom.

His assistant, Fantu Assefa, a young Ethiopian woman, greeted her.

"More film to develop?" Fantu asked, her smile exposing strong, white teeth.

"Yes, miles more," Karen replied. "Stavros not around?"

"He went to the lakes for a couple of days. By the way I saw the contact sheet with the pictures you took of me," Fantu said, obviously pleased. "They came out well."

"Because you're a beautiful model," Karen replied.

She had taken pictures of Fantu in traditional dress made of white gauze with a shawl of the same material, both exquisitely embroidered along the borders. She looked again at the contact sheet depicting a close-up of Fantu's face framed by the shawl's embroidery.

A black Madonna, she thought thrilled by the perfect distribution of light and shadow on the face and the serenity it gave forth.

"I'll make prints for you too," Karen said.

Fantu thanked her, and Karen went into the darkroom to develop both black and white and color film. Eager to see her work, she forgot about time, watching many of the drying prints turn into excellent pictures.

A sob escaped her seeing photos of Anouk standing among shepherd children, then a close-up of her face. Anouk was smiling that wide, bewitching smile that sent Karen's emotions soaring. She decided to make duplicates and send them to Anouk along with two superb shots—one of a reed boat on Lake Tana, another of two women filling their gourds with water at the lake's shore.

It was four in the afternoon when she stopped working and asked Fantu for a manila envelope and a sheet of paper. She wrote: *Remember? I hope we'll soon be traveling again. Yours, Karen.*

She put the note along with the photos in the envelope and sealed it, addressing it to Anouk.

"Shall I mail it for you?" Fantu offered.

"That's okay. I'll drop it in the mailbox on my way home," Karen declined, getting her purse. "I'm off. See you tomorrow, Fantu."

Crossing the street to the cafe where she intended to eat dinner, to her surprise she saw Anouk leaving and called out to her.

Anouk turned.

"Hi!" Karen said when she reached her, every muscle in her body straining forward.

But Anouk made no move toward her as she asked, "How are you?"

Karen's heart was hammering, and for a few seconds her vocal cords tightened. She swallowed and said, "Fine." Remembering the envelope, she held it out. "Here, this is for you."

"For me?" Anouk asked, surprised. "What is it?"

"Just a little memento. But don't fold it."

"Thanks." Anouk held it carefully.

"I heard you've been away."

"Yes."

Karen expected more, but couldn't think of anything to say. She looked at Anouk, longing for more than just a cursory greeting. She felt like screaming, Don't you remember how you held me? I can still feel the warmth of your body, your kisses. Didn't all that mean anything to you?

"I'm going to have a bite to eat and an espresso," she said, trying to keep her voice from trembling. "Why don't you join me?"

Anouk's smile was apologetic. "I'm sorry, I just ate, thanks." She looked at her watch and said, "I have to go. Take care."

Shattered at Anouk's refusal, Karen watched her walk away, then entered the cafe and ordered a double cognac and an espresso, having lost all desire to eat.

Damn it, she fumed, this woman is like a fortress. Yet there were moments when she had let down her guard. She is tender. I have seen a longing in her eyes. So what's wrong? Why is she recoiling just when it seemed like we were becoming more open?

A hot tear dropped from the corner of her eye and she quickly brushed it away.

Meanwhile Anouk sat for a while in her Land Rover with her arms over the steering wheel. Seeing Karen again had caused more impact than she had anticipated. She had not been blind to the longing in Karen's eyes. How she hated having to act so cold, but she didn't want to encourage anything, especially now when she was wrapped up in helping Silke. She was still grappling with how to get the girl away from Marib and didn't need any distractions.

She looked at the envelope Karen had given her suspecting that it contained photos. She carefully opened it. My God, they're beautiful, she murmured. She read the note and kept staring at it while suppressing the urge to run back to the cafe.

She started the car before her desire could get the better of her, and drove to a shop to have the pictures framed.

Karen's new apartment was on the third floor with a view to green mountains. She was glad to have her own place at last, and wished she could show it to Anouk. Spacious, it was a furnished one-bedroom with big windows, adequate for her needs. She didn't have a servant as there was too little housework. Not far away were coffee shops and a bistro where she took her meals when she didn't feel like cooking.

Feeling lonely, she sat on the living room floor sorting photos, noting names of places and categories on the envelopes which she stowed into boxes. When she came across the close-up shot of Anouk she had taken near Lake Tana, she pinned it to the wall above her desk and sat wistfully looking at it.

But a picture was a poor substitute. She wanted to see the real Anouk and there was one sure way to achieve that. She went to the phone and called Sergio to book a flight to Harar, a walled-in town from the ninth century.

"I'd like to fly with Anouk," she told him.

"Let me look at her schedule," Sergio said. "She's available the day after tomorrow."

"That's fine," Karen said, suddenly feeling much better.

But the next day Sergio called her back. "Sorry, Karen, Anouk is unavailable for your trip to Harar."

"Why?" Karen asked, feeling everything inside her shrivel.

"She switched with Murath for some reasons. These things happen; other matters come up. You've flown with Murath. He's a good pilot."

"I wanted to fly with Anouk," Karen said in a low voice.

"Do you want to postpone?"

What's the use, she thought. She'll just switch again. "No, it's all right. I'll fly with Murath."

Hot tears stinging her eyes, she sat down at the desk, took a sheet of paper and picked up a pen. After the fifth draft of a letter to Anouk, she gave up. She crumpled the paper and threw it on top of the other discarded drafts in the waste basket. Why bother? she asked herself, wiping her face. Why humiliate myself and ask for reasons?

Ten days later, she returned deeply tanned from her trip with a bag full of film and fresh ideas for her book. She had not only visited the old town of Harar but also driven to the sprawling town of Jijiga, the only watering place in the immense Ogaden desert. She had stayed in a small hotel and eaten in a ramshackle restaurant owned by an Italian woman, Elsa.

Elsa was a widow, and eked out a living cooking for truck drivers and smugglers who traveled between Jijiga and the Somali coast on the Indian Ocean. Karen had become good friends with Elsa who was full of wild tales about this forsaken place. Elsa took her to a Somali ritual dance, and introduced her to Europeans living in the area with whom she went on hunting trips to see some wildlife and get a taste of this harrowing and lonely desert.

She was unpacking when the doorbell stopped her reminiscing.

"So you're still alive," Nora said, hugging her. "I called several times last week and got no answer."

"I just got back. I think I got some great shots of Harar, Jijiga and the Ogaden desert. We saw lions; I can hardly wait to see my photos."

"Well, you sure got a lot of sun!" Nora said admiringly as she followed Karen into the living room.

"Excuse the mess, but I'm in the middle of unpacking."

"So I see," Nora remarked, looking at clothes on the floor and the couch, the camera and lenses on the desk. Her gaze fastened on Anouk's portrait on the wall above it. "You flew with Anouk again, didn't you?"

"No, not this time."

"Why not?"

"She couldn't—wasn't available."

"But you're seeing each other?"

"I wish," Karen said, trying to sound casual, but suddenly her eyes were brimming.

"Oh Karen," Nora said, putting an arm around her. "Is it that bad?"

Karen nodded, sniffling against her friend's shoulder.

"Poor girl," Nora said, caressing her hair. "Is she already involved with someone?"

"I don't think so—it's complicated. She seemed interested, then became distant. Every time it's worse, I suppose, because I want it all the more."

"Well, it's no use pining away for unrequited love," Nora said, turning practical. "You'll only make yourself sick. Maybe she's afraid of a relationship with an American because she doesn't know what makes us tick."

Karen smiled through her tears. "We don't tick that much differently from other people."

"She could also be self-protective because you're here for a limited time only." Nora got a tissue from her purse. "Here, blow your nose."

Karen obeyed. "You're right. Just because we share a sexual persuasion doesn't mean we're destined for each other—does it? It's just she was such a breath of fresh air for me—her sense of adventure and risk. That's why I've fallen for her; I want that, too. I love to be with her—I have loved what she brings out in me ever since I met her the first day on that desolate shore. She found me! I just haven't been the same since." Karen paced to the window and stared out without seeing anything. "I have to get her to fly with me again somehow."

"Forget it! What you need is distraction!" Nora declared, joining her at the window. "Actually, I came to tell you that you're invited to the Baron's party tonight. He shot a kudu the other day and is having a big barbecue. He specifically asked me to bring you."

"I don't give a hoot about the Baron or his kudu," Karen muttered.

"I know, but it'll get you out of your four walls. You should mix with people instead of staying cooped up here, wallowing in misery."

When Karen remained silent, Nora patted her face. "Come on, girl. Perk up. Anouk isn't the only woman in this world. And if she doesn't want you, it's her loss." She looked at her watch. "I have to pick up my son from school. Anyway, I'll expect you to be there tonight. Promise?"

"Promise," Karen said, half-heartedly.

"I wish you'd call me Kurt," the Baron said. "To answer your question, yes, I'm a passionate hunter. Shot a lion not long ago. A big fellow. Almost got me."

"Really," Karen said, feigning concern.

"Do you wish to come along one day?"

"No thanks. I just got back from a hunt—with my camera—and am way too behind on my book at the moment."

"Are you also too busy to have dinner with me?" he asked, giving her a deep look.

His brazen wantonness annoyed her. "I'm sorry but unfortunately I have a tight traveling schedule. I am preparing for a photo trip to the Omo."

A whiff of cooking meat filtered through the garden and she pretended to be hungry to get away from him. He led her to the buffet, handing her a plate. She took some meat and vegetables and another glass of wine from a tray a waiter was carrying around and joined the Peters at a table. The habitual crowd was mingling with a few newcomers. She waved at the Thompsons, the Milnos and the Donners, who came to their table.

"How have you been?" Mrs. Milno asked. "We haven't seen you at our afternoon teas lately."

"I've been working on my book," Karen said apologetically.

More people came and the conversation veered to the usual small talk. Karen got another glass of wine and ambled away. A pleasant high replaced her torment about Anouk. She felt strong and weak at the same time and oddly enough, found this state almost enjoyable.

The sun was setting and the tiny flies that get lively after sunset were swarming. She saw Sergio arriving and greeting people. He spotted her and approached.

"How was the trip to Harar?" he asked.

"Everything went fine. Murath was a good guide."

"Anouk told me that you're an excellent photographer."

Her heart jumped. Anouk must have liked the photos she had given her. "Where is she?"

"She should be home."

"Will she come to this party?"

"I wouldn't count on it." He sighed, then laughed. "She doesn't have much in common with this crowd. And lately she seems to have a problem—don't know what it is." Friends interrupted, and he turned to greet them.

Karen ambled on, suddenly overcome by a passionate desire to see Anouk. She stole away to her car and drove to Anouk's house, but the Land Rover was not in the driveway. She drove on, feeling foolish and dejected. She had no wish to return to the party or to go home, and continued to drive aimlessly till she reached the other end of town.

Suddenly she slowed, seeing Anouk's Land Rover parked in front of a white stone house. Wondering what Anouk was doing there, she parked the car on the other side of the street, determined to find out. Having watched Anouk slip off to her secret adventures, Karen knew she was onto something.

The front door was open with dim light and the wailing sounds of an Arabic song filtering through a curtain of glass beads. The place was obviously a bar. For a while she observed a few Ethiopian men coming out and getting into their cars. Then an Ethiopian woman appeared and after a moment another one. Karen debated whether or not to go inside.

If Anouk was in there, what was there to be afraid of? Feeling reckless and out of control from the wine, she left the car. Just before entering the bar, her courage ran out, and she hesitated. But someone came up the walk behind her to go in and she had no choice but to walk through the strings of beads.

The gloomy room was smoky. Ethiopians sat at wooden tables along whitewashed walls and at the bar. A hush fell over the room as everyone stared at her. For a moment she remained standing near the door ready to bolt, looking back at the people. Then she straightened her shoulders and boldly crossed the room to the bar. Several men jumped off their stools and offered them to her.

Thanking them, she climbed onto one, and turned to the huge black woman behind the bar. "A scotch on the rocks, please."

The woman frowned. Scotch? with rocks?

Karen smiled. "I mean whisky with some ice cubes. Do you have ice?"

"Ah, I see," the woman smiled back.

While the woman poured the drink, Karen glanced around once more. Anouk was not among the patrons. Overwhelmed to be the only foreigner in the room, she quickly turned back to the bartender who had put the drink in front of her and had a good swallow to drown her self-consciousness.

Conversations resumed, her tension eased and she gazed around once more. Discovering two doors next to the bar, she wondered if

Anouk was behind one of them and, if so, what she was doing.

A new record came on and a few people got up to sway to sensuous Ethiopian music. They were mostly young women and older men, moving against each other suggestively.

She finished her drink and waved at the bartender. "Another one, please." As it was being poured, she said, "I'm looking for Anouk."

The woman's brows arched in surprise. "Anouk?" Jerking her head towards one of the doors, she said in English, "She doin' da hookah."

The hooker? Karen thought, shocked, looking at the door then at the woman.

"Go see." The woman nodded towards the door.

No way, Karen thought.

"You go," the woman insisted, pointing. "Anouk in there."

Aware that the men around her were watching, she slid from the stool, slowly walked to the door, and opened it a crack. The room was even darker than the bar. She could make out men sitting on mattresses arranged in a semicircle. On a brass tray in the middle of the semicircle stood a water pipe and a brazier burning charcoal. The only sound in the room was the gurgling of the water pipe as the mouthpiece went from person to person.

She opened the door a little wider and made out Anouk the same moment Anouk glanced up at the door.

Peering through the cloud of smoke, Anouk couldn't believe her eyes. It was Karen. What in the world…?

With an apology under her breath to her cohorts, Anouk leapt from the mattress and came towards her. "Karen! What the hell are you doing here?" she asked in a hoarse whisper.

"Having a drink," Karen retorted.

Anouk stared at her. "B…but how did you end up here?"

"Same way you did. By car."

"This is no place for you," Anouk hissed.

"Why?" Karen asked. "How about introducing me and letting me join you?"

Anouk took her arm firmly. "I'm going to escort you back to your car."

"I don't want to go to my car," Karen said like a stubborn child. "I want to try that—whatever it is."

"It's called a hookah."

"Oh, hookah," Karen repeated, realizing how she had misunderstood the bartender.

"It's a water pipe and you don't want to try it."

"Why? Are you smoking some drug?"

"Just tobacco. Now let's go." But Karen tried to push past her.

"Karen!" Anouk warned in a low voice, and pressed her against the door to stop her. "You can't come in here."

Karen began to enjoy this. "You're doing it. So why can't I?"

"Because you and I are two different subjects. Now let's go."

Karen pretended to push Anouk out of the way again, to get still closer to her. "I'm not leaving," she said, pressing her body up against Anouk.

Anouk inhaled sharply, then pushed her through the door. "You're impossible!" she said, and walked her to the exit.

"Wait! I owe for two drinks," Karen cried.

Anouk reached into her pocket and threw a few bills on the counter while everyone watched in silence.

Outside, Anouk asked, "Where's your car?"

"Over there."

Still holding her arm, Anouk walked across the silent street.

"The key," she ordered, holding out her hand. Karen got it from her purse and Anouk unlocked the door.

"I guess I just have to find another place like this," Karen remarked slyly.

Anouk took her by the shoulders and shook her. "Karen, this isn't for you! It could be misunderstood by some drunk. You shouldn't be in these kinds of places, or in this area. You could end up in trouble."

"What about you?"

Anouk's eyes rolled skyward. "That's different. I belong here, and I look and talk like they do. The men have accepted me the way I am and certainly don't find me very appealing."

"But I do," Karen said, and pressed her mouth on Anouk's.

Anouk flinched, yet her arms went around Karen like a reflex. With a groan she pulled Karen closer and kissed her hard and hungrily. "Karen," she said, letting go of her abruptly. "This is not…"

"Yes it it." Karen kissed her once more, pressing herself against Anouk. Holding her tight, Anouk covered her neck, ears, throat, and face with kisses, her breath hot and fast.

"Karen, Karen," she whispered, and kept kissing her with a savage passion.

Hearing footsteps, they drew apart, watching a man walk on the other side of the street until he disappeared around a corner.

"You better drive home," Anouk said, chest heaving.

"Yes, with you," Karen said, not letting go.

"Do you think this is wise?"

"I don't want to think. I want to make love to you." Karen kissed her again, pushing her thigh between Anouk's.

Anouk melted and her doubts gave way to an untamed want. "All right," she said in a thick voice. "Follow me." And sprinted to her car.

They stepped into each other's arms as soon as they were inside Anouk's house, their kisses hard and steamy.

"You've been avoiding me," Karen murmured against Anouk's mouth. "I couldn't take it any more."

"Yes," Anouk moaned.

"You switched with Murath because you didn't want to see me."

"Yes."

"Why, for godsake, when this is what we both want?"

Holding her close, Anouk looked at her. "This isn't Philadelphia, a big city where things can be more anonymous. Addis is small and people here thrive on gossip because they have nothing better to do. And they will find out and you'll lose your friends."

"I don't give a damn," Karen cried. "Nora knows and doesn't care. And all the others are none of my concern. Anouk, you are the only one that matters to me. I love you. I think I fell in love with you the moment I met you at Lake Assal."

Anouk pulled her close, buried her face in the hollow of her neck, murmuring endearments and kissing her with a growing urgency.

Kissing as if they wanted to devour each other, they wriggled out of their clothes and moved to the bedroom where they sank onto the bed. Anouk pressed her down and wrapped Karen with her arms and legs as if to take her not only with her mouth but her whole body.

Karen began to shake. "I've been wanting this for so long."

Anouk kept smothering her with kisses, her eager hands touching, squeezing, searching. "You're so beautiful," she said in a choked voice. "Skin like alabaster, a mouth like honey."

Karen cried out when Anouk entered her. She felt heat surge through the entire length of her body and swirl around her brain. Dazed, and holding on to Anouk's shoulders, she began to move.

Eyes half closed, groin on fire, Anouk watched her, afraid she was dreaming this. Her fingers were bathed in Karen's wetness as she kept up her relentless thrusts. Karen's hips moved faster in search of release. Her own desire began to peak and she rubbed against Karen's thigh, her breath raspy and fast.

Karen began to make noise and Anouk slowed. Dizzy and nearly crying, Karen begged. "Please."

Anouk closed Karen's mouth with hers, then whispering endearments into her ear, moved faster against her thigh.

"Anouk, if you don't, I'll die. "

A deep sound escaped from Anouk and she gathered all her movements into several forceful thrusts. Karen bucked, went rigid, and sank back with a long moan.

Anouk slipped her hands under Karen's buttocks, came between her thighs, and began to move. Her eyes were glassy, unsmiling in a growing need.

Karen felt her quiver and arched herself into her.

In her loins Anouk felt a shocking, protracted implosion of flesh that rushed to her core, then jolted and spread in waves to the farthest corner of her being.

Awed by their powerful feelings, they lay in each other's arms. But their breathing had hardly calmed when Anouk moved down Karen, pushed her knees apart, and covered her golden tuft with her mouth.

"Oh, Karen," she sighed.

Karen clawed the sheets as Anouk's tongue explored, sliding behind the hair, between the folds and into her invisible sex, then slowly to the quicksilver of her clitoris. Each slow stroke was a dazzling thrill bringing another swirling tide of lust.

"Anouk!" Karen cried as another orgasm swept over her.

When she was back to reality, she murmured, "I knew it would be fantastic with you."

Anouk smiled, her dark eyes sparkling. "You're fantastic too. Would you like something to drink?"

"Do you have mineral water?"

"Yes." Anouk left to get it.

Karen looked around the room and saw the photos she had given Anouk framed on the wall above the dresser.

"I like the way you framed my photos," she said when Anouk returned with a bottle and glasses.

"They deserved the best. I'm pleased to own them and I'm sorry

I never thanked you." Anouk poured the water, handed her a glass, and settled down next to her.

"Well, you have the rest of the night to thank me," Karen said, smiling slyly.

Anouk grinned back, then drank and put her glass on the night stand.

Karen emptied her glass and put it next to Anouk's, sighing, "I'm so happy we're together. For a while I was afraid it would never happen. You can be quite difficult, you know?"

Anouk drew her close. "Do you think so?"

Nodding, Karen brushed a strand of black hair from Anouk's forehead.

Anouk drew a breath. "I have a lot on my mind right now and didn't think it would be fair to you. " She stopped and chewed her lower lip, debating whether or not to tell Karen about Silke.

"What do you mean?" Karen asked.

Anouk moved away a little and sat with her legs drawn up and her arms around them.

"Come on, don't clam up," Karen begged.

"I'm not," Anouk said in a low voice. "There's something I have to do. Something you might not like because it involves great risk. And for you to understand why I'm doing it, I'll have to go back to my childhood."

"I'm listening," Karen said.

Chapter 12

"I was ten when my aunt, a sister of my father, died," Anouk began in a low voice. "She left an eighteen year old son and thirteen year old daughter. Much to my sister's and my joy, our family decided that Yasmine should live with us.

"Yasmine was beautiful, bright, and a lot of fun, and went to the same school my sister and I did. When she turned sixteen, her father announced he had found a husband for her. She was frightened and begged him to let her finish school and become a teacher which had always been her dream. But her father insisted, telling her that her groom was rich and she should be grateful not to work. A little later we met the man—he was about the same age as her father with a nose like a vulture's beak.

"Yasmine cried and cried, not herself any longer. As the wedding day drew closer, she withdrew more and more becoming a shadow of herself. My sister and I tried to cheer her up, but it was useless.

"The day before the wedding she had to submit to this custom of removing all her body hair—because a woman has to be completely hairless on her wedding night. She lay naked on a table while women applied hot wax to her arms, legs, and genitalia and pulled out the hair, which is quite a painful procedure. We could her moaning and crying.

"The wedding was a big affair and Yasmine looked gorgeous. But we could see the fear in her eyes." Gritting her teeth, Anouk let her head sink onto her knees.

Karen wrapped her arms around her and waited till Anouk had regained her calm.

After a deep breath, Anouk resumed. "A few weeks later she arrived at our house, pale and thin. She had run away from her husband. Crying, she fell into my mother's arms. My mother took her into her bedroom where Yasmine stripped and showed us her body."

Anouk's voice trembled, and her eyes became moist. "She was covered with bruises; her vagina and anus were swollen and raw." Anouk's voice cracked and she took another deep breath going on through clenched teeth, "That pig had raped her over and over. My sister and I cried with Yasmine and my mother stood in shock and outrage. When my father came home and she told him, he was also shocked and called Yasmine's father who came over immediately. Yasmine wanted to show herself to him but he refused to look at her, believing my mother. He seemed shaken but didn't say much and left.

"Of course Yasmine stayed with us. Two weeks later when she had just began to heal, her father came back. Citing the Koran, he ordered her back to that sadist, that pervert, saying, 'a wife belongs to her husband no matter what and she has to obey him at all times.' We couldn't believe it.

"Three weeks later, Yasmine was dead. She hung herself."

Karen gasped. "Oh God, Anouk."

Anouk's head sank back onto her knees and Karen knew she was crying. Not knowing what to say, she just held her.

After a deep sigh, Anouk wiped her face, saying, "I was afraid to grow up after that. I hated every birthday. Then Alifa was married off, also to a rich, older man. But apparently not a sadist. Anyway, my sister had become pretty resigned ever since her brutal circumcision.

"Then I turned sixteen. I can still feel the fear as I waited for my father to make the announcement. But nothing happened and I dared to breathe again, thinking I had another year. But about two months later, my parents told me that they had found a husband for me.

"I sank onto a chair and stared at them, speechless. Then I begged and when that didn't help, I screamed and threw a fit. I was always a bit rebellious and headstrong and sometimes got away with things. Well, this time I didn't. My father slapped me, calling me ungrateful and too willful for my own good. He said that the hand of a strict husband would put me in my place.

"The idea of being touched by a man, especially an older man, was unbearable to me. And the thought of being at the mercy of someone like Yasmine's husband was enough to drive me insane.

"So I decided to escape. I took money from my mother's purse, stuffed a shirt and pants belonging to my brother into my school bag along with my lunch, a toothbrush, some toiletries, a knife and a pair of scissors, and left home as if I were going to school as usual."

"Weren't you scared?"

"Of course, but getting married scared me more. Anyway, I took a tram to the railway station, changed clothes in the toilet where I also cut off my hair."

"In the toilet?"

"Why not? And I did a pretty good job, too. I threw my dress into a garbage can, bought a ticket to Alexandria, and got there in the evening. I knew Alexandria well, my parents have an apartment there, sort of like a home away from home where we spent summer vacations. Of course I couldn't go to that apartment, the concierge would've immediately called my parents. So I walked to the harbor, scared stiff, not knowing what to do or where to spend the night.

"I came upon a few sailboats, some local, some foreign. Suddenly a couple speaking French came out from one of the boats discussing their grocery list and arguing about what time they should put to sea. I still remember that the man wanted to leave at midnight, the woman early in the morning. Anyway, as soon as they were out of sight, I sneaked on board. Only the forward hatch was open, just enough for airing. I squeezed a hand through the slit, unscrewed the lock and climbed into the forepeak. It had a bunk on one side, a sail-bin on the other. I crawled under the sailbags.

"The couple had no idea that I was on board when they sailed off a few hours later. I stayed hidden for a full day before showing myself.

"I cried and told them about Yasmine and myself and that I had an aunt in Dijon where I wanted to go. They were understanding and compassionate and when we arrived in Nice put me on a train after finding my aunt's address through information."

"How did you get into France without a passport?"

Anouk let out a little laugh. "That was easy. We just sailed into the Nice harbor as if we had returned from a day's sail. Nobody knew we had come all the way from Egypt.

"Anyway, my aunt had divorced her Yemenite husband and lived with her daughter, Stephanie, who's my age. She was also compassionate and promised not to write to my parents that I was staying with them. Barely a month later, Stephanie found a letter from my father in which he announced his arrival.

"Stephanie gave me all her savings and, once again, I pretended I was going to school. I took a train to Paris instead where I worked for a family as an au pair. A year later I went to London using

Stephanie's French passport—we look enough alike and were often taken for sisters.

"Finally when I was twenty-one, Hilde, with whom I lived in Duesseldorf, made connections with the Egyptian Consulate—she was great at that—and I was able to get a legitimate Egyptian passport, and my birth certificate from Cairo."

After a long silence, Karen said, "Wow! What do you think your father would have done?"

"I wasn't going to stick around to find out. An Arab father has the right to do what he wants with his family. Some have gone as far as killing their daughters if they suspected they weren't virgins any longer. To save the family's honor.

"Of course there is a law against that nowadays, but the man is usually out of prison within a few weeks, and celebrated like a hero by his family and friends."

"Couldn't you have gone to the French authorities for help?"

"As a minor? Illegally in the country? They would've turned me over to my father right away."

Karen snuggled closer to Anouk. "That's quite a story. So, what is it you have to do that made you want to keep me away?"

"It has to do with Yemen."

"Ah, when you left the country so mysteriously. And a seaplane maybe?"

Anouk smiled. "You're quite astute, I have to say," she remarked, and explained about Silke and what she had done so far.

Again Karen was speechless. Finally she managed to say, "But this is very dangerous! What if you get caught?"

"I have you worried already, don't I? The answer is simple—I can't afford to get caught."

"How will Ulf get Silke through all those roadblocks?"

"As a European working for the government, Ulf has some immunity and won't be checked as thoroughly. He can hide Silke in the trunk. I think that's the least of our problems."

"Wouldn't it be easier to do it with a motorboat?"

"North Yemen just came out of a terrible civil war and everything out of the ordinary is still eyed with suspicion. A yacht would be surrounded by officials the minute it entered Yemen's territorial waters, and constantly under surveillance."

"All right, so Silke will float a mile or so offshore in a small boat. What about currents?"

"They can be calculated, and Silke will have a small compass and flares."

"Hmm," Karen mused. "Is there really no better way to get her out?"

"Tell me a better one," Anouk taunted. "It's the only way. Airports are out too. First, because Silke doesn't have a passport, second, because the minute she's reported missing, all airports will be alerted, especially the Sana airport which will also be patrolled by her husband and his male relatives. They'll figure that Silke's mother is behind the escape, and that Silke will try to leave the country."

After some more thought, Karen said, "You still haven't told me how you're going to get Silke away from the village."

Anouk let out a long sigh. "Because I don't know how yet. That's the most difficult part."

"Silke could sneak out of the house in the middle of the night when everybody's asleep, pretending to go to the outhouse?—And you'd be waiting in a car. You'd be in Sana by the time they all woke up and noticed."

"Fine, but I'd have to arrange the day and time with Silke which is impossible because I can't go near her." Anouk sighed. "I have to make another trip to Yemen to see what I can do."

"I'm coming along," Karen said.

"No way! I don't want you to get involved."

"You can't stop me! If you must do this I won't let you do it alone. I'm sure I can help."

"Don't be ridiculous!" Anouk made an impatient sound. "How can you possibly help? You don't speak the language. You'd have to be cloaked and veiled. You have no idea how restricted the women are."

"I won't mind," Karen insisted.

"Look, Karen, that's very sweet of you. But this is a deadly serious mission which I can't afford to jeopardize. There's no room for slip-ups, and it's hardly romantic."

"Don't underestimate me." Karen gave her a level look. "You've seen for yourself that I'm capable."

"Karen, you couldn't move around freely. Women never walk alone in public which would be considered immodest. They're either with another woman, or a male member of their family, and they must walk with their heads lowered behind the men."

Karen shrugged. "I don't mind."

"You will hate it. No non-Moslem woman lasts long in this country because of all the restrictions."

After some thought Karen asked, "Why is it that Arab men do this to women?"

"Because the Koran teaches that the female is considered dangerous to herself and others, and can't be trusted to her own judgement. The male is superior physically, intellectually, and morally. Allah has preferred the one sex over the other in the matter of mental ability, and in their power to carry out divine commands."

"With all the horrors men have committed and are still committing daily around the world, this is incredible," Karen hissed, barely able to contain her anger.

Anouk remained silent, thinking, I shouldn't have told her. Damn it. I need to be focused, why couldn't I wait until this was over? "Karen," she began.

"If I have to be cloaked and veiled, I could go as your wife," Karen interrupted.

"Oh yes?" Anouk's tone was mocking. "And what would you do walking behind me like a black shadow with your head lowered?"

"You said all those cloaks look alike?"

"Yes."

"In other words, all the women look indistinguishable from each other, except for their height or weight and wouldn't recognize each other unless they talked?"

"Right."

"That means I could walk close to Silke and her in-laws at the market pretending to shop, and when we're well surrounded by other women, whisper to Silke to follow me. As I told you, I know enough German to make a little conversation. Then Silke and I would leave the market as if we were done shopping, while you're waiting in a car. We'd be miles away before her in-laws would miss her."

Anouk looked at her, astounded. "Karen! You've just solved the most difficult part of this venture."

"Now tell me again I can't be of any help," Karen taunted.

Anouk took Karen into her arms and kissed her until she was breathless, then made love to her till dawn.

Two days later, Anouk and Karen went to the Arab shops behind the market where Anouk bargained with the merchants for all the necessary clothes Karen would need in Yemen: a black cloak and veil, a couple of long black skirts and several long-sleeved blouses in muted colors, black shoes and socks.

"Do women really wear all that under the cloak?" Karen wondered.

"Yes, especially the woman who would be my wife," Anouk said. "And I want to warn you that you'll be quite hot in the desert."

"I'll survive it," Karen said, unperturbed.

They walked along a sandy alley past a mosque and narrow Arab stores. Karen, ever hungry for good subjects, shot pictures of old men on donkeys, little girls squatting next to their mothers and a beggar playing a mazenka, a one string fiddle, to whom she gave a few coins.

They stopped at a coffee shop which was a mere nook in the wall and had mocha coffee, then walked on, Anouk lingering in front of a stand with African masks, while Karen went to change film in the shade of a small tree. As she was closing her camera, she heard someone calling Anouk, and saw a beautiful young Ethiopian woman clinging to her. Her pulse quickened when she watched Anouk talk to her, then shake off her embrace. After a curious glance at Karen, the woman walked away, wagging her behind in a seductive way.

Damn, Anouk thought, joining Karen.

Nostrils flared, Karen glared at her.

"Karen." Anouk began.

"You must have a heart like a daisy," Karen quipped. "A petal for everybody, huh? So am I just one of many?"

"Karen, you know better than that."

"I don't. And I know you also have women in the north." As Anouk's brows rose in surprise, Karen said, "Oh, it was quite obvious. And I meant to talk to you about this."

"It's a little after the fact, isn't it? You didn't ask questions when you came to find me."

"I know. I should have. Because I know I can't share you."

"Neither can I share you," Anouk said, motioning for them to continue walking.

"Who are those women? And what do they mean to you?"

"I'm not in love with any of them, if that's what you mean. They're working women, prostitutes if you want, who have given me companionship and sex."

"And how do I know you won't keep seeing them when you're alone?"

"Because since being with you that life is over for me."

Unsure, Karen took a few steps away from her.

Anouk pulled her back. "Don't do this, Karen. Please."

Karen looked at her. "How can you enjoy paying for love?"

"Not love. Sex. And why not? It's a service like any other. I'm human and have needs. And those women have been there for me when no one else was. After all, I couldn't know you'd come along or that you'd stick around once you'd finished with your project."

Still doubtful, Karen went on. "That woman seemed to be more than just a prostitute. I mean she appeared to really like you."

"I'm not going to say I didn't like her. Besides, I treated her better and paid her better than the men do."

"Weren't you afraid to catch some disease?"

Anouk shrugged. "I guess I have been lucky. I have periodic check ups. I'm healthy right now, Karen, if that's what's worrying you."

"Did you ever live with someone?"

"Of course I did."

"In Addis?"

"No, never in Addis. I had several relationships in Europe and one in South Africa."

"Somebody very special?"

"Yes…Diana."

"Why did it end?"

Anouk's voice was suddenly low, her gaze far away. "She died in a plane crash."

"I'm sorry I asked."

"It's all right."

"Does it still hurt?"

Anouk put an arm around her, saying softly, "Diana will always have a special place in my heart. But she is a memory. Now you are that very special one for me, Karen, and I hope that we'll be together, if not here somewhere else, somehow. I love you very much and would do anything for you."

Karen's face softened. "So would I for you."

They dropped into silence while Anouk steered them through the crowd back to her car.

Finally, when they got to the car Karen asked hesitantly, "Was Diana black…? I mean do you prefer black women to white women?"

"No she wasn't. Karen, I don't fall in love with skin color. But living in Europe I met more white women, although I lived with a Moroccan woman in Paris and in London with a woman from Ghana."

"Ghana?"

"Yes, she was studying medicine and after she got her degree she returned to Ghana, ending our relationship. Shortly after that I met Hilde with whom I drove to South Africa. I told you about that when we first met. Remember?"

They climbed into the car and Anouk started the engine. "Anything else you want to know?"

Karen shook her head. "At the moment I can't think of anything."

"Well, so tell me did you have someone special," Anouk asked. "There must have been someone."

"Of course I did, but I never loved anyone as much as I love you."

Anouk gave her a warm look, took her hand and kissed it.

Back at Anouk's, Karen practiced walking cloaked and veiled.

"Now remember, if you must pass a man in the street, you lower your head and look away from him. And don't show your hands." Anouk showed her how to hold the cloak closed under her chin without her hand showing.

"Even the hands must be covered?"

"Yes, unless it's necessary to do something like shopping. And yours are white and would give you away and make everyone in Marib suspicious."

"I'll apply one of those self-tanning lotions," Karen said and walked around the room a few more times. Suddenly worried, she asked, "What should I do when a man talks to me?"

"No man would, with the exception of merchants, of course. Otherwise the rules of decency require that men take no notice of a woman's presence by looking at, greeting or in any way interfering with her. So you're safe."

Karen took off the veil and cloak. "I think I've got it. And tomorrow I'll get my tourist visa for Yemen. I also have to call Nora to tell her I'm leaving for two weeks."

"What're you going to tell her?"

"That you're taking a vacation and I'm joining you." Anouk looked pensive and Karen added, "I have to, Anouk, or she'll think something happened to me and sound the alarm."

Anouk nodded. "She'll want to know where we are going."

"I'll say Kenya. And when everything's over tell her the truth."

"Good enough."

"Have you called Ulf and told him about our plan?"

"I did but I don't trust phones and only told him that he is to meet his American fiancée so he's aware, in case he's questioned by the immigration officials at the airport. I also called Irmgard. The seaplane is on the way. She'll call me as soon as she's made a reservation for Addis."

Four days later, they were on their way to the airport to pick up Irmgard.

"That must be her," Anouk said, pointing out an attractive woman of medium height coming off the Lufthansa plane and walking to the immigration booth, which was cordoned off from the waiting hall.

"I think you're right," Karen said, looking at the fortyish woman with short blonde hair wearing a sporty dark blue pantsuit and white sweater. The woman handed her passport to the official who, after a brief glance, stamped it and handed it back.

"Irmgard?" Anouk called as the woman walked past the cordon.

The woman's tired and drawn face lit up. "Anouk?" She held out her hand which was cool and slender. "So happy to meet you. Stephanie sends her love. They're all holding their breath in France and in Hamburg."

"We're holding ours, too," Anouk said and introduced Karen. "I think Karen and I have a good plan. But let's discuss it at your hotel. How was your flight?"

"Long with one stop in Cairo," Irmgard replied.

They picked up Irmgard's suitcase and drove to the Ethiopia Hotel where they had made a reservation for her.

Irmgard glanced around the room which was like any other modern hotel room, then out the window.

"A very incongruous town with a strange mixture of architecture," she remarked. "What's it like to live here?"

"I like it," Karen said. "The country is beautiful. There're so many interesting places."

Irmgard took off her jacket, sat down in a chair, bidding them to sit. "So, what's your plan?"

Anouk told her.

"That's quite ingenious," Irmgard remarked, her blue eyes suddenly bright with hope. She got a photograph from her purse. "This is Silke at sixteen. This picture was taken shortly before her father abducted her, because that's what it was—an abduction."

"She is lovely," Anouk said, studying the smiling wide-eyed face framed by wavy chestnut hair—a far cry from the photo Dr. Korda had taken of Silke in the hospital. She handed the picture to Karen.

"She inherited your blue eyes," Karen said.

Irmgard nodded. "Unusual, but yes, she did. Like me she is also very musical. She wanted to study music at the conservatory. To think that my girl is confined in a mud hut with goats and chicken and is being beaten and raped…" Her voice broke.

"I assume Dr. Korda has seen you in Hamburg?" Anouk asked.

Irmgard nodded, wiping her eyes. "He told me what happened after I left Yemen and about the sterilization. I never thought my daughter had it in her to fight back that way. As sad as it is and as risky as it was, I have to give her a lot credit for that." New tears filmed her eyes.

Anouk took Irmgard's hands. "Irmgard, Silke knows help is on the way. And she knows me." Anouk told her what happened on her last trip to Yemen.

"I'm so grateful, Anouk. Stephanie was right. Only you could do something like that, being Arab yourself and knowing the customs." She reached into her purse again and dropped a thick bundle of US dollars into Anouk's lap. "You never named a price. If you feel twenty-five thousand isn't enough…"

Anouk lifted her hands in protest. "But I haven't done much yet. You pay me when Silke's in your arms."

"You've already had expenses and I know what you're risking. Anyway, is it enough?"

"Yes," Anouk assured her.

"I promised Silke that I'd move heaven and earth to get her out. We must get her out, Anouk. You have no idea how awful it was when I had to leave Yemen without her. She looked so sick and lost and clung to me, begging me not to leave her. Oh God, forgive me for falling apart." Crying, she pressed her face into a handkerchief.

Karen went to her and held her, murmuring soothing words.

When Irmgard was calm again, Anouk said, "How was it possible for your ex to get Silke to Yemen without you suspecting anything?"

Irmgard's smile was bitter. "Silke was four when I divorced him. He didn't want the divorce and was angry at first. As you know, in his country women can't divorce and it was an affront to his ego. Then he seemed to come around, proposing we should be friends for the sake of our daughter. We ended up getting along better. Even my parents liked him more after the divorce. He even paid some child support, he saw Silke on weekends and took her to the islands in the North Sea during summer vacations. He did not object to her studies and even encouraged her to become a pianist. He duped us all for twelve years waiting for his revenge. All that time he was planning an arranged marriage for her. When he suggested Silke should get to know his country and family, neither my parents nor I saw anything wrong. He didn't even fly with Silke but entrusted her to Yemenite friends, a nice couple, who had lived and worked in Germany for many years and were returning to Yemen to retire."

"Do you think they knew what he was doing?"

"I doubt it. They didn't seem like that kind of people. They were simply to make sure Silke met up safely with her uncle at the Sana airport."

"Stephanie wrote that your ex has vanished?"

"He certainly has. He must've left Hamburg shortly before Silke should've returned from Yemen. I have a feeling he went to his brother in France but I haven't been able to find him."

Anouk studied Irmgard for a moment before saying, "I hope you don't mind my asking this...but why did you marry a Yemenite? I mean...?"

"I understand very well what you mean. I was young and foolish and in love with his exotic good looks and...well...he was a terrific lover. I thought I had found a prince. He was eager to learn European customs. He went to school to learn to speak and read German correctly. I had no idea he would change once we were married."

Anouk's smile was cold, her voice low and intense. "Irmgard, I promise you to do my utmost to get Silke out. That will not only humiliate her husband and his family—there's nothing worse for an Arab man than to have his wife run away—Silke's father will have to return the price he got for Silke. That is, if they can find him."

Chapter 13

Anouk and Karen landed in Sana on a hazy Friday afternoon. Following the stream of disembarking passengers to immigration, they pretended not to know each other. As usual, Anouk wore a light suit and headcloth weighed down by a band of goat hair.

Karen looked quite modest in a knee-length skirt and long-sleeved blouse. She walked ahead of Anouk, her carry-on bag slung over her shoulder, the black cloak over her arm.

The official glanced at her American passport with slightly raised brows. "The purpose of your visit?"

"To visit my fiancé, Ulf Joergensen." She gave him the address.

"What does he do?"

"He's an electrical engineer working for your government."

Stamping her passport, the official warned, "As soon as you leave the airport, you must wear the cloak."

"I certainly will," Karen said, taking her passport and looking him straight in the eyes with a smile, something he wasn't used to from a woman, and which Anouk had told her was a provocation. But she was still in the neutral zone of the airport and knew she could play a little, something she enjoyed doing especially now.

The official didn't return her smile and just waved her on as if she were an annoying insect, his contempt clear.

Anouk, who had observed it all, suppressed a smile and stepped forward, presenting her Ethiopian passport again.

He perused the document. "You were in Yemen not long ago."

"Yes, sir. I teach history and heard that Yemen needs teachers. I will apply for a position at a college here."

After asking her where she would be staying, he stamped her passport and she went to retrieve their luggage.

In the reception lounge Karen and Ulf recognized each other easily. As she made her way towards him, she noticed the hostile looks from men. Now she carefully avoided looking at them, not wanting to push things too far. To her surprise, she made out another European woman sitting on a bench and reading a book, obviously waiting for a plane out judging from the luggage around her feet. She also was uncovered in the neutral zone of the airport.

She shook hands with Ulf who also had a cloak on his arm. "Hello, fiancé. Nice to meet you."

He smiled. "I wish the fiancé part were true. Anouk didn't tell me you were beautiful."

Karen just smiled, concerned about keeping track of Anouk who walked past them with a brief glance.

"I see you came well prepared," she heard Ulf say, pointing to her cloak. He lifted his cloak. "I brought one too, in case you didn't." Then laughed.

"I also have a veil," Karen said, wrapping herself in the cloak.

"No need for European women," Ulf said. "Only the Yemenite women must veil their faces. But that's the only concession made for foreign women. Ready?" He picked up her carry-on bag and led her to his car.

An hour later, they were settled comfortably in Ulf's living room.

"So, what are the plans?" Ulf asked, bringing them drinks.

"First, we have to dismiss your houseboy," said Anouk, accepting a glass.

"I already have and won't take on another till this is over."

"Do the other tenants have servants?"

"I know Manfred downstairs let his go. But the other German and the Dutch might have one. But those boys come from six to eleven and won't come up here."

"We will still have to be very careful. Can your neighbors be trusted?"

"They mind their own business. And Manfred knows all about Silke and has met Irmgard. He would like to help in any way he can. So, this is it then? You plan to take Silke away this time?"

"I'm determined to," Anouk said. "The seaplane is in Asseb on the coast. Irmgard is waiting in Addis." She looked at her watch. "She's staying at my house. We need to call her soon."

Leaning back in his chair and crossing his legs, Ulf asked, "So, what's this brilliant plan you mentioned on the phone?"

"It was Karen's idea," Anouk said and explained the details.

"Very clever," her remarked with a nod to Karen. "As for my

bit—I got the boat, the compass and the flares. And I've arranged a different car for you this time. A tan Land Rover—a fairly common vehicle and color."

They met Manfred after dinner, a stout Bavarian with greying hair and a good sense of humor. He told them how much he missed his wife who had gone back to Germany.

As they went over the plan with him, they reckoned every risk and reassessed every minute detail until there was nothing more to hash out.

"It sounds like a solid plan," said Manfred as he took his leave, "but please be careful. Remember to expect the unexpected at all times. And don't forget I have an extra room you can hide out in when you get back."

Ulf was already gone when they got up in the morning. While having breakfast they studied a map of the country, wanting to be as familiar with the towns and topography as possible. Then they decided to have a look at their neighborhood to give Karen practice wearing her veil and cloak in public.

"Remember to always walk behind me," Anouk reminded her as they were about to leave the apartment.

"Yes, my master," Karen mocked.

"And don't you dare talk!" Anouk laughed, drawing her close and kissing her through the veil.

"Now if you do this to me in the streets..." Karen adjusted her veil.

"We'd be thrown in jail. Even a married couple can't show affection in public. Ready?"

Karen gripped the front of the cloak under her chin from the inside so her hand wouldn't show and nodded. The staircase was empty and they left the building unnoticed.

They spent the day in the medina, the old walled center of the city. Anouk had told Karen that it was one of the largest completely preserved medinas in the Arab world.

At one of the many suqs, Anouk bought a jambiya, a ceremonial dagger, curved and razor sharp, worn by men on their waists. While Anouk bartered, Karen stood aside with her head lowered, wishing she could understand Arabic. Anouk and the merchant were either laughing or yelling. When Anouk raised her hands as if in protest and walked away, the merchant went after her, waving the dagger and talking rapidly. Anouk continued to shake her head. After another outburst of words, money and the dagger exchanged hands, and Anouk and the merchant bowed to each other, smiling.

They walked on, Karen always behind Anouk, taking only quick glances at the charming buildings around her, regretting that she couldn't work with her camera.

It was a warm sunny day, yet her view of the city from behind the veil was dim and hazy. She began to feel encumbered, even encased. The veil also held in the air she exhaled, making her face hot, and after a while, she had the sensation of suffocating. She loosened the veil but it kept stretching over her face; she had also begun to perspire profusely.

They reached the great mosque, famous for its beauty but hidden by straight walls from outsiders. Only the two minarets were partly visible. Anouk could have gone inside, but not Karen. They walked to the main door which was open to have a quick peek into the hall of columns. More busy suqs followed and many smaller mosques, their graceful minarets rising high above the roofs of beautiful tower houses, some built in the Turkish style with several cupolas.

The smell of cooking food drew Anouk to a market stall where she bought four spears of shish-kebab which the cook wrapped in brown paper.

Walking on, Anouk began to eat one and Karen's mouth was watering.

"Sorry," Anouk whispered over her shoulder. "Women can't eat in public. Too bad, because this is delicious."

"Sadist," Karen hissed.

"Now, that's no way to talk to your husband. I'll have to take the stick to you."

"You try that."

"Great Allah," Anouk moaned under her breath. "What have I done to deserve such a wife?"

Walking on, she attacked a second spear, groaning with delight at the tasty meat.

"Don't you dare eat the other two," Karen warned.

As soon as they were back in Ulf's apartment, Karen ripped the veil off her face and took several deep breaths. Then she pulled all her clothes off and attacked Anouk, her eyes spewing blue fire. "You creep!"

Grinning, Anouk caught her arm and drew her close. Laughing, they fell on the couch.

"An Arab wife would never show herself naked to her husband, you know. That's considered very indecent," Anouk reprimanded.

"How do they make love?" Karen asked.

"Dressed." Anouk murmured, kissing her neck.

"You mean...she lifts her gown and he lowers his trousers?"

"Hmmmm...something like that." Anouk's hands had began to travel down her body.

"I need a shower," Karen said. "I perspired like a pig under that cloak."

"Don't tell me I didn't warn you," Anouk said, licking a pink nipple. "And Marib will be worse. You'd better be prepared."

"Anouk...not now..." Karen moaned. "Ulf might come home any time."

Anouk looked at her watch, letting go of her and Karen hurried into the bathroom.

"Better enjoy it," Anouk called after her. "It might be the last shower for a while."

The streets were still silent when Anouk loaded their luggage into the car the next morning, then helped Karen, veiled and cloaked, into the back seat.

"Only men have the privilege of sitting in front," she said.

"What about when women drive?" Karen asked.

"A woman driving? Allah forbid. They'd tear her to pieces."

Once the city was behind them, Karen pushed the veil to the side to make breathing easier and to see better.

They drove through large cultivated plateaus with Anouk relating some history of the country.

"There's no one around," Karen said, looking at a beautiful range of mountains. "Why don't you stop so I can take pictures?"

Anouk drove to the side of the road and they got out. Karen filled her lungs with clean, cool mountain air and shot the scenery. Clouds had accumulated and the first rain drops splashed on the windshield as they drove on. Then the sky opened and the monsoon rain rushed down, making it hard to see and compelling Anouk to grope her way down the mountain.

The rain ceased as they neared the desert. Anouk got out of the car and added mud to the already soiled fenders and license plates to make them illegible, then rinsed her hands with some of the water they had brought.

It became hot so they opened the window. Karen kept fanning her face with a map.

"There's a car coming," Anouk warned, looking at a cloud of dust on the horizon. "You'd better cover yourself."

Karen put the veil over her face and wrapped the cloak around herself, making sure her hands weren't visible.

"It might be a patrol," Anouk said, frowning at the approaching jeep.

"What will they do?" Karen suddenly felt nervous.

"They may check my papers. I'll have to tell them we just got married and that's why I don't have your name on my passport. And with the slowness of bureaucracy I hope it works."

"You sure they won't question me?"

"They'd never talk to the wife of another man. That would be a breach of their moral code. Just keep your head down."

The jeep stopped and two armed Bedouins motioned Anouk to drive to the side of the road. Karen's heart was in her throat and she pressed deeper into the corner of the seat while Anouk talked with the men who briefly looked inside the car, then said something to Anouk and motioned her to drive on.

"Wow," Anouk sighed with relief.

"What did they say?"

"What I thought—who I am, what is my business. I said you were my wife and I was on my way to old Marib for historic research. So we had better go there."

"I'd like that," Karen said, relaxing again. "It might be our only chance because once we have Silke…"

"We're entering the region of Saba now, once a great kingdom ruled by the Queen of Sheba who also ruled in Axum. Old Marib was the capital of Saba and has quite a turbulent history."

"Those were the days," Karen sighed. "Imagine a woman ruling here now!"

They reached the village which was on a hill. Karen looked at its tall, small-windowed buildings, their basements built of stones from ancient monuments with Sabean inscriptions, ornaments and figurative motifs such as ibex heads.

"Unfortunately many of these houses were bombed during the civil war in the sixties," Anouk explained. "And others simply disintegrated through lack of care."

They got out of the car and were greeted by a few children herding goats and yelling, "Baksheesh." Otherwise the streets were deserted. Anouk gave the children a few coins.

The sun was piercing and Karen gasped for breath. They didn't stay long and drove on to the archeological sites along the wadi. Inside the car, Karen ripped the veil from her face. "How can the women bear being covered up in this heat?"

"Careful," Anouk warned. "There's a truck coming."

Sighing, Karen covered her face.

Old and puffing black smoke, the truck was filled with more Bedouins. Anouk lifted her hand in a casual greeting; they waved back and drove past, leaving them coughing and spitting dust.

"These are the remains of Sabean temples," Anouk said a couple of miles later. "You will notice that the Sabean script is very similar to the modern Ethiopian script."

They admired the remarkable buildings, some half-buried in sand; Karen got her camera and took pictures while Anouk stood watch.

"What's this?" Karen asked, looking up five tall pillars and at a sixth which was broken in the middle.

"The local people call it Arsh Bilqis," Anouk explained, "or the Throne of Bilqis. Bilqis is the Yemenite name for the queen of Saba. Of course some archeologists maintain that these pillars belonged to a temple consecrated to the moon god, Almuqah. As always they change the facts when they find evidence that women had once ruled, or that there had been a matriarchy or a goddess, before men usurped the ancient religion and changed female deities into males and threw the world into the chaos it's in."

Karen clicked away. "Yeah, but I understand that more and more digs bring out the truth. Archeology in the coming years will turn history upside down."

"Would you believe that one dig in the Middle East was closed to hide the evidence?"

"I believe it," Karen said, putting her camera away.

The sound of an engine interrupted their contemplation and Karen quickly veiled herself.

Anouk glanced at her watch. "Enough of history. It's time we drove to new Marib and checked into the hotel. But before that I suggest we relieve ourselves behind those stones."

Karen looked at her as if she had lost her wits.

"You'll understand when you see the toilet at the hotel," Anouk said and squatted behind a historic boulder as soon as the truck was out of sight.

Wondering, Karen did likewise.

The innkeeper bowed deeply to Anouk, completely ignoring Karen and said, "You're honoring us again with your visit, sir."

"I need a room for several days," Anouk said, also acting as if Karen were a piece of luggage.

He took a key from a nail in the wall. "You shall have the best. Let me show you upstairs."

"I can find my way," Anouk said. "Just see to it that our luggage is brought up."

He handed her the key. "Of course. It's the second door to your left." He snapped his fingers at a young lad who had appeared.

The minute they were alone in the stifling room, Karen threw off the veil and cloak. "Let's get some fresh air in here," she breathed going to the window and opening the shutters.

Anouk pulled her back. "Don't!" she whispered and quickly closed them after making sure no one had been looking up from the street. "You'll give yourself away. Imagine, a white woman in town. That'd get to Silke's in-laws like wildfire and we'd be watched more than we are already. Besides, women only look through the louvers or they might as well be walking unveiled in the street." She set the louvers so air could come in but no one could see inside. "And we must speak quietly because, being strangers here, there's no telling what ears are listening in."

"I understand," Karen said in a low voice and sank down on the edge of the bed.

Again Anouk pulled her away. "Don't get near that mattress. It's crawling."

Karen shuddered, sat down on a chair and got out of her blouse and stockings. Anouk got the insecticide and sprayed the mattress. The fumes made them cough and Karen went to the window and wiped her sweaty face. "I didn't expect the Ritz. But is there a bathroom where I can wash?"

"Down the hallway. I'll come with you." Anouk wrapped her into a sheet they had brought from Ulf's and pulled a towel and two washcloths from their suitcase. "And not a word. We can't be caught speaking English."

In the bathroom, Karen looked around and swallowed.

"Don't touch anything," Anouk said, handing Karen her robe. "Just watch me. I've got this down to a science." She wetted the washcloth and wiped herself down, then held Karen's sheet so Karen could do the same.

"Where's that toilet?" Karen whispered on their way back to the room.

"You don't want to look at it with a full stomach," Anouk whispered back.

"That bad? Then we should buy some container we can pee in and empty down the tub and the rest we do outside the village."

"Good idea."

Back in their room, Karen made a face at the dead bugs on the floor. Anouk sprayed the mattress one more time, then put sheets and pillows from Ulf on it.

Karen stretched out on the bed naked, relieved to be rid of all her clothes.

"Shameless," Anouk muttered in feigned outrage, getting into a fresh shirt and trousers. "I'm going to the cafe up the street to order our dinner."

"Praised be Allah for your safe return," the owner exclaimed.

"I've returned with my wife and need an evening meal," Anouk said. "Could you prepare it and have it sent to the hotel?"

He bowed. "It will be my honor. For how long are you going to stay this time?"

"That depends on how I get along with my thesis. Maybe a week. I'm also considering moving here. This is a growing area with great possibilities and I want my wife to get familiar with the area and the market."

"We shall be honored to have you as our neighbor."

Anouk bowed slightly. "It will be my joy to live and raise my sons here."

"May Allah grant you many."

"This is delicious." Karen licked her fingers and washed down a mouthful of spicy lamb with beer they had brought from Ulf's supplies.

They sat at the shaky table in their room which they had wiped clean with paper napkins. Warm bread, rice, stew, raisins and figs graced crude clay dishes. When they were finished eating, Karen hid the beer bottles in their luggage; Anouk gathered the dishes and plates and brought them downstairs, asking the owner's boy to return them to the cafe after giving him a few coins.

"Shall I wash your car, sir?" he suggested looking at the Land Rover.

Anouk knew he wanted to earn money, but a clean car was the last thing she needed. "Tell you what—I'll give you two riyals not to wash it."

He looked dumfounded. "Sir?"

Anouk smiled. "You heard right, young man. I'll be driving back and forth to the archeological sites to do research and the car will get dustier and muddier yet."

"I could wash it every day."

"I'll let you wash it at the end of my stay. In the meantime make sure no one touches it."

He pocketed the money. "Yes, sir, thank you, sir."

Karen lay on the bed, glancing at the dirty walls and ceiling which the twilight mercifully blotted out. She closed her eyes and imagined herself on a flower-studded, sweet-smelling meadow, longing for Anouk's touch. A hot breeze came through the shutters carrying an Arab tune. Played on a lute, it came from somewhere nearby, soothing and sensuous and somewhat sad. She could feel her body relax to it. She loved to make love to music that was soft and yielding like her body was now while she waited for Anouk. Surprising how a body could change. During the day it was controlled when she went about her business and at night light and pliable with the antic-ipated joy of making love.

Anouk returned and undressed and Karen held out her arms. Anouk lay in them and pushed a thigh between hers. "You're so ready for me," she whispered. "So beautifully wet." She slipped a hand between Karen's legs to stroke, then enter her.

Karen sighed, matching Anouk's slow rhythm, feeling Anouk wet against her. They caressed and kissed in slow motion, enjoying the tender and seductive play till impatience broke all barriers. Their dallying, their flirting and whispering of loving words, made room for an unrestrained passion which hurled them to their peak.

"You surprise me every time," Karen murmured when she was calm again. "You've made me addicted to you."

"You've done the same to me," Anouk said, as she slowly, tantalizingly, slid down Karen's body and opened her legs to look at her wet sex. Karen felt her body swell in a ripening of new desire that became a throbbing ache. Moaning, Anouk drank the juices, separated folds of skin with her tongue, found the small knob of lust and licked it till Karen quaked and shuddered and was once more engulfed by a wave of exquisite pleasure which catapulted her to another incandescent orgasm.

Spent, they fell asleep in each other's arms.

In the middle of the night, Karen stirred.

"What is it?" Anouk asked drowsily.

Scratching, Karen moaned, "I think I'm being bitten by something."

Anouk went to the light switch by the door.

"Yuk," Karen exclaimed and jumped from the bed, seeing a few bugs scurry into hiding.

"Damn," Anouk muttered. "I guess I didn't get them all." And got the insecticide.

Karen switched off the light and opened the shutters to let more air in. Below, the street was dark and silent. Looking at the star spangled sky, she prayed, "Please, let us get Silke in the morning."

Chapter 14

They woke to the persistent crowing of a rooster.

"I could twist his neck," Karen hissed, scratching welts on her thighs.

Anouk rose and opened the shutters a crack. The street was deserted, the sky turning pink beyond the roofs. After a look at her watch, she said. "Time we got up anyhow."

On their way to the bathroom, Karen whispered, "I have to pee."

Anouk stopped by the toilet. "Go ahead, just hold your breath."

Karen could barely get through the door without recoiling from the stench. Rushing out after relieving herself in a corner, she moaned, barely able to keep her voice down, "I'll never go in there again. We have to buy a container today."

Anouk walked ahead of her into the bathroom and began to wash as best she could.

Back in their room, they dressed in fresh clothes. While Anouk applied soot to her face, Karen poured coffee from a thermos into cups they had borrowed from Ulf and unwrapped biscuits.

Quiet and tense, they had breakfast, listening to the muezzin's song from the mosque as the sun lit up the world. Then Anouk gathered their dirty clothes to take downstairs and have washed and ready for the next day in case they didn't get Silke that morning.

The innkeeper bowed. "May your day be as peaceful as your night was."

"My night was miserable," Anouk retorted. "The mattress is full of lice. My wife is with child and has been bitten and her whining kept me awake most of the night."

He lifted his hand in despair. "Ah, Allah sends us these plagues. But I will get you another mattress."

"Make sure it is a clean one or I will deduct half of what you charge me. I also want you to clean the bathroom and the toilet. By

Allah, they are a disgrace."

A while later they left the hotel, with Karen following Anouk. The Land Rover had not been touched, the license plates were still hard to read. Anouk stowed a bag with Karen's camera, the empty beer cans to dump away from the village and a full water bottle. Then she helped Karen into the back seat.

Anouk drove along several streets while Karen looked at the high walls, then slowed. "This is where Silke lives."

Shocked, Karen gazed at the reed roofs rising from behind the fence. "My God! But why here? Why wasn't she married to someone in Sana...to someone well-off, where at least she might have a bit of art or culture?"

Anouk let out a short laugh. "Art and culture are out for the women even in Sana. And her father wasn't from a family of means if he had to go to Europe for a decent job. He must have family in this region who helped find a husband for Silke."

"So, he may have wanted revenge for Irmgard divorcing him but didn't he care about his daughter? Didn't he realize what it would mean for her to live here after Hamburg?"

"Did my uncle or father care about their daughters? Daughters are to be married off as soon as they're old enough and be off their father's hands. As I told you, the father has the ultimate say over his family. Silke's father had no control of Irmgard, so he made sure he wouldn't lose control of his daughter."

Anouk drove on and parked at the end of the street. They waited and watched as people emerged from different houses, but only four men came out of the gate where Silke lived.

"The father and his sons," Anouk remarked, watching them in her rearview mirror. "One of them is Silke's husband. They all live in the same compound. They must be going to work" She drove on so as not to attract attention. "I guess it won't be today."

"Why don't we check out the market," Karen suggested. "And buy us a pot."

The place was already bustling with people and noisy. They walked from stand to stand, Anouk in the lead. She bought some bread, goat cheese, fruit and an aluminum pot she held up for Karen's silent approval.

"What now?" Karen asked when they were back in the car.

"I don't know," Anouk said, driving along other streets, stopping from time to time as if looking at houses. "We could go look at other historical sites, but first I'd like to talk with a real estate agent about buying property. We need to justify our stay here."

She stopped at a filling station and bought gasoline pumped by a young man from a pipe in the ground. Paying him, she asked for an agent, then drove to a white stone building down the street.

"Isn't this just complicating things?" Karen asked nervously. "Why can't we just go visit the ruins?"

"I could do that without you here. I have to look like I want to settle here and have a reason for you to be along. Just stay in the car. I'll make it quick."

Reassured, Karen nodded. There was no room for argument. She loosened the veil over her face as she watched Anouk disappear. Leaning back, sweat trickled from every pore of her body.

Anouk returned shortly. "The agent is going to show me a number of houses. I told him I wanted you to come along."

They followed the agent's old British Vauxhall which rattled dangerously, belching black smoke, and came to a stop behind it along a nondescript wall of mud bricks.

The agent, an older man with a turban and white beard, showed them into a spacious yard covered with white sand and containing two houses—one of mud bricks and a reed roof, the other of white stones with a roofed terrace and three rooms. The kitchen next to it had mud walls on three sides and a corrugated iron roof. Wooden boxes served as shelves for dishes and pots and pans. Charcoal was used for cooking. In the back yard, out of view and thick with flies, was the primitive bathroom with a shelf and wash basin but no running water. The toilet was an enclosed area covered with sand. As water was scarce and expensive, nothing grew in the courtyard.

Perspiring, Karen followed them around, wishing for the house tour to end so they could drive out of town and she get some relief from being covered. She nudged Anouk from behind.

Anouk glanced at her briefly, but kept talking to the agent for what seemed an age before leading them out of the compound.

"Sorry, Karen," she said, driving after the agent yet again. "I have to look serious and look at one more place. You can stay in the car. I know how hard it must be for you in this heat."

"I will stay in the car." Karen lifted her veil enough to wipe her face. "I wouldn't have anything to say about the house anyway, would I?"

"That would depend on your husband."

Karen adjusted her veil. "I sure do pity the women having to wear this stuff all the time in this climate."

Anouk smiled at her through the rearview mirror. "They only have to wear it in public and they don't go out often."

"I can't imagine being cooped up in those compounds with nothing to do but housework and raising children. Literally the prisoners of their men."

"They don't know anything different." Anouk parked behind the agent again. "I'll make it fast."

True to her word, she returned shortly and drove out of town where Karen could pull off her veil.

"If we don't get Silke tomorrow, I'll look at more houses. You can stay in the hotel," Anouk said.

Karen nodded. "Good. It's too stifling to wait in this car. Where are we going?"

"I thought we could take a look at Sirwah which was the capital of this region before Marib."

They reached the ruins after half an hour. Like Marib, modern day Sirwah was only a shadow of its former self, a small village next to the ruins.

To kill time, they spent the day driving around, stopping in the scant shade of a tamarisk tree to eat their lunch. Before returning to Marib, they relieved themselves behind a broken wall.

When they returned, the innkeeper spoke to Anouk without even a glance at Karen. As if I didn't exist, Karen thought.

The more she lived behind the veil, the more she realized how little women meant in this society. In spite of her mental preparation she began to resent it.

"Your bed has a new mattress," the innkeeper explained to Anouk, showing his gold-capped teeth. "And your clothes are washed. You will find them on the table in your room, sir, as well as your dinner which has been delivered from the cafe."

Anouk thanked him and headed up the stairs with Karen following behind, her head lowered grudgingly.

The room smelled of naphthalene and food. Anouk opened the louvers, then sprayed the mattress to make sure nothing survived before putting Ulf's sheet back on.

They used the bathroom which was in slightly better shape, only the sink having been wiped out. On their way back to their room,

Anouk peeked into the toilet, shaking her head. "Still pretty bad."

"Well, at least they know how to cook," Karen said, enjoying the meal. They shared the last beer which they had kept locked in their suitcase.

After a swig of the warm brew, she sighed, "The first day's behind us. I hope we get Silke tomorrow. I can't wait to get out of here."

"Don't count on anything," Anouk warned.

True enough, the following two days only men and teenage boys appeared from Silke's gate.

"Men going to the market?" Karen asked. "Isn't that below their dignity?"

"No," Anouk replied, driving up and down other streets so not to look as if she had a particular interest in Silke's. "In fact some husbands don't trust their wives with money at all and do all the shopping, maintaining that they get better prices."

Once again they ended up in the market where Anouk bought a picnic—fruit, bottled water, olives, green peppers, bread and cheese.

"What's on the tour agenda today?" Karen asked gamely as they headed out of town.

"I thought a picnic at the Temple of Refuge would be nice. The temple was built around 400 BC as a safe haven for the persecuted. Even the worst criminals could obtain temporary shelter. It was partly excavated in the early fifties."

"It wouldn't do us much good today if they found out we abducted Silke, would it?"

Anouk laughed. "I'm afraid not."

The old ruin provided some shade and they sat on the stones to eat. They were alone and it was eerily silent. Karen took off her cloak, bent forward and poured some of the water they had bought over her head.

"Oooh..." she sighed, "does that feel good."

Anouk also rinsed her head and face, smoothed back her hair, and spread the food on a flat stone. They ate in companionable silence, then Anouk stretched out on another flat stone and drifted into a light sleep.

Karen sat on a stone further away and leaned back against a column. Gazing at the temple ruins around her, she wished the stones could talk about the people who had lived here two thousand years ago. Slowly her thoughts became jumbled and she, too, nodded off.

She didn't know how long she had been dozing or what had alerted her. Anouk lay with her mouth slightly open, breathing evenly.

She looked around for prying eyes and froze. A snake was moving between stones not far from her feet. Tongue flicking, it came closer. Karen shrank against the column, eyes wide, lips suddenly dry.

"Anouk," she whispered. "Anouk."

But Anouk didn't hear. The snake stopped moving and looked at her from eyes embedded in dark green scales, its head slightly raised and swaying back and forth, its forked tongue smelling her.

"Anouk," she called louder, more urgently. "Anouk. Wake up!"

Her plea slowly penetrated Anouk's sleep; she came to and blinked. Seeing the snake, she grabbed her headcloth and threw it over the snake's head.

Karen shrieked and jumped away.

The snake rose higher, blindly stabbing the air under the cloth. Anouk found a sizeable stone and threw it on top of the snake.

Holding Karen, she asked, "You all right?"

"No," Karen said, trembling.

"Sorry. I should've known better. This is a haven for snakes and scorpions. We'd better get out of here."

"I could use a stiff drink," Karen breathed.

"All I can offer you is water." Anouk put the cloak around her. "Let's drive on."

"Let me pee first." Karen found a flat depression, gathered her skirt and cloak and squatted. "I stink," she said in disgust, rising and adjusting her clothes.

"You're not the only one," Anouk retorted.

In the morning, they saw the old woman and a boy going to the market.

"Grandma and her grandson," Karen remarked dryly.

Anouk chewed her lower lip and muttered, "Why isn't Silke appearing? Hope she isn't sick."

She drove to the market where she had become a familiar face. The merchants smiled and chatted with her. One asked if she had found a house yet.

"The news is out," Anouk said, driving back to the hotel.

"I notice the men getting increasingly friendlier with you. What would you do if they invited you to their homes?"

"Make up an excuse."

"Why?"

"I don't want to get too chummy with them. Imagine someone involving me in a conversation just when you and Silke are leaving the market. Besides, they'd extend the invitation to you and you'd have to visit with their women, in a separate part of their homes."

"Do women visit each other?"

"Of course they do. And they love to gossip."

"Spare me!"

Anouk laughed, but her mirth didn't last long. "Frankly, Karen, I'm getting a little worried," she said. "I can't understand why Silke hasn't appeared yet."

"But neither have the other young women. All we've seen so far is the mother-in-law, and the men and boys. I wouldn't worry yet."

"Still...what if something is wrong?"

Karen shrugged. "We have no choice but to wait. What else can we do?"

"Maybe we should drive back to Sana for a few days to clean up and rest..."

"No," Karen interrupted. "We're so close...and chances are that she might go to the market just when we're gone. Let's be patient and take it a day at a time."

"I was also thinking of you in all these heavy clothes. It isn't fair of me to subject you to so much misery."

"Darling, I volunteered, didn't I? And you warned me. So, please, don't worry now. I can take it."

"I love you," Anouk said, looking at her through the rearview mirror.

They had a quick lunch in their room, then Anouk left to meet with the real estate agent. "I'll be back in an hour or so," she promised.

Karen lay down on the bed and tried to read. But the heat made her drowsy and she fell asleep. She woke to knocking on the door, and, at the last, minute stopped herself from crying out, "Yes?"

She looked at her watch. Six o'clock. Where was Anouk?

There was more knocking and the innkeeper's boy saying something. Karen didn't know what to do and wrapped herself in the cloak, then looked for her black socks to cover her white feet. The boy knocked again and kept saying something, his voice louder, more persistent.

The food from the cafe! It suddenly occurred to her. She had learned a few words in Arabic from Anouk including the word 'yes' and hoping it was the right answer, said huskily, "Aiwoa."

The boy said something else, then she heard him walk away. Karen waited a while before carefully opening the door a crack.

The tray with the food was on the floor. After looking left and right, she quickly pulled it into the room and put it on the table.

Where was Anouk? she asked herself again. She said she'd be back at four. Damn it, Anouk. Don't leave me alone here. What if the innkeeper comes to the door to ask something? She paced the room and peeked through the louvers. There was no car in sight and it was rapidly getting dark. Nervous, she had a sip of water and sat on the bed, waiting.

An hour later her anger changed to concern and she began to walk back and forth like a caged animal, wondering if Anouk had been in an accident. Or was stranded because of car trouble.

Still an hour later she was crying, imagining Anouk attacked and robbed. Or in jail because her gender had been discovered.

She dressed and sat on the bed again. Hearing a car, she jumped up and looked through the louvers at a truck driving past. Unable to sit still, she continued to pace, pondering what to do and how to find Anouk if she were in trouble. What if it was something harmless holding up Anouk?

She doubted Anouk would leave her waiting without letting her know, and clenched her hands in a fit of despair.

This was something they hadn't foreseen and planned for—just as Manfred had warned.

"Anouk! Don't do this to me!" she groaned.

She heard a dog bark and raced back to the window. Another car drove up and stopped at the curb to let two men out.

They were discussing something with the driver and suddenly one motioned to her window and they all looked up.

She drew back, horrified, sure that something must have happened to Anouk. Or had the villagers deduced that she was up to something and had her arrested? She grabbed her cloak and sat trembling on the bed, expecting someone to burst through her door at any moment.

When nothing happened, she looked through the louvers again. The car was gone and the two men were walking up the street. She glanced at her watch. Ten past ten! She threw the cloak from her and sat on the chair, debating what to do.

Any move on her side would end this mission. But it would be the same if something had happened to Anouk. And if Anouk was hurt, she wanted to be with her. Yet what if she was wrong and Anouk was only visiting with some men?

"If you are, Anouk," she muttered through clenched teeth, "I swear I'll kill you."

It was close to eleven when she heard a car drive up and ran to the window. Anouk parked the Land Rover against the curb and got out.

Moments later her footsteps resounded on the stone stairs and along the hall in that solid quick rhythm characteristic of her.

"Forgive me, Karen." Anouk entered the room, slightly out of breath. Karen stood next to the bed and glared at her. Anouk walked to Karen to embrace her. Karen stepped back.

"Let me explain," Anouk said.

"It better be good," Karen said in a low voice.

Anouk took off her headcloth. "We had car trouble…"

Karen's eyes widened in alarm. "The Land Rover?"

"No, the agent's Vauxhall. He offered to drive us in his car. He's running out of places to show me and is determined to make a sale and drove to some property behind the fields toward the hills. Then he asked if I minded if he delivered some papers to a relative and I couldn't say no. But it was farther away than I anticipated. Suddenly his engine quit in the middle of nowhere and we had to walk several miles to his relative who was eating his dinner and invited us to join him. So we ate. He finally took us back to Marib on his donkey cart which took an eternity. I know how worried you—"

"You had…dinner?" Karen interrupted.

"Karen, how could I refuse? The man was at table…"

"You had dinner while I sat here and…and…" Karen gasped for breath.

"I couldn't very well ask him to interrupt his dinner and drive me back to Marib, because my wife was waiting. No Arab man would ever worry if his wife was waiting. Wives are supposed to wait and never question their husbands. It's the custom. Besides it would've been an affront to reject his hospitality…don't you understand?"

"No…" Karen hissed, grabbed Anouk by her shirt and shaking her, cried, "You…had dinner…while I went insane…worrying."

"Karen." Anouk tried.

"…about you…" Karen sputtered with fury, pulling harder and

133

harder at Anouk's shirt until the buttons flew off.

Anouk tried to catch her hands, but Karen got hold of Anouk's collar and sleeve and continued shaking her as if possessed.

"Karen! I couldn't help it—"

But Karen wasn't listening and kept attacking her, venting her anxiety of the past hours.

"Stop it! At once!" Anouk ordered, at the limit of her patience, afraid someone might overhear them. Karen kept ripping Anouk's shirt. Anouk caught her wrists and flung her on the bed, lifting a hand to strike her. "I'm warning you, Karen. Stop this."

Eyes glinting, Karen rose to attack her again. Anouk slapped her.

Holding her burning cheek, Karen stared at Anouk in disbelief.

"Sorry," Anouk said coldly. "But you snapped. I should've known this would happen…that you can't handle it." And took off her torn shirt.

"Damn you," Karen said under her breath and propped herself up.

"Watch it!" Anouk warned and continued to undress.

"Nobody has ever slapped me," Karen said. "Nobody."

"Nobody has ever attacked me like you just did! So be quiet, all right? Because if you aren't…" she made an unmistakable gesture with her hand.

Karen shook her head, hissing, "This is incredible…"

She shrank back when Anouk came to the bed and towered over her, her hand twitching, her voice dangerously low. "I mean it, Karen. One more word out of you…"

"All right, all right," Karen said in an appeasing tone and quietly undressed, then lay down on her side of the bed, hurt and glowing with indignation.

Anouk switched off the light and lay down with her back to Karen.

In the morning they went through their routine silently and without looking at each other. Anouk gathered their clothes to be washed and the tray with the uneaten food and went downstairs.

"My wife was sick last night and couldn't eat," she explained.

Nothing in the innkeeper's face betrayed that he had heard anything the previous night. "There's a hospital in Al-Hazm, a mere hour's drive," he said.

Anouk thanked him and returned to their room.

"Karen, we can leave for Sana right now if you're at all unsure of me or what we're doing."

"You had no right to hit me," Karen hissed in a low voice.

"Karen, you got physical first. I apologized when I came in the room but you didn't give me half a chance. I had to calm you down somehow. If we slip emotionally we jeopardize everything—our very lives—"

"You should talk! Going off to who knows where, endangering both of us, getting too familiar with the agent. Enough of this house buying." Karen stared at her hands in her lap. "Anouk, I was scared. I've never been so scared in my life."

"You're right. I did go too far. I was scared, too." Anouk reached for Karen's hand and kissed it gently. "Let's call it quits and get back to our job, hm?"

Blinking back tears, Karen smiled at Anouk, "I'm sorry."

"I am too. I meant it when I said I'd do anything for you, but I'm putting you at too much risk. Look, if we see no action today, I'll tell the agent I'm going to talk my finances over with the bank in Sana. I've already told the innkeeper you're sick. We'll retreat awhile. Come back and try again. As it is Ulf must confirm or delay your flight soon. If you don't want to come back with me then, I'll understand. I'll figure out something."

"You mean *our* flight…he must delay *our* flight."

"Y…yes…yes of course."

Karen shook her head. "I'd go mad waiting at Ulf's—last night would be nothing compared to waiting in Sana. I need to be with you so I know what's going on. We go down, we go down together, not you out on some donkey cart and me here."

"That's fair enough." Anouk nodded. "Now, can we handle it today if we see the women come out to the market?"

"Yes."

"Ready?"

"Ready."

"Make it look like you're feeling ill as we leave. Stumble a bit and I'll help you."

Karen put on her veil and cloak and followed Anouk, stumbling in the lobby so that Anouk had to help her from there to the car.

Anouk turned into Silke's street. As they drove slowly past the gate, two women emerged. Finally!

Watching the women, Anouk said, "The mother-in-law is the short, stocky one. Watch the other one as I drive by. If she looks at us, it's Silke."

Karen's heart beat faster as they passed them. "She didn't," she said, disappointed. "They both looked away. Let's follow them around the market anyway, just for practice."

Anouk found a place to park, walked to a stand with baskets, and averted her face so the women wouldn't recognize her. Karen remained behind her and watched them approach.

Walking after them, Anouk listened to the familiar voice of the old woman as she bargained with a vendor and noticed that the other woman's hand was dark.

More women gathered around the vegetable stand where there was light pushing and shoving. Karen remained close to Silke's in-laws and was often hidden from Anouk who had to remain at a discreet distance. Anouk had trouble keeping track of Karen in the crowd of black cloaks. Karen was definitely doing a good job of blending in.

Boys chasing each other almost bumped into her and she quickly stepped aside, grumbling a curse. When she looked up again, the women had shifted and she didn't know where Karen was anymore.

Damn, she thought, we should've agreed upon some sign. For a moment she followed a few of the taller women, hoping Karen was one of them and would give her a sign or come to her. But the women separated and moved off in different directions. Worried, Anouk followed one group, then another and finally gave up.

Karen, where are you? Give me a sign, she thought, gnashing her teeth. Why are you doing this? Leaving me standing here like an idiot?

Anouk wandered around to be visible to Karen, hoping nothing had happened. She wouldn't know how to recognize Karen and help her. Had someone guessed what they were up to and taken Karen away?

She looked at her watch. Half an hour had passed. I mustn't lose control, she commanded herself.

Many of the women were leaving the market with their baskets full. Anouk made another round, then decided to wait in the car.

As she came up to the Land Rover, she noticed a cloaked figure in the back seat. Getting inside, Karen chuckled. "How was that little stunt, huh?"

Something inside Anouk snapped. "Do you think that was funny?" she said sharply.

She started the car, jammed it into gear and roared away. Boys, dogs, donkeys, goats rushed out of her way. Accelerating, Anouk drove for several miles in her anger into the desert.

"Anouk, can't you take a little joke?" Karen cried, pulling off her veil.

Anouk slammed on the brakes and faced her through a thick cloud of dust. "No, not this kind of joke," she said icily. "Not at a time like this."

Karen shrank back from the fury in those eyes of black stone. "My God, all I did was…"

"…have a good laugh at my expense while I was worried sick over you."

"Well, now you know how I felt last night. And I didn't want to make fun of you. I only wanted to…"

Anouk interrupted her, voice and face quivering with rage. "This has nothing to do with last night. We called it quits on that, remember? I couldn't help what happened but this you did on purpose. You know too little and act like you know too much. You're dangerous."

"Shit! Anouk, who's losing it this time? I only wanted to show you…"

Anouk cut her short, "Don't ever do such a thing again. Don't you dare." And after a deep breath. "I should take you back to Sana."

Stunned, Karen said nothing. She had only wanted to prove how good her camouflage was and how easy it would be to get Silke away without anyone knowing what was going on. And yes, she did want to have a little fun. Hell, there hadn't been much of that for days. Why did Anouk have to take it so badly?

Anouk was about to start the car when she noticed a jeep speeding towards them. "Damn! This might be a patrol!" Quickly she pulled out a map from the door pocket and bowed her head over it.

Frightened, Karen covered her face and pulled the cloak tightly around herself.

The jeep came to a crunching halt beside them.

"Lie down. Act like you're sick," Anouk hissed as four soldiers jumped from the jeep with machine guns drawn.

"What are you doing here?" The soldier in command yelled. "You, get out!"

Anouk took a deep breath and got out of the car, holding up the map. "I took the wrong road out of town to find a doctor…my wife is sick…"

The soldier glanced into the rear seat where Karen moaned, shaking with fear.

He walked around the Land Rover, then stood at the back. "Open it!"

Anouk did. He went through their bag and Anouk sighed with relief that they had disposed of their empty beer bottles.

"What are you doing with these cameras?"

"I'm a history teacher and researching the ruins around here for a book I'm writing. I need to take pictures for that purpose, sir." Anouk's voice was colored with a calm she didn't feel.

His tone became a trifle friendlier. "You are from Egypt?"

"Yes, sir,"

"Let me see your passport."

Her mind racing, Anouk got the Egyptian passport from the glove compartment. She thanked heaven that she had left the Ethiopian one locked in the suitcase at the hotel.

She watched him leaf through it, thinking, If he asks me for my driver's license, it's over. But, after what seemed an eternity, he handed back the passport, saying, "There's a hospital in Al-Hazm with an Egyptian doctor." And showed her the road to take on the map. Anouk almost crumbled with relief and bowed slightly. "Thank you, sir."

He snapped an order to his men and they marched back to the jeep and drove off.

Anouk sank into the back seat next to Karen.

Karen clung to Anouk, her voice tight. "What did they want?"

Anouk held her. "Calm down. It's over." She caressed Karen's head with a trembling hand. "I'll take you back to the hotel."

They drove back in silence. The innkeeper's smile froze and he shrank back, seeing Anouk's grim face as they went upstairs.

In their room, Karen dropped her cloak and veil. Anouk had a sip of mineral water, and before Karen was able to say anything, she left with a curt, "I'll be back."

Outraged, Karen stared at the closed door. She's behaving just like an Arab husband. How dare she?

Arms crossed over her chest, she walked back and forth like a caged tigress. And caged she was. Unlike Anouk, she couldn't just leave the hotel, or drive, or walk around. Or have coffee at the cafe. Hell, she couldn't even look out the fucking window. Tears of rage spilling, she thought grimly, just come back, Anouk, just come back.

The room was stifling and she ripped off the rest of her clothes, flinging them against the wall, then lay down on the bed. Inhaling the mixture of naphthalene and insecticide, she drifted into a fitful sleep.

She woke when Anouk entered the dim hot room and watched her taking dishes from a bag through half-closed eyes. Anouk put them on the table, then took off her headcloth and sat on the edge of the bed.

"I know you're not sleeping," she said in a soft voice.

Eyes flashing, hands clenched, Karen lashed out, "You shithead, how dare you dump me in this room and leave without explanation."

Anouk caught her hands. "Stop it, will you?"

"If you think you can treat me like an Arab wife, I have news for you," Karen spat, trying to break free.

Anouk held her down. "Don't even start. I'm sorry I blew up at you, I really am. I needed to calm down and think without us fighting."

"Right, and you can just walk the streets while I—"

"It's the only choice I had."

At Anouk's tender look, Karen's anger dissolved like snow in the sun, her hands relaxing. "You sure do have a temper."

"Look who's talking."

Karen smiled contritely. "This morning I wanted to show you how well I could whisk Silke away. I didn't mean it as a joke…well, maybe a little. It was uncalled for."

"Yes, I'm in no mood for jokes with things going as they are. I'm too worried about Silke. I'm wondering if she's sick and hospitalized in Al-Hazm again. Or if she gave herself away somehow after my last visit…or that the other women realized I said something in German and she is not allowed to leave the house. I've got to get her out, Karen."

"I know," Karen sighed at a loss for words. After a moment of silence, she asked, "Where did you go?"

"To see the real estate agent. I told him I'd go to Al-Hazm to look around before I make a decision. Then I had coffee at the cafe while the food was being prepared. I paid our bill for this room, by the way, and told the innkeeper what I told the agent." Anouk sighed. "I don't know what to do any longer. We can leave for Al-Hazm after we eat."

"No, let's give it one more shot in the morning before we leave."

Chapter 15

In the morning they left their room willingly. The innkeeper had sent the boy to help Anouk carry their luggage to the car.

"Your car, sir," he reminded her. "I could wash it very fast."

Anouk tipped him more than was customary. "It's all right. I'll still be driving around a lot and the mud and dust protects the paint from the sun."

When she and Karen left, the innkeeper bowed. "If it's Allah's wish, we shall see you again in good health."

"May Allah also be with you and your family," Anouk answered. "And I will be back if I don't find a house in Al-Hazm."

In the Land Rover, Anouk headed once again for Silke's street, drove to the end of it, made a U-turn and stopped.

"There!" Karen whispered minutes later as four women emerged from the gate.

"One of them is Silke, one of the two taller ones. Keep an eye on them." Anouk's voice was colored with excitement. "We've got her," she added matter-of-factly.

They drove slowly after the women. Nobody took notice when they parked near the market as they had for ten days. Anouk pretended to be busy with something inside the car while Karen kept the women in view. For a brief moment she thought one of them glanced at the Land Rover, then they walked past with their heads lowered.

Karen was soon tailing them, staying as close as possible. They mixed with the crowd, Anouk keeping her distance.

Pretending to look at vegetables, Karen observed their hands. One woman carrying baskets had dark hands and kept close to the short, heavy-set woman who carried the purse and bargained with the vendors.

Karen moved closer to the two women whose hands she hadn't seen, then turned to Anouk who nodded slightly.

The women walked to the next stand where a vendor cried out something which drew the buyers around him. Karen was careful to stick to the two taller women whose hands she hadn't seen, wishing they would show their hands so she could be sure. The woman with the old voice talked to the merchant; the one with the basket picked up the goods, saying something to the other two. One replied in a low voice; the other remained quiet.

Is the quiet one Silke? Karen wondered, following them to the next stall. How could she be sure? Maybe it was Silke who had replied. What if none of them was Silke? What if one was a neighbor or a relative?

Don't let your imagination run wild, she scolded herself. Silke must be one of the two taller women, but which one? She threw another brief glance at Anouk and continued to follow the women.

Again it was the older woman bartering, and the other woman putting goods in her basket. Soon they'd be done shopping and leave the market. She had to hurry or it would be too late. Desperate, Karen looked at Anouk who was nearby, but out of the women's sight. To Anouk's inquisitive look Karen shook her head to let her know that she still didn't know which was Silke. She couldn't risk addressing the wrong woman.

Mouth dry with nervous tension, she followed them to a merchant loudly hawking his wares. A whole crowd of women gathered round, and Karen stepped closer so as not to lose Silke. Suddenly there was loud bleating and the bodies parted to let a billy goat run past chased by a boy with a stick. Karen tried to get out of the goat's way but it bumped its head hard into her hip before vanishing in the crowd. "Ouch!" she cried, stumbling and catching herself from falling. Then she froze realizing what she had done. But no one seemed to have noticed her un-Arabic expression of pain in the general tumult.

Karen gave Anouk, who looked concerned, a nod to assure her that she was all right and concentrated on following the women. But the incident had caused a shift in the crowd and she realized to her terror that she wasn't sure any longer if she was following the right women. Then she recognized the voice of the older woman as she talked with a merchant. Moving closer, she noticed one of the women looking at her. Her heart stopped, had her "ouch" been noticed after all? Surely only Silke would recognize it. She decided to take the risk. Bending towards the woman, she nudged her, whispering, "Silke?"

The woman inhaled sharply and Karen whispered,"Come with me," in German and slowly walked away.

To her great relief and joy, the woman followed, brushing against her. "Mama?"

"Irmgard sent me," Karen said in a low voice, not breaking her stride. She threw a quick glance at Anouk who had walked into their line of vision.

"That man…" Silke said.

"Yes, sh…he's with us."

Swiftly, Anouk left the market. Silke walked faster as if to catch up with her.

"Slow down," Karen warned, although she felt like running herself, expecting someone behind them to yell at any moment.

Anouk had the Land Rover idling by the time they reached it. They climbed in the back breathlessly, sitting close, Silke reaching for Karen with a shaking hand. Karen clasped it, her hand shaking just as much.

With an eye in the rearview mirror, Anouk drove away at a normal speed. As soon as she was out of town, she accelerated and tore off as if a thousand devils were after them.

Karen lifted her veil. "Let me see you, Silke."

Silke exposed her face which was pale and thin with big circles under her eyes. Her hair was long and wispy and in need of a shampoo. "Who are you?"

Karen smiled. "Karen Jensen."

"You're American, aren't you? And who's he?"

"He's a woman. Her name's Anouk Turabi. We'll tell you everything later."

Eyes on the road and the rearview mirror, Anouk drove at a high speed, reaching the road to Sana in a long twenty minutes.

Karen and Silke kept looking out the rear window. "There's a car coming from Marib," Karen said.

"I see it," Anouk said, her foot heavy on the gas pedal. She knew Silke would have been missed by now, and that the women would have notified their men who in turn would be turning the market upside down. While the search was on in town, she prayed that Silke's disappearance would not be linked to her and Karen right away.

Silke sat huddled against Karen watching through the back window, rigid with fear. No one talked and the tension in the car was thick.

The car which turned out to be a truck, approached the intersection where they had just turned left, but passed on through, heading north.

They dared to breathe again.

The desert disappeared behind them as the road curved up the mountain. A few trucks coming from Sana passed them, and Anouk hoped they wouldn't remember a dirty Land Rover.

Clouds hung low, and half way to Sana rain hit them in torrents, slowing them down, but washing the car.

"Damn," Anouk uttered shortly before reaching the outskirts of Sana. "I think this is a patrol. Are you covered?"

Karen and Silke pulled their veils over their faces and sat close, holding hands and trembling

"It is a patrol," Anouk said, seeing two soldiers next to a jeep signalling her.

"Do you think they've already been alerted?" Karen asked.

"Impossible. But I'm glad the rain washed the car." Anouk drove to the side of the road, speaking over her shoulder, "Quick, Karen, act as if you're in labor. Silke you're her sister helping her."

She came to a stop next to the jeep and began to talk fast and excitedly. "In the name of Allah, let me drive on. My wife is about to lose my son. I have to rush her to the hospital."

The soldiers threw a brief glance into the back where Karen lay moaning and squirming and Silke sat bent over her and motioned for Anouk to drive on, wishing her "Salamat"—good luck. Anouk thanked them and gunned the engine.

A block away from Ulf's building, Anouk stopped at the curb. "Here's the key to Ulf's apartment. I'll park the car in a side street and will be with you shortly."

Karen and Silke were hugging and crying with relief when Anouk joined them. Ulf wasn't home so Anouk telephoned him at his office.

"We're all back," she said in case an operator was listening.

"All right," Ulf answered and hung up.

Anouk knew that he would pick up the Land Rover and drive it to a friend's garage. She took a deep breath and finally looked at Silke. How pale and thin she was, yet there was joy sparkling through her tears.

Smiling, Silke asked in Arabic, "Are you really a woman?"

Anouk smiled back, pulled off her headcloth, opened her shirt and took off the bandage binding her breasts. "Satisfied?"

Silke gasped, then hugged her. "Thank you, thank you so much for getting me out of there." And broke into more tears.

Anouk held her until the crying was spent.

"I told her Irmgard was in Ethiopia and about our escape plan," said Karen, arm around Anouk.

"Are you familiar with small motorboats at all?" Anouk asked Silke in English for Karen's benefit.

"Yes, I drove motorboats when I went water-skiing with friends in Hamburg," Silke said in halting English and at the memory of it burst into tears again. "I can't believe it...I hope I'm not dreaming..."

Murmuring soothing words, Karen held her as Anouk walked to the window and waited for her to calm down. One big part was accomplished. But the next part would be as tough. She knew it had never occurred to Karen to wonder what would happen once they had Silke and she hadn't divulged anything. She gazed at Karen holding Silke, knowing it would be hard to make Karen accept the next step of this undertaking.

Bathed and in fresh clothes they sat in Ulf's living room that evening. Silke wearing a new blouse and slacks her mother had sent along for her, also looked scrubbed; her hair, cut short by Karen, fell in soft, shiny waves around her face. Her blue eyes were sparkling with joy.

"I haven't felt this clean in two years," she sighed. "I was only allowed a little water to wash with."

Ulf and Manfred listened in awe as she told them briefly about her in-laws and her life with them.

"They hated me," she said, speaking half German, half broken English, "especially the women because I was educated and could read and write. I had brought a book with me from Germany, Thomas Mann's *Die Buddenbrooks*, a family saga and kept reading and rereading it until I knew it by heart. And one day it was gone. All hell broke loose when I wanted to study Arabic. It would've given me something to do, stimulated my mind. With nothing to read or do except household tasks, constantly confined to the compound, I thought I'd go crazy. But even the men can't read and they don't believe in educating women. They made my life miserable whenever they could. And the whole family was after me all the time because I didn't get pregnant.

"The only time I was allowed to leave the house was to go to the market. But they wouldn't let me go every time. So I pretended to hate going so they'd make me." She turned to Anouk. "When you stumbled into us that day and said something German, I thought I hadn't heard right at first."

"Did the women ever comment about the incident?" Anouk asked.

"They called you a clumsy foreigner and said that they couldn't understand half of what you'd said. How did you recognize me?"

Anouk smiled. "Your hands."

Silke laughed. "I was very happy that day because I had begun to lose hope when nothing happened after my mother's visit. You have no idea how I clung to it. I kept looking for you whenever I was allowed to go to the market which was about once every two weeks. But I knew I had to be patient."

"Don't we know it." Karen rolled her eyes. "We were watching for you for ten days."

"Well, don't lose that patience yet, Silke. You will still need it," Anouk advised. "So will we all."

"How are you going to get me to the coast?"

"In the trunk of my company car," Ulf explained. "I already have the boat in safe storage in Al-Hudayda. Nothing fancy but with a good outboard motor. I've tried it out once in the harbor. As soon as Anouk's back in Ethiopia and ready to take off with the seaplane, Manfred will tow the boat to the beach as if he were going on a fishing trip. We'll join him on the beach and put you into the boat. Are you up to it to motor out a mile or so before sunrise?"

"I'd do anything to get out of here," Silke exclaimed, turning to Anouk. "How far is Ethiopia from Yemen?"

"Asseb, from where I'll take off is about a hundred and seventy miles from Al-Hudayda, or an hour by plane."

"What if the weather turns bad?" asked Manfred.

"August is usually dead calm," said Anouk.

"Why August?" Karen asked, puzzled. "It's the nineteenth of July. If we fly out the day after tomorrow…"

"Only you are leaving Yemen in two days," Anouk interrupted.

Karen's eyes widened. "Why?"

"Karen, in Marib they must've figured out by now that this strange teacher and his wife who kept cruising around town in his dirty car and who disappeared the very day Silke did might have had

145

something to do with her escape. Remember, your face isn't known to them, mine is. You can return to the airport as Ulf's departing fiancée, but, like Silke, I can't show my face at the airport."

"Then how are you going to get out?"

"I'm afraid I'll have to trek to the coast and find a dhow across the Red Sea."

Karen cried, "You never—"

"I know, Karen. But what was the point? We needed to concentrate on Silke…"

"I'm not going to leave without you."

"Karen, please…"

"I'm coming along. Remember we agreed we'd go through this together?"

"Karen, they'll be looking for a husband and wife. Besides, the way I'll be traveling I couldn't possibly take you along." Karen tried another protest, but Anouk's eyes turned hard, her voice low, resolute. "You will leave the day after tomorrow."

Karen burst into tears and left the room.

The others sat in embarrassed silence.

Ulf coughed. "Oh, this is very serious then."

"Please excuse me. We're all tired and need a rest," Anouk apologized and followed Karen.

Finding her on the bed with her face buried in the pillow, Anouk lay down next to her.

"You should've told me." Karen's words were muffled.

"What good would it have done?"

"At least I would have been used to the idea."

"Oh, Karen," Anouk groaned.

"I don't know what I'd do if something happened to you."

Anouk took her into her arms. "I promise I'll be careful. Alone I can make it. And I'll feel better knowing you're out of the country and safe."

"What about me? How do you think I'll feel knowing you're in danger?" Crying, Karen buried her face against Anouk's shoulder.

"I'll be all right, Karen. You have to trust me. Please. I'm going to need your trust." Anouk cupped Karen's face, kissed the tears from her face, then her mouth. Desperate, Karen kissed her back.

Slowly they took off their clothes and made love as if it were the last time. Clinging to Anouk, Karen fell asleep exhausted. Anouk lay awake for a long time before she, too, found some peace.

146

Chapter 16

In the morning Ulf went to work as usual and the women recuperated, Silke eagerly looking through magazines Ulf had lying about while Anouk tuned into the radio news broadcasts. Nothing was mentioned in the morning news, but at noon Silke's escape was announced in great detail:

"A young wife has disappeared from the Marib market while shopping with her mother- and sisters-in-law yesterday. So far the family have no clue to the woman's whereabouts, but it is assumed she is in Sana. The abducted woman is originally from Europe and could be trying to leave the country. Patrols have been set up at Sana airport.

"The police are looking for an Egyptian and his wife in a mud-covered, tan Land Rover for questioning. It is believed that the alleged wife might be a man.

"According to witnesses, the Egyptian, claiming to be a teacher, has been in Marib twice before, and the abducted woman's mother-in-law remembers an incident at the market some time ago when he accidentally collided with the women.

"The man in question is tall, brown-skinned and good looking and was last seen wearing a red and white headcloth and a white shirt over khaki pants. He is well-mannered, seems to be wealthy and speaks with a distinct Egyptian accent.

"The police are confident that both suspects and the abducted woman are still in Yemen, and any information leading to their arrest will be well rewarded by the woman's family."

The broadcast finished with the stern comment: "Yemenite law punishes abduction with death by decapitation."

Anouk and Silke exchanged long looks.

"Would somebody mind translating!" Karen said impatiently.

"You translate," Anouk said to Silke in a low voice.

While Silke repeated the news in English spiked with German, Anouk paced the room, then stood by the window, hands in her pockets, brows furrowed.

"Oh God!" Karen exclaimed, covering her face with her hands.

Anouk walked to her and held her by the shoulders. "So? It's only news. We knew this would happen, didn't we?"

"It didn't seem real then. And I didn't know you'd stay behind."

"Well, now you know why I have to. Come on, Karen, we've gotten this far and we will manage the rest."

The following morning they rose before dawn, showered, and went downstairs to Manfred's apartment where Silke was staying. She was up and preparing breakfast for everyone, enjoying the clean and relatively modern kitchen. Manfred appeared, dressed for work. Anouk and Karen were tense and silent and, unable to eat, only drank coffee, while the others ate the eggs, bacon and toast. Manfred bid Karen farewell and left for work.

Ulf looked at his watch, then at Karen apologetically. "It's time we left for the airport."

Silke embraced her. "Thank you so much for what you've done for me. See you soon. Give my love to my mother."

Pale and fighting tears, Karen clung to Anouk, murmuring, "Please be careful."

Anouk nodded, saying softly, "I love you." She kissed her on the forehead. "As soon as you land in Addis, go see Sergio, then call so I know you've arrived safely."

They kissed one last time, ignoring Ulf and Silke, then Karen put on her cloak and followed Ulf who carried her suitcase.

Anouk closed the door and leaned against it, taking a few deep breaths.

Silke studied her. "You're lovers, aren't you?"

Anouk nodded.

"How wonderful," Silke said wistfully.

"You will find love, Silke. With a decent chap in Hamburg. You wait and see." Anouk walked to the living room windows. She could see Karen getting into Ulf's car.

Silke stood next to her. "I don't think I ever want to be with a man again," she said with a light shudder. "My husband raped me every night. He was frantic because he couldn't get me pregnant when his sisters-in-law had a kid every year and his mother had nine. He felt his manhood was at stake because after two years I hadn't borne him a son."

"His manhood," Anouk scoffed, walking away from the window. "Miserable coward. But remember, Silke, the fact that you got away is the greatest humiliation he can suffer. After the dust of your disappearance has settled, he and his family will be the laughingstock of Marib and no father will give him his daughter, or only for an outrageous price. All he and his family can do is claim back the price they paid for you from your father. If they can find him, that is."

Silke's voice trembled with anger. "I swore that if I ever got out I'd find my father. And when I do, I'll have him killed."

"He isn't worth it," Anouk said, thinking about her cousin, Yasmine, who had hung herself and her sister, Alifa, who was probably an old, worn out woman by now.

"He duped me!" Silke raved. "He sold me like some cow for breeding...I lost two years of school..." She broke into tears.

Anouk hugged her. "Silke, you're young and you'll catch up. And because of what you have been through you will be all the stronger. In many ways, this has put you way ahead of your peers."

Silke nodded and wiped her tears.

Anouk took her hand. "Come, let's return to Ulf's apartment."

She carefully inspected the stairs before climbing to the upper floor. Silent and tense, they sat by the phone. When it finally rang, it was Ulf.

"Karen's departure went smoothly," he said.

"Thanks," Anouk breathed with relief.

One of them was safe. Now she only had Silke and herself to worry about.

Karen dried her tears and looked out the plane window. Sana had vanished and there was only mountainous wilderness. A wilderness Anouk intended to cross on foot, by bus, or by donkey cart while being chased by the law. She shuddered and blinked at new tears. She knew she wouldn't be herself till she held Anouk in her arms again.

Leaving Yemen was like leaving a nightmare. Eyes closed she settled back in her seat. When the Ethiopian stewardess gently nudged her and offered her refreshments, she declined, unable to eat or drink, her stomach a tight knot.

To her surprise, Sergio was at the airport. Karen hugged him, crying with relief. "How did you know I was arriving?"

He shrugged. "Ulf called and told me to meet you on this flight unless Anouk sent a message."

"Unbelievable! She had planned this all along." Karen related everything that had happened so far, and what Anouk intended to do.

Face serious, Sergio shook his head. "Nothing will stop her once she has set her mind to something. Don't get me wrong—I feel for Silke and her mother. But Anouk is risking a hell of a lot. And all for a lousy twenty-five thousand."

"It's not the money," Karen sighed. "It's revenge. And she's a dare-devil. I get the feeling she thrives on danger."

"Well, I hope she's careful. I'd hate to lose a good friend."

"Have you seen Irmgard?"

"She called. She's waiting for you at Anouk's house."

As soon as they were at Sergio's office, Karen called Ulf's number and talked to Anouk. They kept it short and businesslike in case the operator listened in.

Driving to Anouk's house, Karen felt exhilarated like a prisoner released from a dungeon, despite her concern about Anouk. No more hot and cumbersome cloak or a veil that hindered breathing and reduced the world to a grey blur. She could drive and walk freely again, be herself. It brought tears of gratitude to her eyes.

Tadessa was sweeping the verandah when Karen drove up and called Irmgard who came running out to hug her.

"Did you get Silke?" she asked breathlessly.

"Yes. She's at Ulf's," Karen said.

Irmgard burst into tears, crying, "Thank God."

A while later they sat in the living room while Karen recounted the story of the rescue once again, and why Anouk had to stay behind.

"I'll pray day and night that nothing happens to her," Irmgard said.

Eyes filming, Karen said, "I'll join you at it. Have you seen the plane in Asseb?"

Irmgard nodded, drying her eyes. "It's kept in a hangar, and a French officer from Djibouti is interested in buying it. I told him I'd let him know when it's for sale."

Chapter 17

Anouk and Silke spent most of their time playing cards while Silke taught Anouk to speak with a Yemenite accent in preparation for her departure.

The evenings they spent with Ulf and sometimes Manfred too. Anouk kept listening to the news which briefly mentioned Silke's disappearance and that the police had no leads.

Anouk was anxious to leave. She assumed that Silke's husband and his brothers, or anybody else from Marib couldn't hang around the Sana airport for more than a few days, poor as they were. And she hoped that the authorities had more to worry about than a missing woman.

To change her appearance, she planned to dress in the Yemenite style and she had Ulf buy the necessary clothing for her as well as change dollars into riyals, which she planned to carry in a money belt. Looking at her fake Ethiopian and Egyptian passports, she debated whether or not to burn them. She wouldn't need either as she intended to sail to Ethiopia with fishermen on a dhow and would simply enter the country, like she had entered France when she escaped from Egypt at sixteen. She didn't really need a passport any longer, because if she were stopped by a patrol it would be over for her with or without these documents. I just can't afford to be caught by a patrol, that's all there is to it, she thought, and decided to burn both passports.

The day she left, she wore a blue striped shirt and dark-grey jacket over a white and blue futa with a belt into which she stuck her curved knife. Her head was covered by a black and white turban with one end loosely hanging across her lower face and tucked behind her ear. On her feet were brown leather sandals.

"You don't look like the man I saw in Marib," Silke said, watching her get ready.

Anouk smiled. "You've also changed. I like that haircut Karen gave you, and you've filled out and look healthier."

"Thanks to you." Silke blushed. "Karen's a lucky woman."

Anouk suppressed a smile as she tied a few things into a red scarf. "So am I."

Silke continued, "I'd love to find a woman like you."

Anouk put a hand on her shoulder and looked her in the eyes. "You will...she's waiting for you in Hamburg. For now, concentrate on your escape. Talk about it with Ulf. How to start an outboard and lighting a flare must become something automatic to you. See yourself away from shore in a small boat. Remember, you'll be very lonely out there."

"I was very alone for the last two years," Silke said. "Today's my eighteenth birthday."

Anouk exclaimed, "Silke, why didn't you say so earlier?"

"I forgot. In Marib nobody observes birthdays. The last one I celebrated was in Hamburg, ten days before flying to Yemen, believing I was going for a month's vacation."

Anouk hugged her and kissed her on both cheeks. "Happy birthday. You know your mother is thinking of you today. Ulf and Manfred will celebrate with you tonight and we'll have a party when we're both safely in Addis Ababa."

Anouk shared a last breakfast with them, then said goodbye. To the men she said, "I hope to see you in Ethiopia one day. It's worth a trip."

Manfred shook her hand. "Good luck."

Ulf said, "I'll call Karen tonight to tell her you're on your way. And I'll be waiting for your call from Asseb so we can agree on the day I shall bring Silke to the coast."

Silke hugged her. "I'll miss you...and our talks and games."

Anouk held her briefly. "Practice everything till you can do it in your sleep."

"Will you call from time to time to let us know how you're doing?"

"I think it's better if I don't. I don't trust telephones. Besides, the way I'm travelling, I probably won't even be near one." She picked up her bundle. "See you soon."

She slipped out of Ulf's building to take her place in the crowds. As she made her way to the bus station, the streets became hectic with traffic and dust.

152

She bought a ticket to Al-Mahwit, a small town which lay on a secondary route to the coast. It was a bit of a detour but less likely to be patrolled, she hoped.

The bus was old, smelling of diesel, people and animals. It filled up with men, two women, cackling chickens in baskets and one goat. The women sat together in the back with the goat which kept bleating and shitting. The chickens were stored under the seats along with heavy luggage. The shelves above the seats were used for lighter things.

Anouk found a seat in the middle next to an old man. She hoped he wasn't the talkative kind and closed her eyes as if trying to sleep. But her senses worked overtime and she couldn't wait for the bus to pull out of the station.

The bus soon wound its way along an unpaved bumpy road, rattling as if threatening to fall apart. Diesel fumes filled the air as well as music from a radio which the driver had at full volume; clouds of dust obscured the view of coffee plantations and picturesque mountainsides.

A military jeep passed them and Anouk's nerves tightened to a snapping point. But the soldiers only waved to the driver and drove on.

They reached the town of Shibam on the edge of the Sana basin with a flat-topped mountain looming behind it.

The two women got off with the goat and some men got off with the chickens, then the bus moved again. Suddenly it jerked and stopped.

Cursing, the driver tried to start the engine, but it wouldn't turn over. The people groaned their disgust. The driver finally gave up and told everyone to get off.

"When will there be another bus?" one man asked.

"Not before tomorrow morning," he was told

"Can you fix the engine?" another yelled.

Waving his hands at the sky, the driver said, "Only Allah knows."

Anouk got off with the others glad to give her ears some rest from the din of the radio and the rattling bus. She walked into the town through the city gate and along high buildings of mud brick in rosy colors. Ending up at the market, she bought some fruit, cheese and bread and wandered back to the bus station. The bus stood with its hood open with four men working on the engine. She joined the other passengers sitting against the wall of the terminal and ate some cheese and bread.

"Where're you headed?" a young man next to her asked.

"Al-Mahwit," Anouk replied. "And you?"

"Kawkaban," he answered. "This your first time in this town?"

Anouk nodded, hoping her accent was good enough. "Anything special about it?"

He grinned. "Ever heard about the historic fart?" Anouk shook her head, so he went on. "In the old times a man fouled up his wedding party by letting out a thunderous fart. Utterly ashamed, he fled, riding his horse all the way to India and settling there.

"Years later and homesick, he decided to return to Shibam, thinking that his shame was forgotten. Arriving at the city's outskirts, he overheard a girl asking her mother about her age. 'You were born on the day of Husayn's historic fart,' the mother told her. Realizing that his fart would never be forgotten or forgiven, the poor man rode away for good."

Anouk laughed out loud.

"Why are you going to Al-Mahwit?" he asked.

"To work for my uncle who has a grocery store."

"Where?"

"I hear it's in the center of town. I haven't seen my uncle for twenty years."

"You speak with the accent of the Marib province."

"I was born there," she said evenly.

"Were you there when they abducted that woman?"

"No," Anouk replied steadily. "But I heard about it in Sana."

"They're a sly bunch, those Egyptians. I'd never trust one."

Anouk nodded. "Yeah, I avoid them like I would a rattlesnake."

The bus driver interrupted them. "We can't fix the bus," he said apologetically. "We called Sana and they'll send another bus by tomorrow at eight."

He left under a hail of protests and curses.

"Shit," Anouk growled.

"I know a cheap hotel here," the young man said. "We could share a room."

"How much would that cost?" Anouk asked.

"Two hundred riyals."

Anouk shook her head. "I only have thirty on me. I'll camp in the terminal."

The man left. Anouk waited a while, then strolled once more into the small town to pass the time. She saw several inns, but didn't dare rent a room in case the police were checking hotels. This was still too close to Sana. Finally, when the sun was low, she returned to the bus station went inside the dirty hall, and settled as best she could in a corner. She wasn't the only stranded passenger. Several men sat nearby against the wall. As the sun slowly sank, some unrolled small prayer rugs, knelt on them and bowed towards Mecca, reciting verses of the Koran.

It got dark and bitterly cold and she shivered throughout the whole night. Aching and exhausted, she went to the toilet in the morning and almost sprang back from the stench. Holding her breath, she relieved herself, then hurried outside to be stopped short. A jeep with two officials had driven up and while one joked with the bus driver, the other came inside the hall, ordering, "Papers, everyone!"

Her sleeve against her face, she retreated into the toilet, and pressed against the feces-smeared partition which hid the toilet from view.

She heard the thudding of heavy boots, then, "Anybody in there?" A grunt of disgust followed, the steps receded and she dared to breathe again, grateful that the stench had kept the official from checking thoroughly.

Fighting nausea, she made sure they were gone before leaving the toilet. Outside, she took deep breaths and slowly recuperated.

Chapter 18

The bus didn't arrive at eight as promised but at eleven and looked little better than its predecessor. This time no women were among the travelers, so Anouk chose a seat in the back to get somewhat away from the people and especially the blaring radio. She soon regretted the decision because dust and diesel fumes from the exhaust pipe blew in through a hole in the floor. Human odors added to the mix as they lost altitude and it became hotter.

Irritated by the bumpy ride, chickens in a basket flapped and jumped, disturbing fleas which landed on her legs. The bus stopped at every hamlet and she was ready to commit murder when she got off in Al-Mahwit that evening.

It was a larger town with attractive buildings and splendid views over the valley, which somewhat eased her savage mood. Taking deep breaths to cleanse her lungs, she looked for a restaurant.

While eating soup, lamb stew and bread and drinking tea, she wondered if it would be safe to check into a hotel. She was desperate for a bath and a good night's sleep and asked the waiter about a hotel.

"Around the corner," he told her.

The hotel was filthy but she was too tired to care. Despite bug bites, she felt better in the morning and studied the map she had brought. She was headed for Al-Makha, a hundred and eighty miles south and only fifty miles across from Asseb in Ethiopia, which could be reached in ten hours by boat. Sailing from any other Yemenite port would take two or more days and she couldn't risk being confined with men for that long fearing they might discover her true sex. If she traveled on the main roads, she could reach Al-Makha in two days. But she didn't dare to.

She had coffee at the restaurant and went to the market to get a bottle of water, fruit, bread, goat cheese and olives. Then she bought a ticket to Al-Qanawis. This time she sat towards the front, next to a middle-aged man whose upper teeth were capped with gold—a sign of wealth.

"Where're you headed?" he asked, giving her a golden smile.

"Al-Hudayda," she replied.

He nodded. "So am I."

Anouk pretended to yawn and leaned back, hoping he would leave her alone.

"You live there?" he wanted to know.

"I'm visiting relatives," she said as the radio came on, making conversation difficult.

The bus wasn't any better than the previous ones, nor was the road which was rippled like corrugated iron and full of holes.

They were leaving the mountains and it became unbearably hot and humid; by evening they reached Al-Qanawis, a brick village, surrounded by reed huts, typical of the region and giving it an African feel.

Figuring she was far enough from Sana and it was safe, she went to the only inn and rented a room with a filthy bed.

It was still early and her room unbearably hot and stuffy, so Anouk decided to go for a walk. The village was small with unpaved streets and she reached its limits in no time and sat under a huge palm, enjoying the quiet. The sky was lit up by stars and she thought she could smell the Red Sea, only thirty miles away. Not far were a few reed huts from which came the soft tunes of a simsimiya—a five-string lyre with a small resonator box, a popular instrument in the Red Sea area.

Curious, she walked towards the huts which were similar to Ethiopian tukuls, yet when she reached them she noticed that they were three times as big.

"Good evening," she heard a man say.

She made out three young men, one with the instrument and answered their greeting.

"You're a traveller," one said.

"Yes," she replied. "I come from Harad and am on my way to Al-Hudayda. Your beautiful music drew me close."

"You're welcome to sit with us and enjoy more," the musician offered.

She thanked him and sat down as he began another tune. She closed her eyes, giving in to the pleasant melody, making her forget

157

all else for a while.

The music ended and she opened her eyes and smiled at them.

"Would you like to come inside my home for some tea?" the player asked.

Anouk bowed slightly. "Do not inconvenience yourself because of me. Your music was gift enough."

"We will all have tea. Come, join us." He clapped his hands and called to another hut for tea, then bid them to come inside. "Get comfortable," he said, pointing to mats.

Anouk was astonished to see that the floor and wall were completely surfaced with mud all the way to the domed ceiling, leaving no visible sign of the reed structure. They were painted with bright colors and lively motifs.

Two boys appeared, one with tea and glasses on a tray, the other with a dish containing figs and another with bint al sahn, an egg-rich sweet bread dipped in clarified butter and honey. Eating and drinking, Anouk answered the men's questions cautiously and with the usual lies. In the end, the host brought a water pipe and they smoked quietly.

It was past midnight when she thanked them for their hospitality and bid them goodbye. Happy for this pleasant interlude and enjoying the cool night breeze that had come up, she strolled back to the inn where she spent the rest of the night on a chair with her feet on a wobbly table.

Miserable and tired the next morning, she studied the map ate some cheese and bread. When she returned to the bus station, she was told that no bus would run that day.

"Are there any taxis? she asked.

"The only one in town already left," the clerk said.

"Where're you going?"asked a man who had been standing nearby. He was short and appeared to be in his forties.

"Al-Hudayda," she said.

"I can take you along to Bajil in my truck," he offered, stroking his thick mustache.

"Allah be praised," Anouk exclaimed without watching her accent.

"You from Egypt?"

Shit, Anouk thought, I'm slipping. "No, the Sudan."

He pointed to his truck. "Let's go."

The route to Bajil was a back road and miserable as was the

humidity and heat.

"What're you going to do in Al-Hudayda?" he wanted to know, offering her a bottle of water.

Anouk took a swig. "I'll be helping my uncle with his grocery store."

"Is it a big store?"

"I hear it is. I haven't seen my uncle for twenty years."

"Doesn't he have any sons?"

Anouk shook her head. "He's cursed with seven daughters, then his wife's womb dried out."

"Ah, Allah is wise," he sighed, "but at times he tests us cruelly."

It was noon when they reached a dreary, industrial town with a cement factory from which the prevailing winds blew clouds of cement. Anouk thanked the truck driver and walked to the bus station. A bus was about to leave for Zabid, a town half-way to Al-Makha. She quickly bought a ticket and hopped on.

Too late she realized that the bus was travelling on the road connecting Sana with the coast and carried heavier traffic as well as military convoys. Sitting on pins and needles, she hoped no patrol would stop them. Her hope was shattered when a jeep with two officers drove up and signalled the driver to stop.

Hot fear dried Anouk's mouth and she looked for a way out, but there was only one door through which the officers entered, barking, "Papers."

Shaking, she watched them going from seat to seat, thinking of what to say.

"Your papers," one of them asked.

"I don't have any," Anouk replied, trying to appear calm and speaking with a lisp to further camouflage her accent. "They were stolen," she added, when he frowned.

"Stolen, huh?"

Anouk nodded, noticing that the bus had gotten very silent suddenly and that everybody was watching.

"You'd better come with us," he said.

"But, in the name of Allah, I haven't done anything," she tried.

His hand went to the gun on his belt and Anouk got up, grabbed her bundle from the rack above and followed them to the jeep.

They ordered her to sit in the back and drove at great speed to the Bajil police station. Anouk cursed her carelessness, knowing that her fate would be sealed if they searched her and found the money belt with the US dollars and riyals, or worse, discovered she was a woman. She was led into a hot office where another officer sat behind a cluttered desk.

"No papers?" he asked, looking at her.

"They were stolen," Anouk lisped. "Along with my suitcase. All I have left is this bundle."

He picked up a form. "Your name?"

"Hamid Said," she answered, watching him write.

"Where're you from?"

"Harad," she replied, feeling perspiration trickle down her back.

"Where were you going?"

"To Zabid. I'm going to look for work there."

"You been in Marib lately?" he asked suddenly.

Anouk met his hard stare. "Marib?" she asked, astonished. "No, sir. Why?"

He rose. "I want you to wait outside."

"What will you do with me?"

"We'll drive you to Sana and, if what you're saying is true, you're free." He dismissed her with a wave of his hand.

Sitting on the bench, Anouk pressed into the dirty wall, her mind racing. They would drive her back to Sana and confront her with someone from Marib, and it would be all over for her.

The officers left to have lunch, and their siesta, leaving her with an armed soldier who was sitting on a chair by the entrance and looking as if he were about to fall asleep and a young man behind a counter, also fighting sleep in the stuffy room. Only a few fat flies seemed alive, trying to get through a grimy window pane.

She walked to the counter and asked, "Is there a toilet?"

The young man pointed down a hall. "The last door," he said, sleepily.

The soldier looked up briefly, then sat with his eyes half closed again. She left her bundle on the bench and slowly walked down the hall and into the small restroom.

Almost insane with fear, she locked the door and looked around. There was one heavily barred window, and above the toilet a small rectangular opening below the ceiling which didn't look big enough for a child to get through. But it was her only chance.

She climbed onto the dirty toilet, gripped the stone sill and, with one foot braced against the wall, pulled herself up and squeezed her head, then one shoulder, through the narrow aperture, leaving some of her skin on the bricks in the process. Twisting and pushing, she managed to get the other shoulder out, hearing her bones crunch against stone. Hanging head down over a small yard, she held onto a pipe going up the wall, and wriggled the rest of herself free, then let herself fall sideways to the ground.

Ignoring the pain in her shoulder and rib cage, she ran out of the yard and along an alley, then into the hallway of a building and out the back into another alley.

The town was shrouded in silent heat and cement dust, and she kept running unhindered along narrow, twisting passages between buildings. Panting, her heart and lungs threatening to explode, she stopped to look around. Hearing the wail of a siren, she withdrew into a building. The siren drew near and she took off her sandals, sprinted up the stone stairs to the roof terrace and looked through the square openings of the stone railing.

But her view to a major street was blocked by buildings. The siren alternately drew near and receded. She heard it for quite a while, then it was still. She hid behind some rubbish in a corner and waited. She knew that they would have the town circled with soldiers and thought of ways to get out.

Maybe the night would bring an answer. She leaned back, feeling the knife in her belt, the reassuring bulge of the money belt. As the sun lost its sting, the town came to life and she heard people and a radio nearby and wondered if she would be in the news already.

Hungry and thirsty and nodding off from time to time, she waited for the night.

It was utterly still when she left her hiding place at two in the morning and tiptoed down the stairs. Treading lightly, sticking to the buildings, she walked to the end of the alley and made out the stack of the cement factory. She headed for it and came to a fence partly covered by dead brush. The factory was a huge building of corrugated iron brooding in silence.

Hugging the fence, she moved quietly to the guard's shack next to the gate and looked through the open door at a fat man on the floor, sleeping noisily. She tiptoed past him into the yard and went toward the building, keeping to the shadow of trucks, sacks of cement and trash. She came to a dusty office with two metal desks, chairs and a file cabinet.

On one wall was a picture of the president, on another a bulletin board and four racks with time cards for about a hundred employees.

She found a bottle of water, drank it dry, then left the office and walked into a big hall full of cement sacks, tools, cases, and five more trucks. She hid there and waited for daybreak.

She jerked awake at the muezzin's call at sunrise. Half an hour later, the workers began to arrive. She waited till the place was swarming, then mingled with the men. Pretending to put tools in order, she let her gaze fly over the yard where three trucks had been lined up and men began to load cement sacks. She strode purposefully to the trucks and helped load the cement.

"You new?" one man asked.

Anouk nodded. "Where's this load going?"

"Al-Hudayda. All three trucks."

"Hey, over there," someone with authority shouted. "You're here to work, not to socialize."

Anouk quickly bent down for another sack before he could realize that she didn't belong. They finished loading one truck and covered the sacks with an awning to prevent them from slipping off.

Two men got into the cab and drove away. She helped load another truck, then climbed onto the bed, pretending to rearrange the sacks.

"Hand me the awning," she said to a worker. When he wanted to help tie it, she said, "I'll do it. Go help load the next truck."

She noticed the foreman walking into the hall, and saw that the workers were busy loading another truck. She quickly tied the awning fast on one side, pulled it across the sacks. Almost lying down, she tied it on the other side, then, after a last look around, she slipped under it and squeezed between the sacks. Trembling and almost suffocating in cement dust, she waited.

Before long, she heard men getting into the cab and the engine start. She waited a while before loosening a tie of the awning to lie with her face in the open to breathe.

They had driven less than a mile when the truck slowed, then stopped and she heard the imperative voices of officials. Heart pounding, she pushed deeper between the sacks and lay perspiring and gasping for air. A beam of sunlight reached her and she held her breath. Someone had untied the awning, and she prayed that no one would think of climbing on top of the sacks or of shifting them.

The sunbeam disappeared and it was dark again. Moments later, the cab doors slammed closed and the truck moved. She crawled on top of the sacks and pressed her face through a rip in the awning and greedily sucked in air.

There were three more patrols on the way to the coast, which they reached in less than an hour. Peering from the awning, she saw that they were on a main street which, she assumed, led to the harbor, the destination of the cement. A park appeared and she waited for a stoplight, then slipped off the rear of the truck.

The park was modern and well-groomed and full of people strolling, sitting on benches or around huge fountains.

She rinsed her face and hair in one of the fountains, brushed cement dust from her clothes and had a taxi take her to the market. There she bought food, bottled water, a jacket, three shirts, three futas, a headcloth, a map, some toiletries and a duffel bag to put it all in. Then she stopped at a market stall and ate lamb stew with rice and vegetables.

She was sipping mocha coffee and pondering where to spend the night when she heard the whine of a siren. A moment later she saw a jeep stop at the entrance of the market and four officials get out.

She grabbed her duffel and slowly walked behind the stall and along an alley to the other end of the market. Hidden by a cloth hanging from poles, she looked back, saw the officials checking papers and hurried through a gate into the Turkish quarter, the oldest part of the town.

She came upon a mosque, entered and joined a group of men who were bowing and prostrating themselves towards Mecca. She sensed that the officials were looking for her, but doubted they would expect her to be in this mosque or disturb the prayers of believers.

It was getting dark when she carefully left the mosque and walked deeper into the quarter which contained some beautiful but rotting buildings. She came upon one that looked as if it would cave in at any minute, and went through a wooden door damaged by moisture and hanging on a rusty hinge.

Cautiously she walked on broken tiles through a hall, scaring a cat and inhaling the smell of mildew in the walls. She called out to make sure no vagrant was hiding somewhere.

But the walls only returned the hollow echo of her voice. She changed into a new shirt and futa, then settled into a corner and waited for the night to pass.

Chapter 19

She was startled from a light sleep, thinking she had heard something, her hand flying to the knife at her waist. The grey light of dawn was filtering into the house and she checked her watch. Five o'clock. She heard it again and rose, holding her breath. The sound came from the next room and she tiptoed to the doorway and looked inside.

"Oh cat!" she moaned with relief, tucking her knife away.

A grey cat stared at her for a moment before whisking into hiding.

She had some water, then carefully left the house just as the sun lit up the sky and the muezzin began his call to believers from the minaret. A few men headed for the mosque. Otherwise the streets were deserted. She walked past the mosque to the market where merchants were beginning to set out their wares.

She had coffee and a honey cake at one stall while observing the slow arrival of shoppers. Listening to the muezzin's song from the minaret, Anouk watched a few men pray in the market on prayer rugs and saw the rising sun suck the pink from the sky and turn it to an aquamarine blue. For a moment she forgot her quandary and felt only soothing peace.

"Another coffee?" the merchant asked, reminding her of where she was.

She nodded. "Why not?"

The market was rapidly filling with people eager to grab the best and freshest of the fruit and vegetables. Nearby, a radio was turned on at full volume, bellowing a heart-rending love song.

Anouk studied her map, wondering which way to go. She was afraid to take a bus, sure that there would be patrols along all the major and secondary roads looking for her. She thought of risking it with a dhow across the Red Sea after all. But after measuring the distance between the Yemenite and Ethiopian coast, she discarded that idea once more. It would be a three-day trip. Dhows had no toilets. What would she do when she had to pee and couldn't do it over-board like the men? She sighed, studying the map, wondering if she should try walking south. She couldn't walk on the major road because of the patrols. But the map showed an unpaved road or track right along the shore and quite a distance from the major road inland. She was sure she would be safe from patrols there.

She was also sure that there were fishing villages along the coast to help her survive. Maybe she could catch a dhow down the coast. Filled with renewed hope, she folded the map and slowly sipped her coffee.

The radio had stopped playing music and was reporting the news, first from the Arab world and Yemen, then the local news.

"The police are still looking for the two thieves who robbed the jewelry store on San'a street in Al-Hudayda last Tuesday," the announcer said. "The man who stabbed his brother-in-law in a fight was detained in Sana yesterday. The brother-in-law is still in serious condition.

"The police are also looking for a man who, it is believed, had something to do with the abduction of the young woman in Marib. The man was arrested on a bus heading to Zabid and brought to the Bajil police station from which he escaped. He wore..." To Anouk's horror, a description of her followed.

"...Special patrols have been set up between Bajil and Al-Hudayda. Any information leading..."

Anouk stopped listening and threw a quick glance at the mer-chant. But he was busy rearranging some boxes and was apparently not listening. She finished her coffee and slowly walked away. She had to get out of Al-Hudayda as fast as possible and bought two more bottles of water, bread, cheese, some fruit and walked to the street, heavy with traffic now.

She flagged down a taxi. "To the fishing port," she ordered, sink-ing into the back seat.

He drove her to the port, the most important of the country, filled with military vessels. It was noisy and abounded with fishermen returning with their catches to sell at the adjoining fish market. Anouk observed them working on their dhows, debating if she should just risk it and ask one to sail her across the Red Sea for what-ever fee he demanded. Looking around uneasily, she kept walking along the quay and was about to approach a fisherman when she saw a jeep with four officials drive up at the other end of the quay.

Her heart lurched and her mouth became dry; she turned and slowly walked back to where the taxi had let her out, hoping that there would be another taxi. As the jeep didn't pass her, she quickly looked over her shoulder and saw that it was driving along the quay at a slow pace while the officials scanned the port and boats. And, to her utmost terror, she made out the official who had arrested her on the bus.

Nothing around her offered cover and she walked faster, leaving the quay and crossing a small square to get back to the main street. Suddenly there was the sharp sound of a police whistle behind her and the roar of a car speeding up. She ran as fast as she could into the crowd and, disregarding traffic, across the street. Horns blared, brakes squealed and angry drivers shook their fists at her. Looking back, she saw, to her relief, a military convoy driving up.

She sprinted onto a side street, then onto another main street and from there into an alley which led to another street where she discovered a funeral procession. She quickly joined them, walking in the middle and stooping to make herself shorter. Four men carried the bier on which lay a body wrapped in white cloth. An imam—leader of prayers—recited a surah. A group of women walked behind the bier, loudly lamenting the departure of the dead's soul, followed by men paying their last respects. Anouk lowered her head further and joined in the prayers, weak from fear, afraid her trembling legs wouldn't hold her up.

The gates of the cemetery were open and the procession filed through the wide bare yard to the freshly dug grave. The body was lowered and laid in an oblong excavation on one side with its head facing toward Mecca while the imam chanted more verses of the Koran. Then the grave was filled and another prayer was offered for the dead after which the people slowly departed.

Anouk pretended to leave and, after a short look around, quickly slipped into a deep niche in the wall with inscriptions of the Koran and hid behind a big stone amphora. The guardian of the cemetery looked around for a last time to make sure no one was left, then closed and locked the gate and left. With a sigh of relief, Anouk sank to the ground and slowly recuperated. Surrounded by high walls, this was a safe place, at least for this night unless there was another funeral. She waited until it was dark before walking around to stretch her stiff limbs and get rid of nervous energy, then discovered another dug grave waiting for the next body. She sat down on a tombstone nearby and had some water and food, watching the moon come up. She was exhausted but knew she wouldn't be able to sleep and just sat, thinking.

They knew now what she looked like and where she was and would draw a tighter and tighter circle around her until they had her. She had no clue how she would be able to leave this city and sank face down onto the ground in despair. But she had to keep her senses. She couldn't give up. Not with Silke pinning her future on her and Karen and Irmgard waiting in agony. She would find a way.

A creaking sound made her jump and look around. She made out a small side door she hadn't noticed on the far side through which two figures moved into the cemetery. She grabbed her duffel, rolled into the open grave and listened, filled with dread.

She heard them walk close and crawled into the oblong excavation on the side of the grave which received the body and protected it from being covered with earth. Her world had shrunk to the size of a grave, it occurred to her as she lay waiting and trembling, praying this wasn't a bad omen. But no one seemed to have any business with the grave and the steps receded. She slid back into the main chamber of the grave which was five to six feet deep and carefully looked over the rim. The men had settled near the opposite wall and were unpacking things from their bags, talking in low voices. Thieves? Checking their loot? Holding her breath, she watched them light a small kerosene cooker and put a pot on. So she wasn't the only one seeking refuge here and there was a small door which was unlocked, unless these men had a key.

She waited to see if the men would leave again. But after they had drunk and eaten something, they lay down apparently intending to spend the night. She watched them for awhile longer, then lay down in the grave, her head on the duffel and, despite herself, drifted into a light sleep with disturbing dreams.

She woke, hearing the men leave at the break of dawn. As soon as they had disappeared, she ran to the side door and tried it. The lock was rusty, the wood around it rotten. After fiddling with the big handle, the door gave and opened. She looked at the empty dark street, then at her map but could only make out that she was in the south of the city. South was where she wanted to go, but how? No ideas came. All she could think of was that she was trapped. At least she had some water, bread and cheese.

By mid-morning she heard someone unlocking the big gate and quickly hid inside the niche. Shortly after, another funeral procession appeared and a body was laid into the grave which had served as her bedroom. As soon as the cemetery emptied, grave diggers began digging two more graves. They're busy dying here, she thought, observing them from her hiding place. Finally they also left. By the time the day had ended and it was dark she had watched two more funerals. She waited to see if she would get more company and when no one had appeared by midnight, decided to sneak out of the cemetery and walk south to find that track along the coast, hoping for the best.

She hadn't quite reached the side door when it opened and a man came in. Seeing her, he stopped abruptly. Surprised, they looked at each other. Short and thin, he carried a sack on one shoulder probably containing his worldly possessions and seemed more afraid of her than she of him. Lifting his hand in an appeasing gesture, he walked backwards to the door.

"Don't be afraid!" she said. "I don't intend to harm you."

He stopped, studying her with wary eyes. "What're you doing here?"

She shrugged. "I...went to a funeral of a dear friend...and lingered by his grave." She pointed to one of the new graves. "The guard must not have seen me and locked me in. I was prepared to spend the night here when I discovered this side door and wanted to try it." She knew it sounded feeble and wondered if he believed her.

He relaxed and came closer, watching her carefully.

"What're you doing here?" she asked, to say something.

"I intend to spend the night," he said. "I have no home and this is a safe place."

"Any more like you coming?"

He shrugged. "Maybe...maybe not. Why?"

"Just curious. I myself have no place either at the moment for I arrived in Al-Hudayda just in time for the funeral, and by now the hotels must all be closed."

He nodded. "So what do you intend to do?"

"I thought I could walk to the bus station and wait for morning."

"Where do you intend to go?"

"Back to Al-Mansuriya where I work in my uncle's grocery store."

"There's a bus station not far from here, but it is also closed now. Anyway, I'm going to settle over there against the wall and make

168

some tea. You're welcome to a glass."

Anouk's mind was working. Maybe he could be of help. "I would gladly accept a glass," she said. "I haven't had anything warm to drink for a while."

She sat down on the ground with her legs crossed and watched him get a small kerosene primus out of his sack and light it, then pour water from a bottle into a beat-up aluminum pot and set it on top of the cooker. When the water was boiling he threw tea leaves into it and, after waiting a while, poured it into two glasses which looked as if they hadn't been washed in a while and were badly chipped.

Anouk swallowed, wondering where the water came from and if it had boiled long enough to kill any dangerous germs. He set a glass in front of her and she blew at the steam, then waited to let it cool.

Also blowing on his tea, he kept studying her and suddenly asked, "How much money do you have on you?"

Taken aback, Anouk held her breath. "Why do you ask?" she finally said.

"I have a friend who's a taxi driver. He could drive you out of town. He doesn't live far from here," he replied without looking at her, and continued to blow on his tea.

Anouk remained quiet for a moment. This proposition didn't come from nowhere. Had he heard the radio news and guessed who she was and that she was hiding? If so, he expected a reward. "How much will that cost me?" she asked, barely able to keep her voice from choking.

"How much is it worth to you to get...back to Al-Mansuriya?" he asked, looking at his tea.

"It would be nice if I could get back there by morning. Tell me your price."

He named an amount equalling one hundred US dollars. Anouk would've paid him a thousand, but she would have been a fool to let him know she had that much money on her.

"A lot of money for a little favor," she said.

He threw her a quick look. "It's not little."

Anouk chewed her lower lip. "What about your friend...that taxi driver? How much will he want?"

"You settle that with him."

They dropped into silence, he slurping his tea, Anouk thinking, it's useless to pretend. He knows.

"All right," she said in a low voice. "Get your friend."

He held out his hand. "The money."

"Not before I'm sitting inside the taxi."

He nodded, drank some of his tea, then rose. "I'll be back."

Anouk poured her tea into a dark corner, set the glass next to his sack which he had left behind, then got a bundle of riyals out of her money belt and put it into her jacket pocket. Pacing around with her arms crossed over her chest, she wondered if this was a mistake. But how else would she get out of this city? It was her only chance and safer than walking. He was homeless, and probably a petty thief who couldn't care less about an abducted woman and simply saw a chance to make some money. And a hundred dollars was a fortune for him. Besides, it was too late to retreat. He had guessed who she was and if she left, could alert the police. He might be doing that right now, it occurred to her. No, she thought, if he's a thief he would avoid the police. And even if he wasn't a thief, if he alerted the police, the reward would not be as much as he was getting from her.

She waited for two hours and had almost given up hope of seeing him again when he reappeared by the door and motioned her to follow him to a taxi in the street. Anouk handed him the money and got inside. Without a word, the driver drove away. A quick glance at her watch told Anouk that it was four in the morning.

Chapter 20

"Where do you want to go?" asked the driver, a short wiry man.

"Just go south," Anouk said in a toneless voice, looking left and right for patrol cars. But the streets were silent and empty. Surely they were stationed at the big intersections outside the city where the major roads headed in all directions.

"I changed my mind," she said, just before they reached the outskirts. "I'd like to go to the coastal road."

If he was surprised he didn't show it and just turned into the road heading for the coast.

"We haven't talked about a price yet," Anouk said.

"I want fifteen thousand," he said, which amounted to three hundred dollars.

"I don't have that much on me," Anouk said, and thought she heard him make a sound. "What did you say?"

"Let's see how far you want to go first before we settle the fee," he said.

"Fair enough."

An hour later, the city was well behind them and they were driving on the sandy track which deteriorated with every mile. The sky lightened as a new day began; the phantoms of the night with their doubts and anxieties vanished. Filled with new confidence, Anouk permitted herself to relax somewhat.

He reached for his bottle of water on the seat next to him, had a sip, then looked at her through his rearview mirror. "What do you want to do out here?"

"Just keep driving," Anouk ordered, realizing he was on guard. "I'll let you know when I want to get out."

He shrugged and continued to drive.

"You from abroad?" he asked after a few moments, looking at her again in his rearview mirror.

Why is he pretending he doesn't know? Anouk asked herself. Or doesn't he? Had she jumped to conclusions because of the radio news at the market?

"Yes, I've lived in several countries, the last was Morocco," she replied as if bored.

The road worsened, the car shook and rattled.

"You sure you want to go on?" he asked, observing her in his mirror.

"Yes," Anouk said.

"You have relatives around here?"

If he wanted to go on with this farce, so be it, Anouk thought, and said, "Yes," yet wishing he'd be quiet and just drive.

"How was Morocco?"

"All right." Anouk gazed at the dunes to her left, the Red Sea to the right.

"Good jobs?"

"Not bad." Did he really not know, or was he just acting, Anouk wondered, beginning to feel wary.

"So you came back here to live?"

"Yes."

"Why did you leave Morocco?"

"Personal reasons," she said, feeling like telling him to shut up.

"What did you do there?"

"Construction."

He kept looking at her in the mirror as she averted her eyes by glaring at the sea. She gazed at the empty land around them and decided to make him stop at the first sign of habitation. But the land continued to spread out with no sign of human settlement.

Would he send the police after her, once he was back in the city? Anouk wondered. Or would he be happy with the money she would pay him and forget about her? She sighed inwardly. She had no choice but to trust her good fortune.

Suddenly the car sputtered to a stop. Muttering a curse, he got out and looked under the hood. Cursing again, he came to her door, and looked through the window. "You understand something about engines?"

Anouk got out of the car. "It may be just a loose wire."

She froze, feeling something hard pushing into her side. "I know you're that Egyptian on the run," he said, prodding her with a pistol. "Your money and your watch."

172

Feeling the blood freeze in her veins, she slid her gold navigator's watch which Diana had given her when she got her pilot's license from her wrist and gave it to him, then pulled the bundle of riyals out of her jacket pocket. "That's more than what you asked for and that's all I have. And I'm not Egyptian or on the run."

So this had been that little thief's plan. To have her drive out of the city with his friend so he could rob her, knowing she couldn't go to the police.

His laugh was cold. "You've got more. Open your shirt."

"That's all I have," she shouted.

Pointing the gun at her chest, he yanked her jacket open, saw her knife, pulled it from the belt and threw it into the car.

"I told you I have no more," she said menacingly.

"You have more," he sneered, and ripped her shirt open, exposing not only the money belt but shifting the bandage around her breasts.

"A woman!" he growled, shrinking back as if she were a cobra.

Taking advantage of his surprise, she kicked the gun out of his hand. But before she could make another move, he attacked her with the fury of a fanatic. Wrestling, they fell to the ground.

He was shorter but stronger and Anouk fought desperately to keep him from reaching his gun a few feet away in the sand, knowing he would kill her and be decorated for it.

Cursing and spitting insults, he grabbed her throat and beat her head against the hard sand until she feared her neck would snap. She got hold of his hair and pounded his ear with her fist, increasing his fury. His face a grimace of hatred, he let go of her neck and went for her hands.

"Son of a whore!" she spat in Egyptian Arabic, jabbing her knee in his groin.

Cursing, he doubled up in pain and loosened his grip just enough for her to get out from under him. But he was fast and threw himself on top of her again and gripped her neck.

Anouk gasped, and behind her eyes whirled a red cloud as she kicked, and clawed his face, fighting for her life.

He grabbed her hair and lifted a fist to smash it into her face. Feeling the hard edge of a stone stabbing into her side, she groped for it and rammed it into his eye with all her might. Blood spurted from a deep gash and he let go of her with a horrible howl.

In utter fear and rage, she kept hammering the stone into his face and head until he collapsed. Wheezing, she rolled away from him, and spat out his blood which had splattered on her face, then vomited until she tasted bile.

She lurched to her feet, her throat aching and her breath ragged, and gazed around, then at him. He lay motionless, his face unrecognizable with blood oozing from deep cuts.

She staggered to the car, got a bottle of water from her duffel and rinsed her mouth. After drinking, she poured some on her face and hands. She found his bottle on the passenger seat, washed the blood off her chest, changed clothes, and stuffed her soiled ones into her bag. Then she stuck her knife back into her belt.

She looked at him again, sure he was dead. Face distorted in revulsion, hands shaking, she went through his pockets, retrieved her watch, and took all his money and identification papers to make it look like a robbery.

The sun had come up and she noticed several dark specks circling in the sky—vultures which would descend upon the corpse as soon as she left.

She picked up the gun, eyed the taxi, and decided to drive it away from the body to delay investigations. The engine started with no problem; she drove for about ten miles until the road disintegrated, and hid the car behind high dunes.

Hiking along the shore, she hoped no one would come her way.

But there was no sign of habitation far and wide as she made her way south on a stony track. By mid-morning, the prevailing winds appeared, whipping up the sea, and blowing sand across the land, erasing her tracks.

In the evening she came upon a cluster of palm trees and stopped to spend the night in their shelter. The wind had died with the sinking sun and the sea was like a mirror. With a cry of gratitude, she dove into the warm water and scrubbed herself, then washed the blood from her clothes which she hung on branches to dry. Finally she threw the gun into the sea and buried the taxi driver's papers.

Refreshed, she ate the rest of the food she had bought the previous day, then lay in the sand looking at the stars and thinking about the implications of what she had done. She didn't feel sorry for killing the man which she had done in self-defense. But she hoped that neither his body nor the taxi would be found too soon or be connected to her.

She was leaving too much of a trail and had to get out of the country as fast as possible, but didn't know how. She also wondered what the thief would do when his friend didn't reappear. Surely he was impatiently awaiting him to split the money. Would he go to the police and report her? He knew that she wanted to head south, but not that she made the taxi driver take this track along the coast.

Two hours before dawn she woke hungry and thirsty and had some water, then trekked on before the heat could slow her down. Her path seemed to follow endless beach. By mid-morning the humidity and heat left her staggering. The Red Sea was a glaring pool of light, the isolation of the coast astounding. She felt confident that no one would think of looking for her here.

But she needed to find a settlement soon to get water and food. At last she saw reed roofs sticking up from behind the dunes, then a track, and a while later an old man came along in a donkey cart, going her way.

"Where're you headed?" he asked in a friendly voice.

"Hays," she answered smoothly, watching him closely.

He remained relaxed, and she assumed that few people in this region had radios to listen to or needed to distrust strangers who came by.

"I can give you a ride to the next village," he offered.

She gladly accepted, then asked him for water.

He pointed to the basket in the back. "Help yourself. There is bread too."

They reached his village in the evening, and he invited her to stay in his hut for the night.

The following morning she was on foot again. By noon the sun had sapped her energy and she rested under a huge palm on the beach, drinking water and eating the figs and bananas she had bought from the old man. Studying her map, she found she was about sixty miles south of Al-Hudayda and seventy miles from Al-Makha.

She continued down the coast and in the evening reached another village tucked behind dunes. Sitting on the beach, she gazed at the sun which hovered briefly on the horizon like a huge red eye before sinking. The wind which had blown like a hot whip all day died down. The Red Sea shimmered pink.

The trek was taking its toll on her; she was tired beyond remembering and had lost weight. Her exposed skin was deeply tanned. After making sure no one was around, she undressed and went in the water for a long swim. Refreshed, she dried herself with her futa, changing into a fresh one and a new shirt when she noticed someone coming from the village. She picked up her knife and stuck it overtly into her belt, watching the young man who approached slowly.

He wore a white shirt over a blue and white striped futa and sandals on his feet. Though not handsome, his features had the softness of a girl's.

"Good evening," he said in a voice that matched his looks.

"Good evening," Anouk replied, noticing that she was a head taller.

"I came to welcome you. Where're you from?"

"Sadah," she answered with raised eyebrows.

"You've travelled a long way. My name is Ali and I came to offer you my humble home, as there are no inns."

"I'm Hamid," she offered in return. "Do you live alone?"

"I do and my house is your house."

"I shall pay you a hotel fee," said Anouk who had planned on another night in the open. But his offer was better and the young man, obviously homosexual, was trying to pick her up. She knew she could handle him.

She picked up her bag and followed him to his home—three round reed huts—the cleanest dwellings she had seen since leaving Ulf's place.

"Welcome," Ali said. "It is an honor to have you as my guest."

"May Allah reward you for your hospitality," Anouk bowed politely, carefully watching her accent and taking in the interior which was decorated with some ceramics and rugs.

"Would you like me to wash your shirt and futa?" he asked.

"Do not burden yourself with extra work. I shall have them washed in Hays."

"Why are you going there?"

"To work for my uncle who has a grocery store."

He nodded, and went to the kitchen which was a smaller hut. She followed and watched him prepare a simple meal of fish, lentils, beans and flat bread on a wood-burning stove. Anouk added the fruit and water she still had. She also gave him money which he refused at first out of politeness.

They ate outside the hut, sitting with legs folded on the white sand in front of a cloth on which he laid out the food. The light of the kerosene lamp seemed dull against the brilliance of the stars.

He told her about himself and that he had a couple of fields, a donkey, a goat and several chickens.

"You're quite handsome," he remarked towards the end of the meal.

"I only like women," Anouk said, realizing that for once she hadn't lied.

He studied her for a moment, then shrugged and finished eating quietly, Anouk wondering whether he believed her. She couldn't help feeling sorry for him, sure that he had no one in this tiny village.

He carried the dishes back to the kitchen. Then they went into the big hut where he unrolled two mats.

Pointing to one, he said, "Yours."

Anouk thanked him and stretched out in her clothes, hearing him do the same. She listened to his breathing before relaxing enough to fall into a light sleep.

A hand travelling up her thigh made her jump as if a scorpion had stung her. She grabbed the knife and held it to his throat, growling, "I told you I only like women and I paid you for my food and bed."

Frightened, he pulled back, the whites of his eyes shining in the dark. "All right…forgive me."

"You touch me again," Anouk warned with a severity she didn't feel, "and the sand will drink your blood."

He crawled back to his mat, but Anouk knew she wouldn't fall asleep again, feeling a match to his loneliness and pain. Shortly before dawn, she left.

She walked for hours until she came to a small fishing port. There she watched a young man mending a sail on his dhow. He was of slender build with a mop of black curls crowning his head.

"How's fishing?" she greeted him.

He looked up. "All right. You looking for work?"

She liked his face and decided to trust him. "No," she said, touching the wooden hull which was beamy with a low water line. "How much would you charge to take me down the coast?"

"How far down?"

"Al-Makha."

"That's quite out of my way."

"A mere fifty miles. I'd pay you well. Just name your price or I'll ask someone else."

He thought for a moment, then named fifteen hundred riyals.

Anouk pretended to be shocked at what amounted to fifty dollars. "I didn't think your price would be that high. You're taking almost all my money."

"It's a long ride," he insisted, "and I won't be able to fish."

"Twelve hundred," she haggled.

"Thirteen."

"All right then," Anouk relented. "But can we go soon?"

"What's the hurry?"

She eyed the sun which was well up, and observed that the wind was good. "I received word from my father that he is gravely ill and wants to talk to me before Allah takes him."

Since respect for one's father is paramount in the Arab world, she had no doubt that such a summons would bring action. Indeed, he bid her to come aboard, then readied the boat.

She sank onto some fishing nets, sighing with relief. While he was busy hoisting the lateen sail, she retrieved the money from her belt.

When the sail filled with wind, he came aft. Thanking her, he pocketed the money, then steered the boat out of the harbor and headed south. The breeze was stiff, coming from astern, and the dhow sliced through the water at a good speed.

Looking at the bloated sail, the young man said, "If the wind keeps up, we should be in Al-Makha this evening."

Anouk gazed at the coast streaming by, then at the western horizon beyond which lay Ethiopia, where Karen was waiting. She missed her so much it hurt, and she wished she could let her know she was still alive. She had had little time to think about Karen or Silke these past days, with her mind being overburdened with her survival. She knew she was reaching the limit of her endurance and wouldn't be able to go on like this for much longer.

Al-Makha, Yemen's second most important port, is also the country's biggest smuggling port, especially booze from Djibouti. Although the Koran strictly forbids alcohol, it is sold secretly, and many Yemenites working overseas use alcohol as a substitute for qat, Yemen's popular and legal drug, knowing Allah is forgiving.

Thin and dark with chapped lips, Anouk looked very different from her former self. She wandered around the small town which was poor but, like so many places, could boast a great past. Caravans of a thousand camels had brought goods from as far as Europe; exports through the town had included fruit, cloth, spices, dyes, pottery and, most important, coffee which the Yemenites had brought from the highlands of Ethiopia and which thrived in Yemen's mountains.

As the craze for coffee swept over Europe in the fifteenth century, prices soared, bringing prosperity to the coffee merchants of Al-Makha who had a world monopoly on the beans. The trade name 'Mocha' coffee survives to the present day. Eventually the plant was smuggled out of the country and cultivated in Ceylon and Java; the monopoly was broken and Al-Makha fell into decline. Coffee is still grown in the highlands but farmers make bigger profits growing qat.

Anouk walked past a white mosque with a graceful, slender minaret built five hundred years before and passed the ruins of the coffee merchants' villas, some still bearing graceful ornaments, other shrunk to sand-covered heaps.

Hungry and thirsty, she went to a cafe and ordered kebab, vegetables, rice and fruit, then enjoyed the famous coffee. There were no hotels and she prepared herself for a night in the shelter of one of the ruins.

First she wanted to check out the small port. She felt a rush of panic when a jeep of soldiers drove by and almost hid.

But they were laughing with each other and not paying attention to anyone. She wondered if the taxi driver or what the vultures had left of him, had been found. She didn't even want to think about whether the link would be made to her, the suspect who fled through the toilet.

Strolling around the harbor, she watched men securing sails and tackle on their boats. They looked like a rough bunch and were surely smugglers she had best avoid. She intended to find another fisherman to sail her to Asseb.

A boy approached her. "Sir, you want a girl? She's from Ethiopia and clean."

"Go away," Anouk said, waving him off.

Eyes full of hope, he asked, "You like boys?"

"No! Leave me alone."

"How about whisky?"

"How about my foot in your ass?" she shot back and he finally sprinted away.

A dhow sailing into port caught her attention. It had fishing nets on the bow, and at the helm, an old man in a striped shirt, loose trousers and a white turban. He sailed to a dock and tied up.

Anouk walked close. "Good evening. I hope the sea was kind and your catch good."

"I can't complain," the man replied calmly.

"Are you going out again tomorrow?"

"I go out every day, but although my bones are getting old, I can't afford to pay for help."

"It is I who would like to pay you. I need to get to Asseb."

He coiled a line. "I don't sail that far any longer."

Anouk touched the bow of his boat. "I'd make it worth your while. Could I invite you to chew some qat in a private place so we can talk?"

She had invited him to the number one activity of Yemenite social life. There wasn't a single man who didn't participate in qat parties where news was exchanged or business discussed. A man avoiding such get-togethers would soon be regarded as a social outcast.

A large, evergreen bush needing little care, qat originated, like coffee, in the mountains of east Africa, and is also grown in Ethiopia. Its tender leaves are chewed, and being a social drug, are seldom chewed alone.

He studied her with eyes that were almost hidden by folds of skin. "All right. I'll offer my house."

Just then the muezzin's voice rose from the minaret, and he went aft and bowed towards Mecca. Anouk did the same on the dock, pretending to pray.

The prayer said, he stepped off his boat. On the way to his home, they stopped at the market where Anouk bought enough qat branches for a six-hour chewing session.

Her host's home was behind a high wall and consisted of five huts, one of which was for receiving guests. Anouk heard voices of women and children, but saw no one else. He bade her sit down on a mat, then disappeared.

She tensed, wondering if he might have heard about the fugitive, and was sending a family member to the police. Nonsense, she told herself, this is a port of smuggling—this man must've done his share.

Her host returned with a boy carrying a pot of tea and some food. Anouk relaxed somewhat, hoping it wasn't a trap. When the boy left, they sat across from each other, quietly eating and drinking, then Anouk put the qat between them, motioning for her host to help himself, and put a few leaves into her mouth against her cheek. She began chewing them to a paste maintaining the lump between her cheek and teeth, and adding leaves till it formed a small ball. Her host did likewise till his cheek was bulging with a wad the size of a tennis ball.

Anouk felt a surge of energy pervade her from the mild, slightly bitter tasting drug, followed by a sense of well-being.

"You're not from this country," her host broke the silence.

"I've lived in Ethiopia for many years," Anouk replied, knowing that it would take some chatting before they would come to the point.

"What brought you to Yemen?"

"My father's death. Allah took him before I had a chance to speak with him for a last time."

He closed his eyes, mumbled something that sounded like a prayer, then said, "You seem to be wealthy."

"I have a store in Axum and am doing well with tourists," Anouk replied, aware that he wanted to find out who she was and if he could trust her.

"Who is taking care of it while you're gone?"

"My brother-in-law. But he has his own business and is eagerly awaiting my return, so are my three sons, and my wife who'll soon give birth to my fourth child."

"Allah has blessed you."

"Yes, he has been good to me."

They fell into silence, and he put more leaves into his mouth. Anouk had reached her limit and just chewed.

"Asseb is a ten-hour sail," he finally remarked.

"I'd reward you well," Anouk said, and offered him two hundred dollars—six thousand riyals, knowing that he had never seen that much money in one bundle.

He stopped chewing. "You could take a plane for that much."

Anouk threw her hands up as if warding off the devil, speaking in the highly charged poetic language molded after the canonical text of the Koran. "May Allah protect me from those machines from hell. Never would I step into one. I only travel by land or by the sea, who carries a boat like a mother a child at her bosom."

He nodded knowingly and kept chewing in silence, then said, "We could leave at daybreak."

Anouk bowed deeply. "Only if it's convenient for you," she said, trying to contain her excitement.

"It is," he answered, and after some more silence asked, "Do you have a place to sleep?" Anouk shook her head and he said, "You're welcome to stay here."

Chapter 21

Karen and Irmgard walked around the busy Asseb harbor, anxiously looking at dhows and boats of all sizes returning from the sea. Then they sat on a low white stone wall by the pier, watching the sun set as they had done for the past twelve days.

"Another day gone by," Karen sighed.

"Maybe tomorrow," Irmgard said.

"I can't stand it," Karen cried. "I hope nothing has happened to her."

Irmgard remained quiet, her face marked by worry and lack of sleep.

"Should we call Ulf again? In case he heard something in the news?"

Irmgard's voice was toneless. "He will call us if there is a problem."

Twice they had called Ulf, who told them everything was ready and that there was no news. Irmgard had exchanged a few words with Silke and wished her a belated birthday, nothing that would make a listening operator suspicious. They checked in with Sergio every day. He too became quieter as the days passed, further fuelling their fears about Anouk.

Waiting day after day was gruelling. Asseb was a small town with nothing to do or see to distract them from their dread. Every day they checked the harbor early in the morning, and again at night as the boats came in. The days were too hot to be outside and they remained in their room, whiling away the time in tense anticipation.

Karen took a deep breath and exhaled. "I never imagined it'd be this awful when she warned me. And she did warn me! She pushed me away repeatedly, tried not to involve me in her life. I thought I was so smart to think of a way to help. I just didn't know it would take so long."

"Neither did I." Irmgard gazed out at the darkening sea. "But let's not underestimate Anouk. She's smart and resilient. It's just taking her longer than we thought. Maybe she's had to hide…"

They had gone over it all before. Karen twisted her fingers into a knot. "I can't stand this waiting much longer." And began to cry.

Irmgard put an arm around her. "Karen, we must remain strong now."

Karen nodded and wiped her tears. Irmgard pulled a handkerchief from the pocket of her skirt and handed it to her.

Karen blew her nose. "I'm sorry. I shouldn't fall apart like this…it's just…"

"Believe me, at times I feel like letting go and screaming. But it would only make things worse."

Karen looked at Irmgard, seeing her innate strength, aware what this woman must have gone through for the last two years trying to find her daughter who was by no means safe yet.

Embarrassed by her weakness, she straightened and drew breath. "You're right."

It was dark now and they returned to the hotel, a white stone building, simple and passably clean.

They wished each other a good night and went to their adjoining rooms. Karen took a shower, then stretched out on the bed, staring at the whirring fan above in the dull detached state that had become her defense against despair.

The sound of an Arab lute seeping through the window brought her back into contact with her surroundings, a painful reminder of Anouk and the time they had made love to such music in that filthy Marib hotel room. She turned and buried her face in the pillow, the ache in her chest so great, she couldn't even cry. Finally she switched off the light on the nightstand and tried to sleep.

There was a knock on the door.

"It's open!" She sat up wondering if Irmgard needed something.

But the figure in the doorway wasn't Irmgard. For a moment she stared confused, almost frightened, and in the next she cried, "Anouk!" And bounded from the bed.

Laughing and crying, she hugged her.

Wordlessly Anouk held her with her face buried between Karen's neck and shoulder.

"You feel so good," she finally whispered. "So soft…"

"Let me turn on the light so I can see you. My God, you're thin and so black!' Karen touched her face.

"I need to bathe. I must smell like an old goat."

"I don't care. You're back in one piece. But you sound tired."

"I am. And I'm looking forward to a long, hot shower."

While Anouk cleaned up, Karen ran to Irmgard's room.

"I heard." Irmgard smiled through tears. "I didn't want to disturb you."

When Anouk came out of the shower, Irmgard hugged her while Karen fussed, "Did you eat?"

"Yes, we caught fish on the way over and had it with vegetables and rice."

Karen wanted to know how and with whom she had sailed, but seeing that Anouk was hardly able to keep her eyes open, refrained from asking.

Irmgard also noticed Anouk's weariness and left. "We'll talk tomorrow."

Anouk went to bed and was asleep before her head touched the pillow. Karen lay down next to her and put a protective arm around her.

"How do you feel?" Karen asked in the morning.

"As if I had died and gone to heaven," Anouk answered, taking her into her arms. "To be with you—in a clean bed—without anyone chasing me—that's paradise."

Karen kissed her hungrily. "I missed you."

Pressed against Anouk, looking into her eyes which lust had turned black, Karen forgot the agony of the past days, giving in to the exhilarating space where there was nothing but her body melded to Anouk's and the pleasure it was giving her.

Anouk heard Karen breathing against her; in her ears was the sound of her own blood. She touched Karen gently, then more urgently, devouring her, possessing her entirely, feeling her awaken in her mouth. Her head was light, spinning, as Karen pulled her deeper and deeper into herself like a tide. When she pressed her swollen sex into Karen's, she no longer knew where she ended and Karen began. She felt herself dissolving like foam, like a small cloud growing until it was enormous, bursting into rain.

Sticky and sweaty, they cooled down in each other's arms, then showered and dressed, Anouk in a shirt and slacks which Karen had brought.

"What's this?" Anouk asked, lifting a package from her suitcase.

"Oh…a gun," Karen answered. "Sergio sent it with me. He wants you to take it on your flight…just in case. He's worried about you."

Anouk weighed the revolver in her hands. "I hope I won't need it. It wouldn't be much use against a patrol boat. Hm, already loaded!" She opened the cylinder, looked at the cartridges in each of the six chambers, then cocked and uncocked the gun.

"You've handled guns before, haven't you?"

"Yes…in South Africa. All the women I knew thought it wise to be armed for self-protection." She took aim at the ceiling fan.

"Ever kill anyone?" Karen joked.

"With a gun? No…just my wits."

Karen frowned. "What do you mean?"

Anouk just smiled. "Let's have breakfast. I'm starving."

Irmgard was waiting for them in the dining room. "I called Sergio. He's relieved to hear you made it and sends his best. As soon as you're back with Silke, he'll send a plane to pick us all up."

"Good," said Anouk settling down at the table and ordering a breakfast that would have astounded a Sumo wrestler. Over their tea and toast, Karen and Irmgard watched her in amusement while she ate and regaled them with her odyssey through Yemen. She didn't tell them about the taxi driver, never wanting them to know how close to failure she had come. She could see that the part about being caught without papers was bad enough.

After breakfast, Anouk took care of business, talking with Sergio first, then putting a call through to Ulf.

"Glad to hear from you." Ulf worked at sounding neutral but she could hear the relief in his voice.

"Could the shipment be ready not tomorrow but the morning after?" she said to make it absolutely clear.

"Certainly."

"So soon?" Karen asked as she rang off.

"I want to get it over with. I want to get back to a normal life. All of us do, Silke most of all. They're more than ready in Yemen. Why wait?"

Karen sighed. She, too, wanted this to be over. But she had hoped Anouk would give them time to recover before throwing herself into the final phase.

They drove in Karen's rental car to the hangar to see the plane.

Anouk looked at the little silver bird with its compact fuselage and sparkling wings.

"Is it not suitable?" Irmgard worried when Anouk didn't say anything.

"It's perfect. I can hardly wait to test it," Anouk said, and made arrangements for the plane to be put in the water. Then she drove to the airport to announce her flight.

The Ethiopian captain, who knew her well, exclaimed, "A seaplane! Since when are you flying those?"

"I did in South Africa and recently at Lake Tana. I'm testing it. Later today I'll fly it around the harbor, and for the next two mornings I'd like to take a spin along the coast before a French captain takes it over. That all right?"

He grinned. "I'll make it all right. We haven't seen you for a while. You still with Sergio?"

"Yes. I've had a lot of flights to the north these past few weeks."

He handed her a copy of the flight plan and authorization. "I'll notify the guys at the harbor. Have a good flight."

Papers in hand, Anouk thanked him.

It was the night before the big day, and the three women went for a walk on the beach. The stillness was supreme, unreal, carrying the blurred rhythm of the surf. They walked where the sand was wet and and packed down.

"By the way, do you have papers to get Silke back to Germany?" Anouk asked Irmgard.

"No problem there. I was told that with Silke's birth certificate they would issue a passport for her at the German consulate in Addis."

Strong starlight illuminated the shore and sea and no clouds smudged the sky.

"We'll have good weather," remarked Karen.

Irmgard looked at her watch, saying apprehensively, "In six hours Silke will motor away from land. Do you think they are already at the beach camping?"

"I'm sure," Anouk said reassuringly, thinking about the coordinates where Silke would leave the shore.

"What about the winds that come up every day?" Irmgard worried.

Anouk put an arm around her. "They come up by mid-morning. I'll be back with Silke by then."

Irmgard sighed deeply, leaning against her. "If you don't find Silke...you know she won't go back..."

"Yes, I know."

They were up at three-thirty and had coffee from a thermos they had ordered from the hotel the evening before, along with cheese sandwiches. The sky was dark with brilliant stars. The weather hadn't changed.

Getting dressed, Anouk was tense, going over every detail in her mind. Karen knew it was best not to talk to her.

At four-thirty, Karen drove them to the harbor. It was deserted and dark with here and there a lantern flickering on a fisherman's boat. Not a breath of air rippled the surface of the water and Karen swallowed an anxious question.

A figure rose from the dock to which the plane was moored, and Anouk said something in Arabic, then paid the young man for watching the plane.

She embraced Irmgard, then held Karen who whispered, "Be careful."

"Now, don't be a pessimist."

"I'm just a worried optimist."

The plane swayed under Anouk's weight when she stepped onto the pontoon. Inside the cabin, she put a bag with the thermos, sandwiches, and the gun on the co-pilot's seat. Familiar with the instruments after her test flights, she turned the switches and checked the controls. The engine ignited, the propellers jumped to life. At a sign from her, Irmgard and Karen untied the mooring lines, then waved after the departing plane. Anouk knew they would wait at the dock until she returned.

She glided past ships to an area big enough for take off. The water was glassy and she spun around to create waves, then headed straight into them. She felt the pontoons getting onto the 'step,' hydroplaned to gain speed, and rose into the paling night.

It was five o'clock.

The eastern horizon turned crimson as she soared towards it, the black sea slowly changing to grey.

The engine purring like a kitten, she sailed along, constantly watching the condition of the sea, the direction and speed of the wind. But the weather was perfect with ceiling and visibility unlimited.

She cruised along at a good height on this first part of the flight. Behind her the African coast was lost in haze; before her stretched the Red Sea. Yemen was still invisible.

Glancing at her watch, then at the map next to her on which a red cross marked the spot of Silke's take-off, she figured that Silke should be leaving the shore by now. So far the sea showed no white caps which would make a small boat hard to find. As soon as Silke saw the plane, she would light the flares.

The sun was coming up from behind the rim of the world and the sea turned ink blue. With the world lit up, her tension loosened; she poured herself some coffee and ate a sandwich.

Seeing the Yemen coast appear on the horizon, she felt her heart speeding up and lowered her flight altitude, craning her neck in all directions for planes or ships below. But smooth and blue, the sea rose and fell unmarred.

Twenty minutes later, she made out the white stripe of beach and lowered her altitude further.

She flew towards the spot where she assumed Silke should be and circled it. She flew in wider circles but no speck smudged the water's surface.

"Come on, Silke," she muttered. "You must be here. Light those flares."

After a few more spins, she headed to the beach from where Silke was to take off. Flying dangerously low, she skimmed the coast and saw a few reed huts tucked behind dunes. Then, to her surprise she saw a tent, a car, and two men standing at the shore, looking up. Ulf and Manfred! They waved and pointed at the sea. She waved back, dipped her wings and hurried away from land.

She hadn't expected them to stick around once Silke was in the water but could appreciate that they had wanted to see her arrive. She hoped for their sake she hadn't attracted anyone's attention to their camp by flying so close to the beach, that not having been part of the plan.

At least she knew now that everything had worked out on their end and that Silke was out there.

But where are you, Silke? Light those damn flares!

Sweat oozed from her pores and she wiped her face against her arm, then her hands on her slacks. Almost brushing the water, she flew south. The coast behind her shrank to a faint line. Sky and sea were empty. She was still alone.

She checked her chart again, changed course. Flying higher, she drew more circles, straining to see below.

Had they underestimated the currents?

Silke! Please! Use those flares, she moaned, licking her dry lips, and veering west against her doubts that Silke would be that far out. Again she circled at different altitudes, then looked at her watch. Twenty minutes had gone by since she had started her search and she had to consider the fuel.

Fear rose seething hot.

What if I can't find her?

Silke would die out here. She would not go back, as Irmgard said.

Anouk swore; this had been her idea and she was responsible. She had been so sure her idea was good. If she failed, she would never be able to face Irmgard or anyone else, and would fly around till the last drop of fuel was consumed. She wouldn't go back either.

Desperate, she opened up the throttle to have another spin—and saw the boat.

"Silke!" she cried relieved.

In the next instant she realized that it couldn't be. Trailing a thick churn, indicating high speed, this boat was big and coming from the area of Al-Hudayda. She had been detected.

She pulled up her nose and changed course to fly further out when a red flash burst forth from the deep blue south of her. Goose bumps tightening her scalp, she watched another flare shoot up and another. She lowered her altitude and headed for it.

Frantically waving a white scarf, Silke knelt in a small boat, heeling from side to side, looking pitifully small. Her hair was cut even shorter, and she wore a shirt and slacks, looking like a teenage boy. Anouk smiled reassuringly, waving back as she prepared for a landing. The conditions were perfect with a three to four foot chop. She levelled the plane, grazing the waves and slowly cushioned down, letting the 'step' on the bottom of each pontoon cut gently into the water. She cut back on the throttle, kept the motor idling.

Gliding next to Silke's small vessel until the right pontoon almost grazed it, she saw the speedboat holding course toward them.

Anouk slid into the co-pilot's seat, opened the narrow door and threw Silke a line which she had secured to a seat strap on her end. "Tie this to your boat. Hurry, we're getting company."

Silke's face was a mask of fear. "I just saw," she said, catching the line and winding it around a cleat with shaking hands. "I've seen you for a while but you were too far away and I couldn't get two of the flares to light."

"The current took you further south than we thought. Don't worry, we'll make it." She held out her hand. "Step onto the pontoon and hold on to the wing strut."

As soon as Silke had a firm hold on the plane, Anouk pulled Silke inside, then untied the line to set the boat adrift before she shut and secured the door.

The speedboat was rapidly descending upon them.

"They must think we're smuggling," Anouk remarked.

Silke remained silent, fearfully watching the boat.

Anouk maneuvered the plane further away from the small boat, pulled out the gun and fired into the outboard motor. It exploded and sank taking the stern of the boat with it. Within moments the rest of Silke's boat to freedom was gone too.

"Why?" Silke licked her dry lips.

Anouk headed into the waves. "I didn't want them to get the boat because it could have been traced to Ulf and Manfred."

They felt the pontoons breaking from the water, easily gliding over it. Moments later the plane was airborne. The speedboat had almost reached the spot where the boat had gone down. With glee Anouk waved at the three uniformed men, swerved around, and headed back to Asseb.

They heard several cracks from a gun over the engine's drone.

"They're shooting!" Silke cried, craning her neck as she looked out the window.

Anouk glanced across Silke to see. "Let them. We're already too far away. Rejoice Silke! We made it!"

Instead, Silke collapsed against the seat unable to speak, shaken by dry sobs of relief.

Anouk took her hand and held it.

Slowly Silke calmed down; the tension she had been under eased. "Thank God I'm out of there. I thought that day would never come. It's like waking from a two year nightmare." Tears filmed her eyes. "How's my mother?"

"Anxiously waiting for you at the dock in Asseb." Anouk let go of Silke's hand, and pointed to the back seat. "There's coffee in the thermos."

Silke shook her head. "My stomach's a tight knot. By the way, Ulf and Manfred say hello. They were great."

"I just saw them at the beach. I hope they saw me land so they know I found you. But they may have broken camp and gotten out of there. My flying over them might've drawn attention to them. We'll call them tonight." Anouk looked at Silke. "You look like a boy. Who cut your hair?"

"Manfred. Ulf bought the shirt and pants. We thought it would be better if I went to the beach as a boy in case the locals saw us. Two older men going camping and fishing with a young woman would have looked a bit strange. It also saved me from wearing that damn cloak."

"Good idea. How did the trip to the coast go?"

"Ulf had me hiding in the trunk at first. There was one patrol but the minute they saw the government seal on the car, they hardly looked at Ulf's papers and waved him on. The rest was easy. Manfred had taken the boat out of storage and put into the water at Al-Hudayda and motored to the beach to make sure the motor worked all right. The locals think Europeans are crazy anyway and left him alone. And when Ulf and I arrived in the evening, he was sitting in front of a tent and roasting fish on a fire."

Anouk laughed. "And I bet he was drinking beer."

Also laughing, Silke said, "Of course. And shortly before day-break they made me practice with the outboard motor and we went through how to light the flares again. Then off I went. They told me they'd wait till you arrived. I was pretty scared. But the thought of staying in Yemen scared me more. And I trusted you."

"Was there any more news after I left Sana?"

"Yes, once. They said they had caught a suspect who had no papers, but that he got away. Was that you?"

"I heard that news at the market in Al-Hudayda," Anouk said, but didn't tell her what happened after.

"We were so worried about you, and had the radio on all the time. My mom and Karen also worried. They called us twice. But we were afraid to say anything over the phone and kept it very short."

"Any news about a taxi driver near Al-Hudayda?"

"Not that I heard. Why?"

"I had a little problem." Anouk throttled back. "Here's the coast of Asseb. We're almost home."

Silke look at the scenery below which differed little from the sandy coast she had just left.

They flew over the harbor, now alive and busy with people and boats leaving and returning. As Anouk headed straight in, all activity seemed to stop as everyone watched the landing of this strange plane.

Karen and Irmgard watched from the dock, anxious to see if Silke was sitting in the co-pilot's seat. As the plane taxied closer, they shielded their eyes to see better.

"She's got her!" Karen shrieked, hugging Irmgard whose shoulders began to shake.

The plane glided next to the dock and when the propellers had stopped rotating, Karen moored it.

Impatiently, Silke threw her door open, struggled from her seat, and jumped onto the dock and into her mother's arms. Crying, unable to get a word out, they held each other in a tight embrace, oblivious to the curious onlookers.

Smiling that wide, mischievous smile, Anouk also climbed out and stepped onto the dock.

Karen pulled her close. "You did it! By God, you did it."

"We all did it," Anouk said softly.

"But from now on no more of these extreme adventures, promise?"

Anouk nodded, her dark eyes sparkling. "I'm more than ready for a quiet life. And while you're working on your book, I'll take up knitting."

Karen burst into laughter. "No...I don't think I could stand it."